BLIND REEF

Recent Titles in the Mariners Series from Peter Tonkin

THE FIRE SHIP
THE COFFIN SHIP
POWERDOWN
THUNDER BAY *
TITAN 10 *
WOLF ROCK *
RESOLUTION BURNING *
CAPE FAREWELL *
THE SHIP BREAKERS *
HIGH WIND IN JAVA *
BENIN LIGHT *
RIVER OF GHOSTS *
VOLCANO ROADS *
THE PRISON SHIP *
RED RIVER *
ICE STATION *
DARK HEART *
DEAD SEA *
BLACK PEARL *
DEADLY IMPACT *
MARINER'S ARK *
BLIND REEF *

* *available from Severn House*

BLIND REEF

Peter Tonkin

This first world edition published 2015
in Great Britain and the USA by
SEVERN HOUSE PUBLISHERS LTD of
19 Cedar Road, Sutton, Surrey, England, SM2 5DA.
Trade paperback edition first published 2016
in Great Britain and the USA by
SEVERN HOUSE PUBLISHERS LTD.

British Library Cataloguing in Publication Data

Tonkin, Peter author.
  Blind Reef. – (A Richard Mariner adventure)
  1. Mariner, Richard (Fictitious character)–Fiction.
  2. Mariner, Robin (Fictitious character)–Fiction.
  3. Kidnapping–Egypt–Sinai–Fiction. 4. Refugees–
  Egypt–Fiction. 5. Sea stories.
  I. Title II. Series
  823.9'2-dc23

ISBN-13: 978-0-7278-8533-3 (cased)
ISBN-13: 978-1-84751-637-4 (trade paper)
ISBN-13: 978-1-78010-697-7 (e-book)

To Cham, Guy and Mark,
as always

Except where actual historical events and characters are being
described for the storyline of this novel, all situations in this
publication are fictitious and any resemblance to living persons
is purely coincidental.

All Severn House titles are printed on acid-free paper.

Severn House Publishers support the Forest Stewardship Council™ [FSC™],
the leading international forest certification organisation. All our titles that
are printed on FSC certified paper carry the FSC logo.

Typeset by Palimpsest Book Production Ltd.,
Falkirk, Stirlingshire, Scotland.
Printed and bound in Great Britain by
TJ International, Padstow, Cornwall.

ONE
Blind

The reef's name in Egyptian Arabic is *Sha'abrur Siyul* and that's what the Red Sea sailors call it. But the divers call it Blind Reef. It is located near the heart of that dangerous little archipelago of reefs and islands strewn across the mouth of the Gulf of Suez close to the African shore. The divers call it Blind Reef because in most conditions it is completely submerged, invisible to the watch-keepers of the passing vessels and unknown to any except the local fishermen and the divers themselves.

Under normal circumstances Blind Reef is too far below the surface to be a hazard to shipping. But now it is approaching low water, and the sea level in the Gulf is as low as it ever gets. Tonight, in fact, the tide is so low that the ship-killing tip of the coral head can just be seen gleaming in the moonlight, steely in the shadowed troughs between the great, silver-backed waves that roll relentlessly out of Suez and into the Red Sea south along the mountainous coasts of Egypt and Saudi Arabia towards Sudan, Eritrea and the horn of Somalia. And these neap tides will last, perhaps, for a week or so.

Blind Reef is a popular dive destination because it offers a range of experiences. At every level there are caves and tunnels in the rocks of the reef, as well as colourful and bustling outcrops of coral on its flanks, upper reaches and all the way up the sturdy spire that, tonight, just reaches to the surface itself. At any time of day or night, in any season and at any depth, it is like diving in a colossal, beautifully stocked aquarium. At almost every time of year, boats, dive tenders and RIBs sail out of El Gouna and Hurgada on the African shore to the south of it. They pick their way carefully through the lethal maze of reefs to surround Blind Reef. From dawn to dusk, men and women of all nationalities and every level of experience explore the beautiful environment.

Which is why, on this particular midsummer night, Richard and Robin Mariner have chosen to sail the hazard-free open waters across from Sharm el-Sheikh at the southernmost tip of the Sinai Peninsula and are planning a night dive which will allow them to explore Blind Reef in the certain knowledge that only they and Ahmed, their dive master, will be there, and that the only dangers their dive boat *Katerina* will face come from the massive tankers and container vessels running north and south to and from Suez. They feel secure in the knowledge that, unlike the reefs, the massive ships will give plenty of warning of their presence, even though the only source of natural light is the low, fat desert moon that is rising above the distant glow of Sharm, away back along their wake. And therefore, except for their torches, they will effectively be diving blind.

The Blind Reef's grey sharks do not need sharp eyesight. They have a range of senses that allow them to feed off the shoals of tuna running past the islands, following the great ships to and from the Suez Canal no matter whether they can actually see them or not. They sometimes work in groups to trap big jackfish and giant trevally against the reef walls before tearing into them with fourteen rows of self-renewing teeth. Tonight, however, the social group of half-a-dozen males and females which has been lazily hunting parrotfish, napoleonfish and warlike goliath trig-gerfish during the day splits up into individuals and settles to the serious business of feeding in the stygian, lightless water. Below them, away in the icy depths to the south, the first of the deep-water tiger sharks come cruising inquisitively upwards, the smallest of them a metre longer than the largest grey shark. In the darkness, it is the squid, cuttlefish and octopi which are most at risk – especially those that move erratically and come too far out from the safety of the sparkling phosphorescence of the reef. Or those which give off a phosphorescent signal themselves.

For tonight, under the huge desert moon, Blind Reef and the waters all around it seem to catch phosphorescent fire and burn in silent majesty. All is silent – except for the throb of the Mariners' dive boat's motors as the sleek *Katerina* sails up to the reef and drops the dive RIB which powers onward, with Richard, Robin, dive master Ahmed and *Katerina*'s first officer, Mahmood, aboard. While the three divers are below, Mahmood will keep a lookout in the RIB and Captain Husan will keep watch from *Katerina*'s bridge where the beautiful vessel's top-flight electronic equipment can scan the environment almost as effectively as the sharks' extraordinary senses, which are so much more acute than those of the people who are about to swim down among them.

'The blind diving the blind, eh?' joked Richard, raising his voice over the buzz of the RIB's outboard as they powered away from *Katerina*.

'Oh, very funny,' answered Robin, rolling her eyes and shaking her head so that the moonlight glittered off her hair, turning the curls to silver gilt. She finished zipping up the dive vest over the high-cut Speedo one-piece she was wearing without a rash vest. The action presented the vanishing spectacle of a cleavage that might have flattered a turn of the millennium *Baywatch* star. Apparently unaware of her husband's ardent gaze, she reached down to make sure her dive boots were ready for her to slip on her long, black fins.

Richard dragged his eyes away from her, scanning their surroundings, surprised at how swiftly the powerful, elegant and dazzlingly illuminated *Katerina* had fallen behind the RIB's phosphorescent wake. A breath of wind that seemed to be coming from a furnace stirred Robin's curls further, and brought the smell of fuel from the outboard together with a fine dusting of sand. Hot winds had been coming and going across the Sinai Peninsula for days because the *shamaal* was blowing strongly down the vast deserts of Saudi Arabia to the east. Richard looked back at his wife and smiled. The moonlight that was already making her hair a distraction gleamed off the length of her bare legs, turning them into a life-sized erotic Cellini sculpture in silver.

Where Robin was all black and silver, Richard was mostly midnight blue from the top of his blue-black hair to the tip of his blue-patterned fins. He was wearing a blue-panelled wetsuit top over a blue rash vest – in spite of Robin's teasing about his sensitive skin – and blue Speedo shorts. Like the rash vest, these were a source of amusement for his wife, but he consoled himself with the thought that while she looked like a swimwear advert, he looked like a proper diver. Though, to be fair, not as much of a professional as the slim, swift-moving dive master Ahmed in his well-worn O'Neill one-piece.

Richard glanced back at Robin, who was now strapping a Maniago Shark 9 dive knife and sheath to her calf, looking like a character in a James Bond film. Even in the moonlight, the blue eyes set deep beneath the black curves of his brows glittered like shards of ice. Then he looked down, mimicking her actions in his own way. He preferred his Aropec K1 quick-release knife, and strapped that immediately below his knee within easy reach of his right hand. He shrugged his twelve-litre tank more comfortably into place and pulled the regulator over his head, making sure the pipes to the mouthpiece were clear and his octopus emergency oxygen tube was also clear. He closed the straps and clipped on the quick-releases before adjusting the fit. He didn't need to cinch a weight belt around his trim waist, as Ahmed was doing, because his wet suit top was the new design with quick-release buckshot weight built in. He did have a belt, though, from which hung a pair of scuba emergency diving shears and a big Beaver Alu underwater torch with a powerful white light beam capable of an impressively lengthy reach. Richard reckoned he would need to be a juggler to use everything he was carrying at once. Or an octopus. On that thought, he leaned forward, slipping his fins over his dive boots, working on another witticism.

Before he came up with one, however, the need to keep up with the others meant he had to put his regulator in his mouth and take a breath or two of cold compressed air. It tasted of stale rubber, as usual. He checked his octopus line again, blowing a burst of cool air against his cheek, just beneath the long white scar that ran along the sharp crest of his cheekbone like the duelling trophy of a nineteenth-century Prussian aristocrat. He took out his regulator before it made his mouth too dry and spat into his face mask. He swirled the spittle round before rinsing it over the side, sparking a cloud of phosphorescence, and easing it over his head and face to hang round his neck. He reached for the head torch that matched his big Beaver dive torch and slid it into place just above where his face mask would sit on his forehead. When everything was in place the torch and face mask would clip securely together and give him light across a sixty-degree angle with a range of up to ten metres, depending on water clarity. Twice the range of a grey shark's day vision, but less than a third of the big Beaver's reach. Maybe not so blind after all.

'Ready?' asked Ahmed, his English perfect and his voice surprisingly deep and resonant for such a slight man. What he lacked in chest-size was more than compensated for by the proud jut of his nose, Richard reasoned.

'Ready,' answered Robin and Richard at the same time.

'One last thing,' said the dive master forcefully. 'Remember we are in the deep ocean here and night time is feeding time. There is very little danger but there is some. If you see sharks, don't panic. Just take care around them and don't trap them against a reef wall. We have discussed the threat display of the sharks we might meet, especially the grey reef sharks and, on the off-chance, tigers. Be aware of barracuda also. They can grow to two metres long and you will most likely see them hanging out at the edge of the light, keeping an eye on things. They won't attack unless provoked. Moray eels won't come out of their tunnels, but be careful if you are close to a reef wall. The biggest ones can be three metres long, but we don't have many that size here. Remember the simple rule: open mouth means no danger. Closed mouth is attack mode – keep clear. We're not going deep enough to come across the big bottom-dwellers like mantas and stingrays. That only leaves the also-rans. Spiny fish – don't touch. Lionfish sting worse than jellyfish and scorpions. You know what fire coral looks like from our reef dives at and around the Blue Hole up in Dahab. But remember, there isn't anything that's likely to attack you unless you provoke it. If we stay together and move slowly we'll be fine. And . . .' He held up his left forearm. There was a waterproof whiteboard strapped there. 'Write a message if you can't remember the signal. OK?'

'OK,' said Richard and Robin in unison.

'Check dive computers, then,' ordered Ahmed.

The three of them looked down at their wrists. They were all wearing new top-of-the range Suunto systems that Richard had brought out with him. It was the first time in ages that he had worn anything on his left wrist other than his Rolex Oyster Perpetual in its battered but still waterproof steel casing. The Suunto dive computers were designed to monitor depth, time and tank pressure; dive time remaining, compass heading and orientation. They also told the time. The systems had been pre-programmed on a laptop and fed to the wrist computers. All they needed to do was switch them on together as their last act before rolling back off the inflatable RIB's side and into the stygian, moon-silvered water. The systems would sound alarms if they dived too deep, spent too long or came up too fast; they would monitor – several times a second if necessary – their breathing rate, calculating with depth and pressure, how much air they had in their tanks and how long it would last for.

'OK. Throttle back, Mahmood,' said Ahmed. 'Masks on . . . OK? Regulators in. And over we go. As we discussed and rehearsed. Robin first . . .'

Richard pressed the start button on his dive computer as he watched Robin curl into a foetal position, holding her mask and rolling backwards to enter the water with the back of her head and her shoulders in the lead. A spray of eerily glowing droplets soared out like a skyrocket exploding. No sooner had the silver-foaming surface closed over her than her torch came on, shining through the water like the blade of a Jedi Knight's lightsabre. For a moment she was framed against the diffused green-yellow brightness. Black torso silhouetted in utter darkness, head and legs lighter, brighter, heart-stoppingly delicate and vulnerable.

'Right,' said Ahmed. 'You're next, Richard.'

The water hit Richard on the back of his head as he rolled back out of the RIB, and there was that inevitable moment of disorientation which came through sensory overload combined with the sensation of falling slowly, upside down. The water was cool but not cold. It chilled his scalp and filled his ears in an instant as he looked up through the bubbles towards his knees and his flippers above them. It slid beneath his wetsuit and covered his legs with goosebumps. It tugged at his face mask, tried to loosen his grip on his regulator and twisted the flexible length of his fins. The sound of it thundering into the channels of his ears stopped abruptly, at about the same time as the roaring of bubbles that he seemed to have pulled down from the surface along with himself. Then there was only the steady beating of his heart and the rhythmic *suck-hiss* of his breathing. He blinked, seeing the tiny maelstrom that had filled his mask with silver and phosphorescence suddenly go gold as his head-torch was automatically switched on by contact with the water. His knees and fins gleamed.

He stretched out, flipped over, pushed his mask against his nose, cleared his ears and sank towards Robin, who was waiting just below him, already hanging vertically in the water as agreed. He joined her, circled his right index finger and thumb in the sign for OK and looked up for Ahmed. No sooner did he do so than he found himself surrounded by inquisitive zebra-striped fish that all seemed to be about the size of his palm. As far as he remembered, these were sergeant majors – though he had no idea how they came by the name. Out of nowhere, an icy current closed around him, cold enough to make him catch his breath. It required a conscious effort of will to keep control of his breathing. He blinked, shaking his head, and found himself at the heart of a shoal of tiny glassfish like a sparrow lost in a raincloud. He pulled the big Beaver torch off his belt and switched it on. The beam shot out like the beam of a lighthouse, reaching the better part of ten metres, thirty five feet, ahead.

Above the bewildering kaleidoscope of movement, Ahmed sank gracefully to join them. No sooner did he do so than the glassfish vanished. The warm water returned, like a tepid bath. Richard felt his body relaxing again. The dive master gestured with his torch and there, in the distance, framed against the shadows at the farthest edge of the light was the steely silver glint of a barracuda's flank. Richard also zeroed the big Beaver's one hundred lumens on it and it lazily sank back towards the shadows it had come from. It was impossible to tell how far away it was, however, and therefore how big. But the simple fact of its presence was sinister enough.

Ahmed pointed below, apparently unconcerned, and the three of them levelled out, side by side, then angled downwards and began to fin gently through the seven metres – twenty feet or so – that separated them from the top of the reef. As they descended, their torches and Richard's wide-beamed head light began to pick details out of the gloom. Clouds of fish swam around the reef itself. Almost at once, like the glassfish and the zebra-striped sergeant majors, they began to catch the light whirling against the glimmering gloom like shooting stars. Anthias and damselfish, seemingly in their thousands, looking exactly like the goldfish their twins, William and Mary, had kept in their big aquarium as children – right up until they left for university a few years ago, in fact. Then, amongst them, flashes of darker but still iridescent colour. The purple and indigo, gold-tipped bodies of tangs, and Arabian angelfish, the same colours striped with white across Red Sea bannerfish; all of them still seemingly the perfect size for a child's aquarium.

They were down close to the top of the reef now, deep enough for Richard to be clearing his ears again, while the white light of their torches caught the kaleidoscope of iridescence that was the coral. He knew the basic types, though even less about their names than the names of the fish that teemed around them. There were brain corals, tree corals, finger and fan. Hard corals and soft corals. Coloured corals and plain. He remembered an illustrated article he'd read in preparation for an earlier dive and tried to match the corals here with the pictures in his photographic memory. But, as he approached the edge of the reef, he became distracted by the range of larger fish moving in and out of the depths and the shadows. He recognized napoleonfish, parrotfish, groupers, snappers, jackfish and trevallys. A devil scorpionfish moved across the reef top, apparently pulling itself along with prehensile fins. A pair of big brown-striped lionfish cruised behind it, their spines halfway between knitting needles and stilettos, tipped with poison. But then, with a lift of excitement, he saw, deep within the floral tentacles of a huge sea anemone, a pair of orange-and-white-striped clownfish. He ached to take out his regulator and call to Robin, 'Hey! I think I've found Nemo!'

But as he glanced up towards her he saw, way over Robin's shoulder, past the column of bubbles that rose rhythmically above her head, at the outer edge of the long blade of his torch beam, the first sinister, sinuous swirl of a grey shark's flank. He looked at Ahmed, close beside her, swam forward and touched the dive master's shoulder. Ahmed glanced at him and made the OK circle with his index finger and thumb. Richard gave a mental shrug as the shark vanished, glanced at his dive computer and saw that he had the better part of twenty minutes' air left, including decompression stops. He paused and fell a little behind the others, waiting for his pulse rate to ease. And it was the rhythm of his pulse thumping gently in his ears, perhaps, that alerted him to the throbbing of a boat's motors, echoing, amplified, approaching rapidly through the waters above him.

No sooner had this new element entered the equation than Richard was struck forcefully from behind. He whirled in the water, searching for his attacker. There was apparently nothing there. No steely barracuda, no granite grey shark. Only the blue and gold of a triggerfish, twice as broad as his hands and twice as large as his head. Even before it dawned on him that this was actually his assailant, it threw itself forward once more. Without thinking, Richard rapped it across the beak of its nose with the torch. It turned away, just missing him, but spinning at the end of its run to come back in like a bull at the *corrida*. Jesus, thought Richard, calm down, fish; what did I ever do to you?

As the triggerfish began its run, Ahmed's hand descended gently on Richard's shoulder. The dive master was gesturing towards the spire that towered above them now, joining the reef top to the surface. Robin was already finning towards it, the beam of her torch illuminating the cliff wall of its side. There was an opening there – the mouth of a cavern or a tunnel. It lay in the opposite direction to the shark and well clear of the earlier barracuda. As long as it wasn't already occupied by a giant moray, it would give them a place to regroup. And as long as the triggerfish stayed away. This time it was Ahmed who dealt with the bellicose fish. He kicked it away with a gentle fin, sending it charging off towards the reef top.

As Richard finned determinedly after Robin towards the cave mouth, he suddenly realized that, during his fight with the triggerfish, the sound of boat motors had become louder, closer. And there were at least two boats by the sound of things, racing across the night-dark ocean ten metres above their heads. What on earth is going on up there? he wondered.

Robin reached the cave mouth and slowed, shining her torch into every internal crevice before she finned carefully in and turned, hanging upright in the cave mouth. Richard swept past her, too confident in her survey of the place to even hesitate. The cavern he plunged into was the size of a large room. There was plenty of room for three divers – especially as, if this had been a room, they were all hanging like bats off the ceiling. Richard turned towards the cave mouth as Ahmed eased in past Robin, and the three of them hovered there, looking out across the reef like characters in a legend or a fairytale, trapped in a prison cell halfway up an enchanted tower.

The image had no sooner occurred to Richard than the racing of the boat motors high above came to a climax. There was a screaming rumble that ended in a grinding *bang!*. The fish around the tower flicked away and ran for the shadows. Even the triggerfish were gone in a swirl of meaty yellow flank. The coral spire shook as though an underwater earthquake was starting. Sand from the cave floor stirred into clouds, billowing in and out around them. Richard's eyes lost clarity of vision, as though he were in a picture that was suddenly out of focus. The water itself seemed to reverberate as though they were trapped inside a drum during a drum roll. His eardrums stretched agonisingly. His eyes flooded with tears. Rocks and coral debris rained down past the cave mouth. Ahmed held up his left forearm, shining his torch on the whiteboard there and Richard had to blink several times before he could focus on the words the dive master had written on it:

Ship wrecked up on the reef spire. Danger. Take care.

Richard looked at the three most vital words on Ahmed's whiteboard. *Ship wrecked . . . Danger . . .* 'No shit, Sherlock,' he said to himself.

One way and another Richard knew a lot about shipwrecks and the dangers they presented. He had been involved in various incidents: the break-up of huge super tankers, the sinking of damaged submarines, the pitch-poling of Olympic standard multi-hulls, the destruction of priceless gin palaces like *Katerina*. He had been aboard a waste disposal vessel whose ill-stowed, leaky deck cargo had dissolved the protective coating round the nuclear waste in her holds, then eaten through her hull. He and Robin had been trapped aboard a Russian cruise liner, storm bound in the Southern Ocean, whose computer control systems had all failed, one by one. He had even saved the crew of an ocean-going three-masted schooner which had broken her back on Wolf Rock in the Western Approaches to the English Channel. What he knew about shipwrecks was that the various immediate dangers – to the crew and passengers, to those nearby, to the rescuers and to the environment, varied depending on the size of the vessel, the composition of her hull, the nature, toxicity or explosiveness of her cargo. Even apparently innocent lost cargoes could have unexpected consequences. He was all too well aware of the fates of containers full of bath-time ducks, beachwear flip-flops and Lego bricks and figures, lost years ago and still turning up on coasts all over the world. Also crucial were factors such as the number of people aboard, the effectiveness of those in command and how well they were all practised in emergency routines.

The state of the sea . . . The time of day . . . The proximity of help . . . The mood of the Gods . . . The disposition of the Fates . . .

Richard pushed past Ahmed and hung just beneath the lintel of the cave mouth, looking towards the distant waves, shining the long bright blade of the Beaver upwards. They were fifteen metres – fifty feet, down. The beam faded twenty feet short of the surface. But even so, it was suddenly full of tumbling wreckage. The first thing that plunged into the brightness was an outboard motor. Its top was big, black and cuboid. It had *Yamaha*, amongst other things, written on the side in faded paint. The long stem leading from the motor housing down to the propeller was snapped off short. Richard remembered the crunching sound. That would have been the propeller chewing itself to pieces on the coral head and snapping off, he thought, just after the reef tore the hull of the vessel wide open. But one outboard meant the wrecked boat was probably not much larger than the *Katerina*'s RIB. Ten- to twelve-seater max . . .

But then the twin of the first motor came tumbling into the light, even as the first span down towards him, trailing fuel like bright brown blood. And that upped the ante quite considerably. Twin motors like that could power a sizeable open boat, five to seven metres long and two to three metres wide. So he reckoned whatever had just ripped its heart and bottom out on the top of the spire must be around seven metres or twenty feet long, able to carry a dozen or so people if it met American Coastguard safety rules. But America was a long way from here. As, in all likelihood, were the coastguards.

But maybe not – for as the second motor came spinning after the first, Richard heard the whine of high-performance propellers closing from the same direction the wrecked boat had come from. No sooner did he register this than the much closer motors powering *Katerina* and the RIB added their turbulence to all the rest as they moved in to help the survivors, of whom there could be upwards of twenty, he thought with a frown that threatened to break the seal between his mask and his forehead. He glanced down, reversing the angle of the Beaver's beam, grimacing as it showed him what lay beneath. The motors were going to impact with the top of the reef six or so metres beneath the tips of his flippers. Well, there was nothing they could do about that. He angled the beam of his torch upwards once more, and gasped. Gasped so deeply that he damn near swallowed his regulator.

The next heavy metal object heading for the top of the reef sixty-five feet below the agitated surface was a surprisingly substantial anchor. It dragged a tangle of bright orange anchor cable behind it. And enmeshed in that tangle were three men, all fighting to get free. But their hope of doing so seemed slim in the extreme. Richard knew only too well that the cable wrapped around them was all-but unbreakable. Even his knife and his shears would take time to cut through it. He looked down once more, his mind racing. The first Yamaha hit the reef top with a sound like a flipped coin landing on a marble table and tottered there, miraculously upright, until a swirl of south-running current, the last of the lowering tide, took it and it fell drunkenly on to its side with a muffled metallic crash.

Richard looked upward again and was in action at once. Behind the entangled men came the entire bow section of the boat, a gently curving arrow-head some six feet long and reaching towards seven feet wide. Its broken and coral-torn edges gleamed in the torch light, revealing a metal hull beneath the thin paint and the thick weed in which it was covered. From the looks of things it even had a metal deck section-cum-bow seat under which all sorts of things had been stowed. Equipment came tumbling out as it sank. Anonymous bags and boxes. More anchor rope. Fishing tackle. For a moment it looked as though the helpless men would be simply crushed beneath the weighted, broken bow section, but then the south-running current took it and moved it, as though it were a solid sail, southwards. Even so, boxes of tackle, bundles of possessions and even jerry-cans of fuel continued to vomit out of it as it sailed away like a leaf on a breeze.

Richard threw himself forward, finning outwards and upwards. The moment he moved, he found Robin at one shoulder and Ahmed at the other. Whatever else might be going on above or below them, nearby or further away, they had one simple priority here. Their immediate responsibility was to rescue the men tangled in the anchor cable before they drowned. But no sooner were they in motion than the situation changed. One of the three managed to disentangle himself. He swam for the surface with powerful strokes, clearly desperate for air. But it seemed that his departure also removed some buoyancy from the tangle above the anchor, for as he departed, the two men still trapped in the orange toils began to sink more swiftly.

One, ensnared by his ankle, was still struggling to pull himself free. The other, who appeared to be enmeshed up to his knees, had apparently given up. Or, thought Richard, who knew almost as much about lifesaving as he knew about shipwrecks, he was on the verge of drowning. An unusual breadth of experience had taught him that the *not waving but drowning* image was the wrong one. Drowning people did not splash about and scream for help as bathers joking around tended to do. They quietly surrendered to the overwhelming inevitability of their situation and most often slid down almost secretly. Silently slipping away to their deaths, as often as not utterly unobserved by those closest to them.

He started finning towards the apparently comatose man as fast as he could, therefore, with the other two at his shoulder. The torch beam showed a skeletal ebony torso dressed in a ballooning white vest and a reed-thin waist above hips just wide enough to support baggy shorts. Arms like black branches stood out from broad shoulders, apparently reaching up towards the surface. Legs that looked little thicker than Richard's arms reached down to the heart of the Gordian knot which the anchor cable had made of itself. The apparently sleeping face was African, if almost skull-like, reminding Richard of mummies he had seen in museums in Cairo and London. Cavernous eye-sockets, broad, slightly flattened nose. Sunken jowls that emphasized the sharp lines of cheek- and jaw-bone. Yet it was a young face, strikingly handsome and heart-wrenchingly vulnerable. Something in it – youth and vulnerability perhaps – reminded Richard of his own son, William.

No sooner had Richard completed this almost instant summation than the second man also managed to break free. He started stroking desperately for the surface, desperately but increasingly sluggishly. A glance at his dive computer informed Richard that his destination was more than fifty feet away – more than half the width of an Olympic swimming pool above a man who was already out of air. No chance. He completed an almost instantaneous mental calculation and reached for Robin. She could get the survivor up from this depth using her octopus emergency oxygen line. She wouldn't want to go, but it had to be her because the last man was going on down past eighteen metres and was going to end up on the top of the reef beside the Yamahas before they could cut him free, by the looks of things, and Richard intended to go down with him to share his oxygen while he used the shears and the knife as best he could. Ahmed, as dive master, was not about to leave a situation like that either, so Richard could rely on his help, too.

Not for the first time, he found to his relief that Robin had read the situation exactly the same as he had. When he tapped her shoulder, pointed to the vanishing figure and gestured upwards with his thumb, she nodded once and was off, finning resolutely upwards, leaving a trail of buckshot in her wake as she lightened her load. He watched for an instant longer – one that was nearly fatal in a range of ways, as it turned out. For he saw, beyond the surface high above her, a star-bright point of light. To penetrate this depth, he knew, it could only have been a flare. And it must have been falling down towards the sea. No sooner had he registered its existence than it was extinguished – plunged into the water, he thought. But the moment of its death was the instant of something else's birth. Suddenly there was a sheet of wild, unsteady brightness covering the whole of the surface thirty feet above Robin and the man she was trying to rescue. The wrecked vessel must have covered the water all around it with petrol and the flare had set the sea alight. A strange sound echoed down through the restless, south-flowing water. That, combined with the buzzing of the motors, the thrashing and shouting of the terrified, burning survivors, and the unusual brightness of the burning water, was enough to bring the big grey reef sharks cruising inquisitively upwards, and the large tigers close behind them.

A strange, sharp metallic *chink!* redirected his attention downwards. The anchor had landed on the reef. Ahmed was already swimming down towards it, the pool of his torch beam illuminating the drowning man as though putting a strange, underwater ballet under a spotlight. Without a second thought, Richard powered after him. As he went, he cleared his ears and was struck immediately by a strange beeping sound. It took him a moment to realize it was the alarm on his dive computer. He looked at it. Its simple display warned him that he was diving too deep and getting dangerously short of air. Well, he knew someone who was down deeper and a good deal shorter, he thought grimly, and disregarded it altogether, plunging after Ahmed with all his might, heading for the dying African.

It was a matter of moments before the pair of them were beside the young man. Richard reached for his octopus tube, but Ahmed shook his head and gestured down at the cordage. With his Speedo shears and his Aropec K1 Quick Release knife, Richard was much more likely to do to this Gordian knot what Alexander did to the original. And the widely experienced dive master would be best suited to perform the simple – literal – life-saving.

As Richard settled down on the reef top in a way he would never have done under normal circumstances, he saw that Ahmed had decided not to use his octopus. Instead he was gently inserting his regulator into the young African's mouth. He pressed the button on the side. A stream of bubbles exploded from the nostrils of that slightly flattened nose. Then the boy's body jerked and the bubbles vanished – sucked deep into that skeletal but sizeable chest. The cavernous eyes blinked blindly. Richard felt his knees gently hit the sandy reef top, thankfully clear of lionfish, spiky sea urchins and fire coral, and went at once to work.

He followed the thin legs down past bony shins to ankles and feet that were apparently immovably entrapped in coil after coil of the bright orange rope. He saw immediately that part of the

problem was the young man's footwear. Most of the men he had
seen recently wore either flip-flops or trainers. This guy was
wearing hiking boots; good solid Timberlands by the look of it.
They were old but serviceable. And probably pretty expensive
regardless of what part of East Africa the boy had bought them
in. Still, in a matter of life and death . . . He pulled the K1 out
of its quick-release sheath and tried to get some purchase on the
laces. And the kid all-but kicked him in the face – would have
done so if his feet hadn't been tied down. Richard looked up.
The youngster was shaking his head wildly, bubbles exploding
from his mouth as he tried to talk the better part of twenty metres
under water.

Have it your way, thought Richard, giving a pantomime nod
to show he understood. Those must be some pretty special boots
. . . He snapped the knife back in its sheath and reached for the
shears at his belt. Even though they were brand new, razor sharp
and expertly wielded by a man who knew ropes and knots, it
still took some time to cut the big, bulky boots free. Long before
he severed the final bright but obstinate strand, Richard's dive
computer was emitting its alarm again. He didn't need to look
at it to know he was too deep, had stayed too long and was
dangerously short of air. But he was a relentlessly 'cup half full'
character. And the plus side in this situation was that the computer
was programmed to time him for a five-minute stop at ten metres
and one- to two-minute stops at fifteen and seventeen metres on
the way up. However, he doubted Ahmed and he were going to
linger over decompression stops. If they were going to get this
boy home alive then it would have to be up and out in short
order – and sort out the side-effects later.

And so it proved. The minute the last strand broke, Ahmed
simply dumped his dive belt and gave a very positive thumbs up
sign. In this instance it meant *hit the surface as fast as you can*,
though the last time Richard himself had used the gesture that
forcibly had been on the news that both his children had received
first-class honours degrees. He grabbed the young man's upper
arm, just beneath his bony shoulder, ripped the release cord to
dump his buckshot weights and powered towards the surface,
pacing Ahmed stroke for stroke. As they went up past ten metres
they collected Robin, who was waiting there at the dictates of

her dive computer and buddy-breathing with her guy. She was using the octopus. And was not, apparently, too disturbed by the grey sharks cruising inquisitively nearby.

Richard's dive computer was getting really angry with him by the time his head broke the surface alongside Robin's, Ahmed's and the men they had rescued. He looked around, disorientated. Shocked by the brightness. For the sea to the west, towards the African shore, was still on fire, the flames pushed back by that furnace-hot wind blowing westward out of Saudi. The yellow flames illuminated the smashed rear section of what appeared to be an open, metal-hulled fishing boat. What little remained of it was sitting at a crazy angle on the top of the reef spire. But it wasn't destined to stay there for long by the looks of things – certainly not if the restless, south-running rollers had anything to do with it.

Beyond the wall of fire, he could just make out the bridge and upper works of a vessel which looked pretty official and military. Coastguards out of Hurgada or El Gouna, as likely as not. And they were not coming any further this way – certainly not until someone put the burning water out. He span clumsily round, pulling Ahmed and their new friend with him. There behind them and blessedly close at hand was the RIB with Mahmood at the throttle, though the twelve-seater was looking a little crowded. Still, not to worry, Richard thought cheerfully. For just behind the RIB was *Katerina* herself, all lit up like a Christmas tree as Captain Husan brought her gently to the rescue.

TWO
Pressure

Richard's first thought was *I wonder how long it'll be before decompression sickness hits.* He glanced at his dive computer, so disorientated that he was mildly surprised not to see his Rolex. In among all the warning signals flashing there he saw the time. 01:10. Seventy minutes since the dive began. The deepest depth recorded was twenty metres. He had come to the surface in three minutes from that depth whereas the computer would have preferred at least fifteen including decompression stops. The back-lit readout further informed him he had remained at his maximum depth for the better part of a quarter of an hour. Moreover, twenty metres was a maximum depth, five metres deeper than planned. Those were the two most concerning factors – time at the extra depth and the uncontrolled speed of ascent.

He wondered what that combination would mean with regards to the manufacture of nitrogen in his bloodstream and the possible locations of bubbles of the stuff in his arteriovascular system and heart, in his joints, in his brain and beneath his skin. Only after these thoughts had flashed through his brain did he begin to register his immediate situation. He spat out his regulator and breathed fresh air. Like the unexpected currents, it was surprisingly cold all of a sudden. And blowing out of Africa, seemingly. He raised his right hand – his left was still supporting the rescued youth – and was about to switch off his head lamp when he realized that it made a useful beacon to guide either the RIB or *Katerina* to their immediate location. He opened his mouth to call to Robin when the situation took a severe turn for the worse.

Someone started screaming. With a shock that oriented him immediately in the here-and-now, Richard realized that there was someone in the water less than a hundred metres west of him. Someone who had not yet managed to swim over and join the others aboard or around the RIB. Someone who was too late now, for he had been caught up in the wall of fire that the new westerly wind was blowing down on them. A black head, silhouetted against the yellow dancing flame wall, was suddenly ablaze, unsettlingly like the head of a giant match. Ahmed shouted something inarticulate, let go of the rescued youth and struck out with a powerful crawl. He had taken four strokes when the burning head was jerked abruptly beneath the waves. The surface of the water was bright enough to show a sinister swirling. The burning man had not just ducked beneath the surface. Something had pulled him down.

'Sharks!' shouted Robin. Richard twisted in the water, and there, immediately behind them, its approach masked by the roaring and the confusion, was Mahmood's RIB. Strong black arms reached down over the inflated gunwale and the safety line looped along the top of it to pluck Robin and her survivor out of the water. Richard pushed the slack body he was supporting forward and it too was pulled aboard, though his Timberlands got tangled in the line.

Richard swung round, shouting, 'Ahmed!'

'Here!' came the sonorous reply, surprisingly close at hand.

'The RIB's full,' shouted Robin, her voice unusually high-pitched with strain and worry. 'Hang on to the safety lines and we'll tow you to *Katerina*!'

As they were side by side in the water, Richard and Ahmed clung on to the same side of the RIB, trusting Mahmood to keep it running straight and true. Robin was squashed between two seemingly comatose young men but was close enough to reach over and put her hand on top of Richard's. 'Don't worry,' she said, her voice brittle but trying for light and breezy. 'I'll keep an eye out for sharks.'

'It's not the sharks I'm worried about,' said Richard. 'You just keep an eye out for that bloody great triggerfish!'

Katerina's square stern offered two main modes of access. There was a ledge that folded down to sit immediately above the water, backed by a low wall which presented an easy step over on to the after deck. Mahmood nestled the RIB against the lowered ledge and the passengers packed within it climbed out and staggered aboard like a plague of zombies, dead-eyed, exhausted and lost. Most of them limping, a couple of them crawling and at least two being half carried, half dragged. On either side of the ledge there was a ladder. Richard and Ahmed used this to climb aboard, then they sat on the low wall with their feet on the ledge while they discarded their face masks and fins then began to shrug off their tanks. Robin helped Richard and, once he had secured the RIB, Mahmood helped Ahmed. In a locker by the diving equipment store there were three terry towelling robes. They shrugged these on and used them to dry themselves as best they could.

Within five minutes, the four of them were pushing their way gently through the men they had pulled out of the sea and climbing up on to the bridge. The slim, slight, dynamic figure of the self-styled Captain Husan was standing at the wheel, uncharacteristically inactive, his hand on the throttles and the helm doing little more than keeping *Katerina* in position against the twin pressures of wind and tide. And Richard could see why. The wall of flame showed little intention of subsiding.

The coastguard vessel was on the far side of it and the coast-guard captain was calling through the open link on the radio in accented but fluent English: 'Unless there is a pressing reason for you to return to Sharm, I would prefer you wait here until I can take the men you have retrieved aboard. It would mean less paperwork and fewer complications if they were all processed together at the coastguard base in Hurgada. I will not risk running my vessel through the fire, however, and almost every other course open to me – other than returning to Hurgada – is blocked by reefs. I repeat, therefore, that I require you to wait . . .'

'That will not be possible, I'm afraid, Captain,' answered Richard, taking command of the situation. He covered the mic and asked Husan, 'What's his name?'

'Captain Mohammed,' answered Husan shortly.

'Captain Mohammed, my name is Richard Mariner and I am in command of this vessel. We have some badly injured survivors here and only limited medical assistance on board. Furthermore, several of our people involved in the rescue are in acute danger of developing decompression sickness within the next thirty to sixty minutes – as indeed are some of the men we have brought aboard. There are two decompression chambers in Sharm and none so far as I know in Hurgada. We are going to Sharm at once, therefore. But we will of course alert the coastguard, police and immigration officials as well as the local hospitals as we approach. Our voyage, such as it is, is already registered with the harbourmaster at Sharm.'

'Very well,' answered Captain Mohammed after a brief pause. 'If you have genuine medical emergencies aboard.'

'Thank you, Captain. Speaking as one myself, I must confirm that we need to be in Sharm as soon as humanly possible.'

'Very well, *Katerina*. I too will be in contact with the authorities in Sharm. I should warn you, however, that the facilities you plan on using are by no means cheap. If you are going to pay for all the treatment you seem to be envisaging, you or your insurers had better have deep pockets. Goodnight and good luck. Over and out.'

'Right, Husan,' said Richard as he broke contact. 'Back to Sharm with all possible speed. Mrs Mariner and I will start assessing the injured – unless and until we get hit by decompression sickness ourselves. Mahmood, I suggest you get on to the authorities in Sharm and warn them when we will arrive and what we are bringing in with us. Check the prices, but bottom line is we will pay anything needed. Ahmed and I will need decompression, as will the man we rescued. That alone is the better part of seven hundred and fifty dollars an hour from memory. Use that as a base figure and work from there. And now I think of it, Mrs Mariner will need to join us too, to be on the safe side, along with the man she helped. The third man from the anchor, if he's aboard, should be OK in terms of the bends – or decompression sickness – because he didn't breathe any compressed air. But we need to assess who has what other injuries from the wreck itself, and who has suffered chemical burns or toxic ingestion from the fuel that was spilt. There can't be any burns from the fire, thank heaven, because as far as I know all the people Mahmood took aboard were out of the water before that flare set it alight. No shark bites either, with luck. That's it for us. Captain Mohammed can work out the rest when he gets his boat and his group of survivors back to the coastguard base in Hurgada. Then he and the authorities in Sharm can get started on the paperwork. When you've reported all that could you come down and give us a hand with the wounded?'

'That's all well and good,' said Robin as Husan brought *Katerina* round in a tight loop, reversed her course and began to power due east towards Sharm with the wind at her back. 'But where are these people from? And where were they going?'

'They're from East Africa,' answered Husan. 'And they're either going to El Tor on the Sinai, a little north of Sharm, or Alsorah across on the Saudi coast. They're almost certainly being smuggled.'

'Smuggled?' echoed Robin. 'But where on earth to?'

'Tell you what, guys,' interrupted Richard. 'This is a conversation we can have while we're doing elementary triage on the people we just brought aboard.' As he spoke he was in motion and Robin followed him as he ran down the companionways. 'If they speak any English or Arabic we might even get some input from them as we work. But from the look of them,' he added as they stepped on to the aft deck and found themselves the subject of a dozen blank and hopeless stares, 'if we don't start helping them soon, the only place they're going to be smuggled into is the graveyard.'

Robin nodded. Richard was right. As ships' captains – still very occasionally exercising command – they tended to keep their First Aid certificates up to speed. Richard in particular kept his up to Accident and Emergency level. When he told Captain Mohammed there was no medical help aboard it had been as close to a bare-faced lie as she had ever heard him come. Especially as *Katerina* boasted a pretty well-equipped little sickbay, though nothing like the facilities their twelve guests were going to need by the looks of them. Or anything like a decompression chamber.

But Robin was nothing if not single-minded. As she and Richard went through the rescued men, performing elementary triage, she quizzed Ahmed and Mahmood – when he joined them – and her surprisingly knowledgeable husband about the nuts and bolts of people smuggling in the Middle East. The triage was basic but simple, allowing maximum time to discuss the history, theory and practice as there was little enough to debate about medical matters. But before the conversation or the treatment began, Richard stood for a moment in silent thought as he tightened the white towelling belt of his terry robe and ordered his immediate priorities, planning what they needed to accomplish during the next half hour or so with the same meticulous foresight with which he planned a voyage or an important action. There were twelve men aboard who needed to be dealt with. They were all young men of African descent in varying states of distress and malnutrition, dehydration and sunstroke. Of the twelve, two were comatose. These were the men Richard and Robin had each brought up drowned to within spitting distance of their coffins. They had been carried aboard and laid on the side-benches. They needed to be checked, then moved to the medical facility and checked in greater detail. Two others were in little better shape, having been on the verge of sunstroke before they had been thoroughly doused in petrol, some of which had found its way into their stomachs and lungs; including the third man attached to the anchor – the one who had pulled free first. They were the ones who had crawled aboard and lay collapsed on the deck now, little better than the pair on the benches. Ahmed and Mahmood would have to support or carry these four men below first to await Richard and Robin's further attention in the sickbay while they continued the first assessment of the others here on deck. The next four were walking wounded – variously cut, battered and bruised from being thrown about in a metal boat that was breaking into a sharp-edged wreck on a coral head as keen as a bundle of razors. Looking more closely at the various wounds, some of which were still bleeding, Richard found himself surprised that the sharks had not attacked earlier and in greater numbers. These men also would have to be dispatched to the sickbay to be washed, disinfected and bandaged – either Richard or Robin could have stitched them up, but he decided to leave something for the hospital doctors to do. Looking around the deck, he was relieved to see that the last four were drenched on the one hand and dehydrated on the other – an interesting combination like something out of the *Ancient Mariner*, battered and bruised but neither skin nor bone seemed to have been broken, so they could be safely left on deck to catch their breath and to drink as much of the Hayat bottled water from the chiller as they could stomach.

Richard bent first over the young man he and Ahmed had released from the anchor. 'There's nothing we can do for this poor bloke in the short term. We'll have to get him decompressed the same as the rest of us, then into hospital. I think I'll give the guy who's swallowed petrol some oxygen to help his breathing. But really and truly we need them all down in the sickbay.'

The sickbay was overwhelmed almost at once. Its two beds were occupied by unconscious bodies and the two chairs beside them contained the men using the oxygen who were varying their breathing through the plastic face masks with sips from big plastic bottles of ice-cold Hayat water. A part-opened pack containing a further dozen bottles stood on the floor between them. Richard and Robin could just about fit in, but the wider they opened the doors to the medicine cupboards and the more equipment they got out, the more cramped it became. A line of four variously wounded men stretched down the corridor, therefore, with Ahmed keeping an eye on them until Richard could start tending to them.

No sooner had Richard started to clean and bandage the wounded than he found himself thanking heaven he had decided not to stitch them up, because all of a sudden he found he couldn't move his fingers very well. He actually stopped working on a gashed forearm for an instant and looked at his hands as though they belonged to someone else. He tried to bend his fingers. Winced with pain and stopped. It was as though a crippling case of arthritis had set into the joints of his hands with amazing rapidity. Frowning, he fell silent for the time-being and concentrated on trying to make his recalcitrant and increasingly painful digits do what he needed them to do. It suddenly occurred to him that he should have perhaps got dressed in more than a robe at an earlier stage, while he could still move. As he realized this, Husan's voice came over the tannoy. 'We're there, Captain Mariner. Sharm el-Sheikh marina. And I believe there is a welcome committee waiting for us on the dockside.'

There were two ambulances waiting for them under the day-bright dockside security lights, with two Terradyne Ghurka long-bodied armoured police vans and a white Ford Explorer SUV police car parked beside them. The ambulances and the Ghurkas were all positioned with their rears facing the dockside, doors open and motors running. Two pairs of hospital orderlies in cotton whites stood holding stretchers. Two pairs of policemen in protective vests stood holding what looked to Richard like Heckler and Koch UMPs with thirty-round magazines. Standing unmoving in the doorway that led out on to the deck, he changed his focus consciously without moving his head, taking in the nearer view on board. The four relatively undamaged men on *Katerina*'s deck, surrounded by empty Hayat water bottles, were all trying to make themselves look invisible. Hardly surprisingly, he thought. It was pretty unlikely that the ambulances were meant for them. Unless they put a foot wrong. Then, by the look of things, an ambulance would be the least of what they'd need.

Robin joined him and the pair of them came out of the bridge house and on to the deck, side by side, like the old people figured in a German mechanical clock. Richard paused and looked around carefully once more, taking in the view and calculating dreamily, wondering, suddenly, whether some of the nitrogen bubbles had migrated from his knuckles and knees up into his brain. An image of his blood fizzing like warm champagne rose unbidden to his imagination. He shook his head, careful of the twinges in his neck, shoulders and back. And focused. The hospital was just at the rear of the dock facility. They wouldn't even have to cross the road. The police station was a little more than a kilometre distant up behind the City Hall on El Benouk Road, not far from Anastasia Asov's cliffside villa in the old Elseid district high on the hilltop, overlooking *Katerina*'s own private dock in the next eastward bay.

As the gangplank was snugged into place by a couple of extremely nervous-looking harbourmaster's men, the rear door of the SUV opened and a tall, slim officer in immaculate khaki uniform stepped out and walked down. The men with the guns came smartly to attention and the men with the stretchers shifted from foot to foot a little apprehensively. All of them watched as Captain Husan and Mahmood secured the plank's lower end to *Katerina* and stood back. Richard gritted his teeth and made his way across the deck and up on to the dock, moving like a rusty robot. Robin followed him, both far too stiff and sore to even dream of changing out of their terry towelling robes and into something more formal, and both thanking God Almighty and Anastasia Asov that *Katerina*'s gangplank had handrails on either side of it.

As soon as they were on the dock itself, the officer came forward and saluted courteously, taking them both in with the gesture before turning towards Richard. Richard had an instantaneous, oddly indelible impression of a long, lean face with kindly, dark brown eyes beneath quizzically raised eyebrows and a wide, thin moustache between a straight nose and a generous, humorous mouth. The jaw was square and the teeth as white and perfect as a film star's. 'Captain Mariner,' he said smoothly in perfect English. 'I am Major Ibrahim of the Egyptian Police Service. I have been in contact at some length with my colleague Coastguard Captain Mohammed of the Swiftship Class 93 patrol vessel *Taba*. I am fully apprised of your situation and that of the men you have rescued and brought aboard. I see from your deportment that the decompression sickness has begun to take hold. I will keep formalities brief, therefore.' He glanced down at Richard's hands knowledgeably. 'And I will require no signatures at this stage.'

Major Ibrahim's wise eyes swept the dockside and *Katerina*'s increasingly crowded deck below it. 'I am a diver myself and appreciate your situation. It is my intention to allow you and everyone aboard your vessel who is hurt or wounded in any way immediate access to the hospital. Anyone *not* requiring immediate hospitalization will come with me up to El Benouk where I have secure accommodation and a police doctor waiting. During the next day or so as you recover, I or my colleagues from Immigration and Security will interview everyone we hospitalize tonight. And to ensure that everyone remains available, we have arranged a secure ward and I will leave a detachment of my men as guards. Yourself, Mrs Mariner and the crew of your boat, who are here quite legally of course, will only need to give witness statements and you will be free to go about your business when you have done so. You will not be held anywhere. Except in the decompression chamber.' The ends of the moustache lifted in a gentle smile. 'And you will not have to consider repatriation of course, until your visas run out. The others will join their friends in El Benouk as soon as they are well enough, and their cases will be assessed from there. Now, have you any questions?'

Richard might have and Robin certainly did. But they both felt as though a power drill was piercing every joint their body possessed, including the joints that controlled their jaws. Even the act of breathing was becoming agonizing. Speaking was currently out of the question. And both were becoming light-headed, almost on the verge of narcosis. 'I'm sure you do,' continued Major Ibrahim, nodding. 'But this is clearly not the best moment to ask them. The situation in which we all find ourselves will not have altered significantly when you get out of the decompression chamber some time tomorrow. We can address any matters you wish to raise then. In the meantime, I will take charge of the situation.'

Major Ibrahim gestured to the hospital orderlies, who came forward with the stretchers and, with the assistance of some colleagues from the back of the ambulances, helped Richard and Robin to lie down. The last thing Richard saw as the pair of them were loaded into the first ambulance was another set of stretcher-bearers hurrying down the gangplank followed by yet more men in white. They were closely followed in turn by the men in the bulletproof jackets with a lot more well-armed colleagues from the backs of the armoured cars.

Richard and Robin were soon joined in the first ambulance by Ahmed and, a little later, by the two unconscious men. Meanwhile, the five of them were separated from the two with lung and airway damage on the dockside. Those two joined the four with more superficial wounds. The five with decompression sickness were clearly to travel in the first ambulance, the other six in the second. As he had said he would, Major Ibrahim took the other four up towards the Central Police Station on El Benouk Road. Captain Husan and Mahmood would then take *Katerina* round to her private berth beneath Anastasia's villa, Richard reckoned. But everything other than his personal experiences began to take a back seat in his mind after the doors of the ambulance closed and the five-minute ride to hospital got under way.

Richard had hardly registered that the ambulance doors were closing and the vehicle was in motion before it stopped and the doors were opening again. Abruptly, he was surrounded by lights, bustle, strange faces and white coats. The specialist doctor on call introduced himself as Dr Zabr as he went about assessing the situation of the first five arrivals swiftly and with a practised eye. He prescribed Ibuprofen as he talked through the triage with a younger colleague and the male nurses manning the decompression suite. Under the circumstances, the anti-inflammatory was injected. A pin-prick that, in comparison with the agony in their joints, they could literally hardly feel. As he and the others were wheeled through to the hyperbaric section, Richard lost sight of the six walking wounded from the second ambulance, bound, no doubt for assessment and more advanced treatment than he and Robin had offered, and then the secure ward under police guard.

As the five of them were wheeled through to the hyperbaric area, Dr Zabr's conversation with his young colleague – courteously conducted, like the introduction, in English – thoroughly refreshed his understanding of decompression procedures. The three who were awake were type two patients in the international triage system, Dr Zabr was explaining, but because they had taken so long to get here, he was happy to treat them as potential type three casualties like the two unconscious men, who might well be at serious risk of permanent damage or even death. Joint pain such as the three waking patients were experiencing – and the tell-tale welts and skin rashes evident when their robes were opened – could well lead to dangerous spinal or pulmonary damage, which was already threatened by the pain they were experiencing moving their heads and breathing. Even if the type three victims had not necessitated the use of the decompression chamber, it would hardly have been appropriate at this stage to insist on the more usual type two treatment of repeating the dive – this time being careful to observe decompression stops dictated by the dive computers. It was a procedure often recommended in less serious type two cases because, unlike decompression in the hyperbaric chamber, it was free. That was as far as the conversation got before they were at the chamber itself. The three who could – just about – walk, were helped inside. The other two were rushed in beside them. And it was at this stage that Richard began to look around himself once more, made more alert by the resurgence of knee pain when he bent his legs in order to sit down.

The decompression chamber, entered through a round, pressure-proof bulkhead door, was surprisingly neat, bright and well fitted out. It was long and spacious, more like a waiting room than a treatment area, with comfortable chairs, piles of magazines and even some books. It was tubular, however, and in spite of its size felt a little like a submarine. The nautical effect was further emphasized by the fact that there was a series of round windows resembling port holes in one wall that looked out into the control room. All in all, had he been more like his old self, however, Richard would have been making wisecracks about Hobbits and their holes.

Once he was seated and the Ibuprofen began to kick in, Richard became dreamily detached once more, watching as both doctors and the medical staff placed Robin and the other patients inside speedily and efficiently, indicating the oxygen masks that were available to help with breathing, settling them over noses and mouths, pulling elastic fittings behind their ears and strapping or clipping monitors to wrists and fingers so that blood pressure, respiration and heart rate could be monitored from outside while compressed air gently elevated the pressure in here at about the same speed as the pressure in an airplane cabin was varied after take-off and before landing. Pressurizing any faster would endanger their eardrums. Eventually the overall pressure would rise to the equivalent of three atmospheres – the ambient pressure at twenty metres underwater. And then, slowly, begin to reduce.

Before Dr Zabr closed the door and began the procedure, his young colleague entered the chamber and sat in the last spare chair. 'I am Doctor Adel,' he said quietly. 'I will stay with you throughout the procedure in case there is any emergency. I suggest you keep the oxygen masks in place – though I know they are not very comfortable – as breathing oxygen helps to rid the nitrogen from your systems. The entire procedure will take about six hours, so I suggest you relax.' He picked up a magazine and began to glance through it.

Neither Robin nor Ahmed availed themselves of any of the reading material, Richard observed, the oxygen giving him a short-term surge of energy and focus. Doubtless because, like him, they were finding every attempt to move any part of their bodies excruciating. And the pain seemed to be most intense where it had first manifested itself – in the knuckles. Though, he thought, in his case his knees ran his hands a close second. Both knees had been injured in a terrorist incident some time ago, and had been repaired with sufficient titanium to set off

security alarms at every airport he ever travelled through. The
bends seemed to have targeted the injuries with particular force.
Dreamily, he considered that, in his case at least, the term 'bends'
was wildly inappropriate. It was trying to bend his fingers, toes,
hips and knees that really caused the most acute agony. As the
air pressure began to rise, however, the pain began to recede,
attacked not only by the reduction of nitrogen bubbles but by
the gathering effect of the anti-inflammatory drug. And, perhaps
not too surprisingly, given the nature of their adventure so far,
the stress, the pain and the mildly narcotic effect of the Ibuprofen,
once the pain was reduced to bearable levels he found himself
beginning to nod off.

Richard jerked awake, unusually disorientated. Blinking owlishly,
he looked around himself, registering the featureless, clinical
brightness of his surroundings. Some partially recalled memory
deep in his subconscious felt mild surprise that he could move
so freely and without pain. But he was cold. The wetsuit top and
rash vest beneath it were clammy. In spite of the robe they were
wrapped in, his legs were covered in goose bumps. The Speedo
boots felt like lumps of ice – and the shorts felt little warmer.
The next thing after the chill that he registered was the fact that
he was ravenous. Visions of thick bacon and sausage sandwiches
dripping with butter, mustard and HP sauce filled his head.
    It was these mouth-watering fantasies that helped him
remember where he was. He had been dreaming occasionally of
bacon, sausages, pork chops and crackling since he arrived in
the strictly Muslim country where such things were utterly
forbidden. He glanced at the dive computer on his wrist. Isolated
from the rest of his equipment, it told little more than the time,
which was seven a.m. local. His waking mind raced. It must have
been nearly three by the time they reached the hospital. The
young doctor – what was his name, Adel? – had said the procedure would take six hours, and yet he felt absolutely fine after
four. He reached up – glorying in the pain-free movement of his
fingers, wrists, elbows, shoulders – and removed the oxygen
mask from his numb ears. He reached out as though preparing
to embrace a giant and stretched luxuriously. Better than fine, in
fact. Rejuvenated. Almost reborn. He had never felt so alive and

full of fizzing vitality. He looked around himself. Robin and Ahmed were also sound asleep – as was the young doctor. Richard found himself smiling indulgently, overflowing with cheery good-nature. In this kind of mood, he thought, I could give Father Christmas a run for his money.

'*Sah!*'

The whispered word came as a complete surprise. So much so that he almost supposed it to be part of the returning sensation to his numb ears and not a real sound at all.

Until it was repeated, more urgently and slightly more loudly. '*SAH!*'

Richard looked across the chamber. The young man with the baggy white vest he had cut free from the anchor was awake and half on his right side, his torso raised, supported by his right arm. Huge dark eyes framed with thick, full lashes stared at him with a desperate fierceness. 'Sah!' spat the boy again, frowning with the effort, as though he was enraged with the entire world.

Even after an adult lifetime in command of ships under all sorts of circumstances, it took a moment more for Richard to realize the young man was calling him *sir*.

'Yes?' Something in the man's look and tone made Richard answer in the same almost-whisper as he was using.

'Sah. See. *See!*' Long, delicate black fingers were pulling desperately at the baggy vest around his middle.

Intrigued, but still not quite certain of what was going on, Richard stood and took a step towards the gurney. He realized his right hand was still attached to the equipment that had been strapped and clipped on to it four hours ago. But the way he had reached out before stretching made him confident there was enough play in the wiring to let him cross the chamber without taking it off if he was careful. Silently on his Speedo dive boots, pulling at the wiring on his right hand with his left fist, he crossed to stand by the young African's side.

The fingers bunched the thin white cotton and pulled it up to his armpit, revealing a cavernous belly and a set of ribs that were separated by deep, dark valleys. Loose and low around his hips, which stuck out like mountain peaks, he was wearing a thick black rope knotted just about tightly enough to keep his baggy khaki shorts up. His skin was a deep, dull brown, mottled with bruising, scratched, scraped and welted. None of which really registered with Richard, whose gaze was simply arrested by the fact that between the black rope and the bowed ribs the man was wearing a makeshift rubber body or money belt. Its very existence was a surprise to Richard, who thought he must have seen or felt anything the man was wearing at some stage of the rescue. But clearly not.

And the implication of the young man's action – let alone of the pleading expression on his fine boned face – was clear enough. Major Ibrahim or the men from Immigration and Security would search everyone taken aboard *Katerina* and brought here because they were at the very least illegal immigrants – whether they were being smuggled or trafficked in the first place. And anything they found was likely – no, certain – to be confiscated. But no one was likely to search Richard, Robin or Ahmed. And, to make things simpler still, Richard was wearing a baggy terry robe beneath which he could almost have hidden the young African – let alone his money belt.

He met the young man's desperate stare and nodded once, decisively. As the long, dark fingers hurriedly started to loosen the belt, Richard look a swift and secretive glance around. Robin, Ahmed and Dr Adel were all sound asleep. There was no one at the portholes through which the people in the control room could look in. The African on the second gurney also seemed deeply unconscious. Richard undid his robe left-handed and eased it open. The desperate young man pulled the money belt free – it was little more than a cleverly adapted combination of inner tubing from a tyre and more black rope. There was no way to see what it contained but it was clearly desperately important.

Richard took it, assessing from the feel of it what the chances were that it had got water in it during last night's adventure. It felt light and therefore he assumed it was probably dry. He crossed back to his seat and rolled up his dive vest – something made easier by the fact that he had dumped all his buckshot weights. The blue panelling ended at about navel-level. There was a broad black band which had contained the weights reaching on down to his hips. With fingers made clumsy by the clip-on attachments and wristband, he nevertheless managed to loop the belt round his hips over his rash vest and knot it tight. When he rolled the black band down again, the money belt beneath it simply vanished, black on black. And when he tightened his robe once more no one would ever have suspected that it was there.

The young man, having watched all this with incredible, agonized intensity, collapsed back on to the gurney and put his left arm over his eyes. The gesture was so defeated and hopeless that Richard, still in Santa mode, got up once more and crossed to stand beside him. 'It's all right,' he said gently, as though speaking to his own son. 'We'll get through this. You'll be OK.'

The painfully thin forearm came off the emaciated face. The huge eyes gazed up at him, their pupils so dark as to seem almost black. Their whites jaundiced and veined. The sculpted lips parted, revealing uneven teeth stained from a lifetime chewing *khat*. 'Nahom,' he said. His voice was thin and weak, yet somehow almost steely and determined.

Richard thought he sounded so goddamned *young*. 'Eh?' he enquired.

The left hand rested like a spider on his chest. 'Nahom,' he said again.

Richard caught on at last. He pointed to himself, his index finger extended by the clip on its tip. 'Richard,' he said.

'Ree-*kard*.'

'Close enough, Nahom, old thing,' he said.

The black spider pressed on the vest draped over that cavernous, skeletal chest. '*Nahom*,' he said again.

'Nice to meet you—'

'You making new friends?' interrupted Robin's voice, a little croakily.

'Yup. Seems the chap Ahmed and I rescued is called Nahom. I don't know what your new friend's called yet . . .'

'How're you feeling?'

'Hundred per cent, actually. Tip-top. Tickety-boo.'

'You and Bertie Wooster.'

'Very funny. What about you?'

'Surprisingly fit, all things considered. D'you think I'll set off all sorts of alarms if I pull this stuff off my hand?'

'Might alert someone, I suppose.'

'Which could be a good thing. Any idea what they told us about lavatory facilities in this thing?'

'No. That is, no one mentioned anything about—'

Dr Adel stirred. 'There is a toilet available for urgent use,' he said drowsily. 'But it is not what one would call *private*.'

'So I'd have to rely on four men and a husband closing their eyes and ears. I think I'll hold it, thank you very much.'

'Very well,' said the doctor amenably. 'Under the circumstances, I'll check everyone and see whether we can equalize the pressure earlier than planned.'

They were out of the hyperbaric chamber just after eight. While Robin went to check the plumbing, Richard went to a phone zone and called Anastasia's villa, making contact with Sasha, the housekeeper, who agreed to send a car for them at once and bring Richard's wallet so that he could settle the hospital's immediate and longer-term financial demands.

Then Richard oversaw the movement of Nahom and his companion into the secure ward with the other six. Although Major Ibrahim's men were conspicuously on guard at the door, there was little sense of threat or incarceration in the bright room, which didn't even have security netting on the windows, perhaps because all that was visible through them was the four-lane highway and, beyond that, a grove of scraggy palm trees and then the desert. It was hardly breakfast time, thought Richard grimly, and it was already as bright as burning magnesium out there – thirty degrees Celsius or so, in the shade. If you could find any shade.

He turned back and caught the attention of a ward orderly. 'Do you speak English?' he asked.

'Of course, sir.' The man was faintly surprised to be asked.

'I am sure the food in this fine hospital is of the highest standard—'

'Of course it is, sir—'

'But it will still be *hospital food*, if you understand me. Is it possible to make special arrangements for these men, and for their guards if needs be . . .'

'Well, I am sure that something could be arranged, should it prove necessary.'

'Send any bills to me, Captain Richard Mariner, at the Villa Shahrazad.'

'Ah. Mademoiselle Asov's villa.'

'You know Mademoiselle Asov?'

'I'm sure everyone in Sharm knows her – or knows *of* her. And everyone knows of the Villa Shahrazad.'

Richard nodded once. 'Good. But that doesn't cover the hospital charges. Can you show me to the finance office?'

'Of course.' The orderly showed him to the hospital's finance office, where Ahmed was waiting with his wallet, and lingered while he made the necessary arrangements. The office was as ultra-modern as the rest of the hospital, and Richard was careful to make sure he was not overlooked by the security cameras as he keyed in his PIN number. But he failed to notice the one slightly old-fashioned element of the place – a convex mirror high in the corner behind his back, which, as it happened, gave a perfect view of what his fingers were doing.

Five minutes later, Richard, Robin and Ahmed were walking across the forecourt to the air-conditioned white Mercedes S-Class saloon which was Anastasia's Sharm el-Sheikh run around. If they were at all embarrassed by the fact that they were all still dressed in towelling robes, they did not show it. 'I am looking forward to the biggest breakfast Sharl the chef can rustle up for us,' Richard announced, pushing his wallet deep into the right-hand pocket of the towelling robe. 'Something really epic.'

As he spoke, Robin slipped a wifely arm round his waist. 'My God!' she said, shocked. 'No big breakfasts for you, sailor! In fact, I think a bit of a diet is called for. From the feel of things down round your tummy, you've put on about ten pounds in weight since we arrived out here!'

'Ah,' said Richard. 'About that . . .'

THREE
Sharm

Nahom's money belt lay on the dining table amid the remains of the largest breakfast that Sharl the chef had prepared in five years. Eggs cooked in every manner possible, tomatoes, chicken and beef frankfurter sausages, beans – baked or boiled. Freshly baked bread and toast made from yesterday's batch. Croissants and a range of conserves. Cold meats of every sort and preparation that did not include anything *haram* or unlawful. A dazzling array of fruit, from mangoes and melons, to oranges, tiny sweet bananas and dates. Coffee, a bewildering variety of teas and hot chocolate. And – tempting Robin almost beyond endurance – a range of confections largely fashioned from millefeuille, coconut threads, sponge cake, almonds and honey.

Robin looked down at the belt lying like a black snake in the middle of the colourful leftovers then, her eyebrows raised quizzically, she looked around Ahmed, Husan and Mahmood. 'What do *you* think?' she asked. The conversation had been going back and forth since the first piles of pancakes and omelettes had arrived. Richard, Robin and Ahmed had used the brief time Sharl had taken with his initial preparations to change into day clothes. And in Richard and Robin's case, replace their dive computers with the Rolexes Mahmood had brought up with their clothes from *Katerina*. Husan and Mahmood were still in the clothes they were wearing last night.

'I don't know,' said the captain, speaking for all of them. 'Mister Richard?'

Richard was standing nursing a steaming cup of Jamaican Blue Mountain high roast Arabica at the huge French windows. He was slow to answer, entranced by the view that encompassed a broad, flagged sun-filled balcony ending in a mock-classical porphyry balustrade, topped with terracotta *jardinières*, reaching from side to side along the edge of a cliff overlooking the private anchorage a couple of hundred feet below, the private beach beside it and the whole panorama of the ink-blue bay and rose-red headland beyond. He turned back with some reluctance to the matter in hand. 'I think we keep it safe but leave it sealed,' he said decisively. 'When Nahom gave it to me it seemed clear enough he didn't want Major Ibrahim finding it, opening it, interfering with it or confiscating it. I guess the same would go for us.'

'But what do you think is in it?' Robin persisted.

'Money. ID of some kind, maybe. What would you need if you're being smuggled somewhere?'

Captain Husan stood up. Like Richard, he was a man of action and thought best on his feet. He eased his belt and settled his jeans on his hips. Then he paced across to the French windows to look down on his tiny white command hundreds of feet below, his flip-flops slapping the dining room's marble floor. His wiry frame topped Richard's shoulder – just exceeding Robin's five foot eight. His hair was a virile cluster of tight-curling black waves, gleaming with pomade. His square, determined chin was cleft in the middle. His expression, even when wrestling with a problem that was as much practical and legal as it was moral and ethical, was cheerfully good-natured. He enjoyed something of a reputation as a smuggler himself – just the kind of man a slightly shady Russian oligarch would want in charge of a superfast cruiser, thought Robin. And certainly the man most likely to know what someone being smuggled across the waters around the Sinai would need.

'Currency,' he said. 'Probably US dollars. Almost as good as gold and nowhere near as heavy. Ten thousand is the going rate, as far as I know. ID if he's being smuggled somewhere to work. Two sorts. Genuine papers for use in emergencies and fake for use when he gets where he's going, unless he's part of a chain that guarantees to supply ID on arrival. But that's not likely – that kind of chain is usually run to get girls and boys into the sex trade. Contact names and addresses for when he gets wherever he's going. Probably written by his contact in the language they use at his destination. You'd be surprised how many people turn up at the Israeli border only speaking some kind of Somalian Arabic, asking for directions to somewhere in Jerusalem.'

'Sounds logical,' said Richard.

'Convincing,' agreed Robin. 'Is that it?'

'And I suppose there's a chance he'll have some kind of cell phone,' Husan continued. 'Depends whether he's going where he's going just as a loner or whether there have been others from his tribe, village or family who have already gone through and/or others waiting at home to follow him.'

'Is that usual?' asked Robin. 'Whole families trying to get through one after another?'

'It's been known,' answered Husan. 'These people are desperate, almost always because of circumstances they can't control. They aren't stupid or helpless or hopeless. They are, by and large in my experience, fearless, intelligent, ruthless, highly motivated and astonishingly adaptable. If they could take the planning, guts and determination they put into trying to get a new life and put it all into any kind of legitimate commercial exercise, half of them would be millionaires. So, if one of them finds a route out that works for them, they'll try and get the message back so other people can follow them.'

'But, to get back to the original point,' said Richard, putting his coffee cup down on the laden table beside the blood-red dregs of Robin's Hibiscus tea. 'What's the best thing we can do with Nahom's belt until we find out what's going to happen to him?'

'We know what's going to happen to him,' said Ahmed. 'I'm right, aren't I, Captain Husan? Whether his papers are genuine or fake, whether he has them to hand or says he lost them in the wreck, it won't make much difference, I'm afraid. They'll either find out where he came from and send him back there or they'll keep him here and put him in a prison or a camp.'

'Like the Sudanese they used to hold in Al-Qanater Prison.' Husan nodded. 'Abu Zaabal Prison and Shebeen Al-Kom. There are plenty of places. If he's stuck here he could apply for refugee status. Egypt is signed up to both the 1951 Refugee Convention and the OAU Refugee Convention.'

'But that's not too likely, is it?' Mahmood observed. 'He wasn't crossing the Gulf as a refugee. He was being smuggled. Unless he's actually one of the smugglers, of course. Either way, he's an illegal immigrant no matter how you look at it.'

'What can we do to help him?' wondered Robin.

'Legally? Nothing,' answered Husan. 'You can visit him in hospital. Try to find out what his plans were. What they are now – if he wants to tell you. And if he speaks enough English to communicate – I guess you don't speak any East African languages. If he's Sudanese, for instance, he could speak any one of fifteen separate languages independently of the three different types of Arabic. How is your Arabic, by the way?'

'Not good,' admitted Richard.

'Better hope he's from Eritrea then. At least English is one of their national languages – along with Italian, Arabic and some local tribal dialects. Then, if you can manage to understand each other, you will have to decide whether you want to help him with whatever he's planning to do now. Whether you want to help him badly enough to start breaking the law yourselves.'

'This is hardly legal, Captain Mariner,' observed Major Ibrahim. 'And I can scarcely imagine how you have arranged it in the time you've had.'

Richard tried to read the officer's tone as the pair of them looked at the trolley full of food which had been brought from one of the restaurants at the nearby Jaz Mirabel hotel to the door of the secure ward, only to be held there like a terrorist suspect, under the guns of the guards. A waiter, in immaculate white with the hotel's logo on his breast, stood listening with lively interest, apparently following the discussion and every now and then flicking a more nervous glance towards the guards and their Heckler & Koch MP5s.

'I shall allow it through this once,' continued Ibrahim smoothly, 'on the assumption that there are no metal files or wire-cutters in those delicious-looking loaves of bread – or that the pile of hardboiled eggs there does not conceal a weapon of any kind. And that whatever lies beneath this dome does not double as a map of an escape route.' He raised the dome in question to reveal a pile of pancakes dripping with honey. 'But suggesting that my guards can share in this bounty comes very close to being bribery.'

'*And*,' added Dr Zabr, whose tone was unmistakably offended, 'while I can only applaud your good intentions, you may want to consider one or two facts, Captain Mariner. First, the hospital's kitchens are second to none and our dietary experts not only feed our patients but use the food as an element of their treatment. Furthermore, it may not have occurred to you but at least part of what is wrong with these young men is that they are severely malnourished. Rich food as represented by those honey cakes, for instance, might very well make them violently sick.'

There was no mistaking the amusement in Major Ibrahim's tone now. 'It is always our good deeds that get us into trouble is it not, Captain? Doctor Zabr, allow me to suggest that you select those elements of this wonderful feast that are least likely to complicate the treatment of the men in this ward – the dishes of melon, say, the grapes and the dates. Perhaps an egg or two and a loaf of bread. Some coffee, perhaps; and is that hot choco- late? Then anything which might be unsuitable here will, I am sure, find an appropriate place amongst the meals prepared by your dietary experts for patients elsewhere in the hospital.'

Five minutes later the Jaz Mirabel waiter wheeled a depleted trolley into the ward with Richard at one shoulder and Major Ibrahim at the other. While the ward nurses checked the prefer- ences of the eight patients in the twelve-bed ward and began to carry the food and drink over to their beds, Richard and the major continued their conversation.

'What is your primary purpose in this visit, Captain?'

'Of course, I want to see how the patients are progressing . . .'

'An understandable urge. There is, is there not, a bond that forms between rescuer and rescued? Much like that I have observed between guard and prisoner.'

'Indeed. And, of course, I wish to find out what I owe the hospital and settle the debt so far . . .'

'Perhaps when Doctor Zabr is a little calmer . . . Though in fact it will be the finance department you will need to speak to in the end, after the good doctors have completed their recording of the treatment so far, the costs incurred to date and made an estimation of what will be needed in the future – which is one of the aspects I am here to check on, of course. The eight men in this ward . . .' he glanced around the gaunt, wide-eyed faces with their bulging cheeks and working jaws, '. . . will, in due course, be joining the four I am currently holding in my own secure facilities. But I need to know how soon I can begin the transfers to El Benouk. Talking of which, I am looking forward to having a less informal chat with you, Mrs Mariner and the crew of the vessel involved in last night's rescue. And that, finally, is the other aspect of my visit. I need to check with the doctors which of these men is strong enough to be interviewed, and when I can go about starting those interviews.'

'You can't wait until you have them up at your police station on El Benouk Road?'

'Alas, no. Captain Mohammed and I find ourselves in an interesting situation, you see. All of the men he has interviewed in Hurgada and all of the men I have interviewed here so far assure us that they are helpless victims of a ruthless confidence trick. They are all innocent Eritreans, who in all good faith have paid local men there quite large sums of money to bring them to Egypt where legal employment has already been secured for them. Or so they claim to have been assured. And there was, apparently, detailed and convincing documentation to prove what they had been told. Unfortunately – and this is as true for the men in Hurgada as well as for my four up at El Benouk Road – they lost all of their paperwork, IDs and money in the wreck. They all maintain this story in the face of the patent facts that there is no such employment and that, even if there was, this is not the way to go about securing it. And finally, as we seem to have rescued everyone except one unfortunate victim of shark attack, logic dictates that at least some of the men we have in Hurgada and here must be the people smugglers who set this all up in the first place.'

'How will you be able to tell which is which?' asked Richard. 'Given that no one is likely to admit to a crime that would get them a good long term in prison, even after their situation as illegal aliens has been sorted out here?'

'Experience over many years suggests,' said Major Ibrahim, his quiet voice suddenly cold and extremely serious, 'that the smugglers responsible for all this will be the ones with the money and the phones. Probably hidden in waterproofed money belts.'

'Do you think there's any way we can open it without him knowing?' asked Robin. The table was cleared of breakfast things now. The black snake of the money belt lay in the middle of it. Richard and Robin were alone, and talking in low voices, as though they were up to mischief and didn't want to be discovered. It was early afternoon. Richard had just returned from the hospital and the pair of them were due at the police station at four o'clock local time to give their statements to Ibrahim in person.

'I don't think so,' answered Richard after a short pause. 'And I'm still not sure I want to go through the poor guy's private things.'

'But from what you say, this *poor guy* might well be one of the smugglers!' snapped Robin. 'I know we've formed a bit of a bond – because of the rescue, the decompression . . .'

'The fact that he looks to be about the same age as William and Mary . . .'

'Whatever. But the simple fact is that we don't know him from Adam and if everyone who was up to no good actually *looked* evil then there'd be a great deal less trouble in the world. Didn't you get a chance to speak to him?'

'Not in private, no. He was still pretty woozy to begin with, and I'm pretty sure his English is almost as limited as my Arabic. And in any case, after that back-handed telling-off about the ways hotel food can undermine security as well as good medical practice, both Ibrahim and Zabr stayed really close.'

'Even so, you have to be getting some sort of impression. Is Nahom a smuggler or was he being smuggled?'

'I'll bet he's an innocent guy trying to get to a better life, though I'm certain Ibrahim has him pegged as a smuggler. Perhaps as the leader of the group. But the problem is that I'm still not sure whether our charming Major was playing mind games with me or not.'

'Looks like one of them is. Either Ibrahim or Nahom.'

'Could he *know* about the money belt?'

'Ibrahim?' Robin shrugged. 'You mean one of the four guys he has in custody at the police station has already put some suspicion in his mind?'

'That, or maybe the decompression chamber has video.'

'It may have but I doubt it. Especially as if Ibrahim had footage of you taking Nahom's belt as you say you did, you wouldn't be back here in Villa Shahrazad chewing the fat with me. You'd be up in a cell chewing the fat with the other four guys he has under lock and key. You're sure no one was watching when Nahom gave it to you?'

'No one I could see. But to be fair, if he suspects Nahom had a belt then it's not really a problem that would take even *one* pipe for Sherlock Holmes to solve, is it? I mean, everyone agrees Nahom was unconscious all the time he was aboard *Katerina* so he can't have done anything with it before he came ashore. And everyone was packed in together so no one had a chance to just take it without being seen. Ibrahim and his guards watched him being brought off *Katerina*, put in the ambulance and then being transferred to the decompression chamber. He didn't wake up until the decompression was complete. The people from the hospital would have turned it over the moment they found it. And they *would* have found it, either when they were getting Nahom ready for treatment after he came out of the chamber or for bed. So that's where the transfer must have happened – in the chamber. And, given the suspicion, they'll have searched the chamber – which is hardly overstocked with hiding places. So if someone said Nahom had a belt and it's not on his person or it's not in the chamber, then the next most likely thing is that you or I took it. I'm the first one Ibrahim saw, so I'm the one he started with the mind games.'

'OK,' said Robin. 'So the bottom line at this stage seems to be do we open it and go through it before we go across to see the laughing policeman? Or do we leave it until after the interview and see whether he gives anything further away.'

'Or whether he plays even more mind games.' Richard shrugged.

'But, for all his cheerful charm, he strikes me as someone who doesn't miss much,' warned Robin.

'So if we open the belt before we go and find anything suspicious in it then we might as well just take it with us, because he'll see from our expressions that we know more than we're saying.'

'From the sound of things, he knows that already, lover.'

'But if we leave it for the time-being at least we won't be any deeper in trouble than we are now.'

'True. But if we're not going to open it or take it, then where on earth are we going to hide it?'

'Is it usual for a major to conduct witness interviews?' asked Robin, her face a picture of innocent enquiry. She looked around

Ibrahim's office. It was a spacious, air-conditioned room with windows looking back over a hedge-lined parking lot with bougain-villeas in full pink flower. The windows were closed; the netting fly-screens outside them were closed also. And where the frames provided thick lines of shadow, the netting was packed with long-bodied, red-tailed hornets sheltering from the sun. The only sounds were a muted rumble of traffic and the whispering of the air-conditioning unit.

'It depends on the investigation,' answered Ibrahim. 'And on the witness.'

'Well,' said Richard, 'we feel very flattered anyway.' He leaned back in his chair, apparently completely at ease. His gaze wandered away over the certificates and photographs on the wall. Everyone from the President to the Chief of Police by the look of things. All staring accusingly straight at him.

'A feeling that may, sadly, be short-lived,' continued Ibrahim blandly.

'How so?' He had Richard's full attention now.

'I'm afraid you will not be interviewed together.' As he spoke, Ibrahim pressed a button on his desk console. A distant buzzer sounded. 'I will take down the details Mrs Mariner remembers about the incident and its aftermath. I have a colleague who will take your statement in another room, Captain.'

More mind games, thought Richard grimly, focusing on Ibrahim's bland smile. The door behind him opened. 'Fine,' he said cheerfully. 'Can't wait. Lead me to him.' He was still smiling amenably when his interviewer came right in to stand between him and Robin. And the smile hardly flickered at the surprise he felt when he saw her.

'Sergeant Sabet will take you next door. She and I will compare your versions of the incident later.'

She stood at five foot three. The white uniform made her look a little on the plump side, but there were clearly several layers of it. Her name badge was printed in English and Arabic: *Gamila Sabet*. The headdress that concealed her hair framed a round face which would have been almost girlish were it not for the deter-mined dimple in her chin and the way her espresso-dark eyes somehow also managed to contain a hint of steely intelligence.

'If you will follow me, Captain,' she said in quiet but perfectly modulated English. 'This need not take too long.' Richard hadn't heard a tone like that since childhood visits to the dentist who promised, *Now this won't hurt at all.*

Half an hour later, Richard really was beginning to feel that the sergeant was starting to extract information which, like teeth, he was unwilling to part with. In her smaller, cramped office there was no air conditioning. A pedestal fan blew slightly cooler air at Richard, who crouched on an uncomfortable chair that was rather too small for him. The windows behind the sergeant stood wide open and only the dusty netting kept the restless hornets out of the room. On the other hand it allowed the snarl of traffic, the fine dust on the brick-kiln breeze, the odd mixture of smells represented by hot tar, petrol and bougainvillea and the restless buzzing of the hornets all to enter the room.

Sergeant Sabet had prompted him to establish the facts of the rescue as he remembered them, but he was getting the increasingly disturbing feeling that she already had all of the information she needed and was checking it against what she had been told – with a decided spin on the facts, perhaps even a hidden agenda. To begin with, she seemed certain that the men were all from Eritrea. That the wrecked boat, designed to carry twelve, had been carrying twenty-four. Twenty-four passengers. And an unknown number of smugglers – or traffickers – who were currently hiding themselves in the crowd of survivors both here and in Hurgada. The four men held in this police station overnight, together with the thirteen under the control of Captain Mohammed in Hurgada, had all been keen to explain what was going on and what innocent part they had been playing in it.

Sergeant Sabet was typing everything he said into a laptop as he said it – as well as making a recording of the conversation. He hadn't thought to ask about having a lawyer present. He hadn't thought he would need one. Now he was beginning to wonder, though he had no idea whether the Egyptian legal system would have allowed him one in any case. But he could have done with one. Particularly as the way her eyes were moving over the screen made him wonder whether his evidence, Robin's evidence and the statements of some of the others were being presented in parallel on multiscreen, so they could be compared at once, point after point. An increasing amount of the sweat on his upper lip was not a direct result of the heat.

'And this man, Nahom,' she said again, gently. 'You noticed nothing unusual about him as you were freeing him from the anchor and bringing him to the surface?'

'What do you mean, *unusual*?'

The flash of her gaze told him she found the prevarication immediately suspicious. But her tone remained gently probing. 'He wasn't carrying anything? Nothing about his person?'

'Not that I noticed . . .'

Again with the prevarication. The gentle curves of her eyebrows rose. The sweat on his lip gathered. She gazed at him for a moment like a tabby eyeing up a juicy mouse. 'You have to understand,' he persisted, thinking *you're in a hole – stop digging!* 'It was a race against time. He was drowning. We had to get him to the surface first, then on board *Katerina* and into hospital as fast as we could. We all got the bends because we had to come up so fast. There was no chance for chats or changes of clothes. And anyway, he was deeply unconscious all the time. Until he woke up in the decompression chamber.'

'Ah, yes. The decompression chamber. He woke up, you say. No one else seems to have registered that—'

'It was quite brief. He scarcely did more than stir. He was awake when I went back later that morning. Major Ibrahim . . .'

'Has told me what happened later. But at the moment, you are the only witness we have as to what happened when this man Nahom first woke up in the decompression chamber. Did he say anything to you?'

'Nothing I understood. I don't think he speaks English and I don't speak much Arabic.'

'And you were the only person he could have been speaking to?'

'I don't understand.' And he didn't. He frowned, trying to see what she was driving at. Licked his lip without thinking, tasting the bitter salt.

'The other man, the one Mrs Mariner brought to the surface. His name, apparently, is Aman, though like Nahom he has no papers at all, so could actually be *anybody*. Was *he* awake? Could Nahom have been talking to him? Giving him orders?'

'No.'

'You sound very certain all of a sudden. Why?'

'The other chap, Aman, you say? He was absolutely unconscious. I'm sure.' But now that Sergeant Sabet had raised it, of
course, he wasn't sure at all.

'And Nahom just said things you didn't understand . . .'

'Certainly nothing that made sense. He may have just been
speaking nonsense as he began to come to . . . Gibbering . . .'
Gibbering like me, he thought.

'Gibbering. Nonsense. Yes, I see. And he didn't try to communicate with you?'

'No.'

'Or give you anything?'

'Look, Sergeant, we've been over this. I saved the man's life,
took him aboard my boat, got him to hospital and I'm trying to
help all I can. I did not search him or try to interrogate him. I
didn't see him talk to anyone else until this morning when Major
Ibrahim, Doctor Zabr and I went into the secure ward with the
food I had sent over from the Jaz Mirabel and saw him talking
to the nurse, telling them what he would like to eat. That's it.
That's all. What is the problem?'

Sergeant Sabet sat silently for a moment, her gaze flicking
from one section of her screen to another. Then she looked up
and focused on Richard. Her brown gaze held his bright blue
one. There was silence, except for the whirring of the fan
and the buzzing of frustrated hornets. And she allowed the moment
to last before she answered, 'No problem at all, Captain Mariner.
Thank you for all your help. You have advanced our enquiries
quite considerably. If you think of anything else that might help
us further, please get in contact.' She slid a card across the table
top towards him. 'And if we come across anything else we need
clarified, we'll be in touch with you. You and Mrs Mariner are
free to leave. Did your car wait, or can we offer you a lift?'

'We have to open it,' said Robin. 'I'm sure they think Nahom is
taking us for a ride. I mean, could he really be one of the smugglers? Perhaps even the leader? That's what Ibrahim seemed to
be driving at while he interviewed me.'

'Someone certainly seems to have given them that impression.

But there seems to have been eighteen or so statements so far either here or in Hurgada. And some of those statements must have come from smugglers pretending to be smuggled . . .'

The conversation, which had started in the Mercedes on the run back from the police station, followed them through the echoing corridors of Anastasia Asov's palatial villa and spilled out on to the balcony where they looked down on *Katerina* a couple of hundred feet below as they talked. The balcony was the most private place in the villa except, perhaps, for the bathrooms. Still talking, they walked side by side to the balustrade. On the top of each section there was a terracotta *jardinière* secured to the marble. Cascades of flowers poured inwards, adding colour and fragrance to the already heady sights and smells of the balcony. As though by common consent, they moved to the right, where the *jardinières* stopped and a teak gate in the balustrade opened on to a short bridge that ended at the top of a private lift designed to spirit the owners and their guests, eight at a time, to and from the private beach at the cliff foot far below.

Richard was tempted to step in, go down and turn right, away from the private beach with its sunbeds and palm-frond sunshades and walk to the equally private marina where Husan and Mahmood were back aboard *Katerina*. Their advice had been invaluable so far. But his experience with Sergeant Sabet had started alarm bells ringing in his head and he really did not want either man to get deeper into this business – at least until he had a better idea what they were dealing with. Especially as the worst that was likely to happen to them as tourists was to have their visas withdrawn and be sent back home with a judicial slap on the wrist. But matters would be different for local people getting mixed up in something that might turn out to be quite seriously illegal. What was the phrase in British law – *aiding and abetting*? Anyway, between them, Robin and he would be able to remember quite clearly what the captain, the mate and the dive captain had told them already.

'If he's being smuggled or trafficked,' Robin said, breaking into Richard's thoughts, but extending them as though they had a psychic link, 'then he's likely to have some money, but not much; a couple of sets of documents – one possibly genuine and one almost certainly false. An address or two – probably written in Hebrew on the assumption that even after the action in Gaza during the summer 2014 he's still hoping to be smuggled in through whatever tunnels are left between Egypt and Israel. And that's about it.'

'On the other hand, if he is a smuggler or a trafficker then it's likely just to be money – mostly US dollars, but also whatever currency he's been collecting off his victims—'

'And a phone. Don't forget the phone. So he can call the families back in Africa and up the ante with a little rape and torture.'

'That seems pretty definitive, doesn't it?' As Richard spoke, he lifted the last *jardinière*, which was not quite as firmly secured as the others, and pulled Nahom's money belt out from underneath it. 'So, let's find out, shall we?'

Robin insisted on looking after their diving kit herself, so everything except their tanks was piled in a big marble bathtub in the master suite's en suite. But of course, all they needed was Richard's Aropec K1 dive knife. Robin laid the black rubber tube along the broad edge of the marble tub, holding it tightly, like an eel that needed skinning. Richard pulled the blade from its quick-release sheath and leaned forward, eyes narrow. The rubber inner tube had been packed with whatever it contained and then sealed shut with waterproof duct tape, into which the rope ends had been pushed. The whole thing looked pretty solid and utterly waterproof. But it was going to be impossible to open it without leaving obvious traces. Richard hesitated for a moment longer.

'Come on,' said Robin impatiently. 'You need an air-drawn dagger?'

'Thank you, Lady Macbeth,' he answered. 'Remember how that little enterprise turned out.'

'It's a rubber inner tube,' she snapped. 'It's not the King of Scotland.'

'Yeah,' he answered. 'And you're not in contact with several witches.' But he drove the point of the knife into the bulge of duct tape securing the rope end nearest her right fist.

'Don't worry, darling,' she whispered. '*A little water clears us of the deed.*' And on her word, he pulled the knife point along the length of the makeshift money belt.

The belt opened as though he had slit the belly of a snake,

the contents bulging out, glistening. 'Where on earth do you get cling film – or cyan wrap, as our American friends call it – in Eritrea?' Richard asked.

'The same place you get duct tape, dummy,' snapped Robin.

Richard pulled the shiny bundle free and carried it outside to one of the shaded, secluded balcony tables. Robin and he sat on the sides of two sunbeds, leaning into the shadow of a canvas-topped umbrella. The cling film proved stubborn, but at last Richard managed to pull it apart. Then, silently, they worked together piling up the contents on the smooth oiled teak top of the table.

'Oh my goodness,' said Robin, her lack of salty language reflecting her shock and concern, 'this does not look good.'

'No,' agreed Richard tersely. 'This does not look good at all.'

In front of them on the table there was a pile of Eritrean *nafka* notes, mostly in large denominations. A pile of Egyptian pound notes, again, mostly two hundred and five hundred denominations. A pile of US dollar notes in twenties, fifties and one hundreds. And a state-of-the-art Samsung Galaxy almost as cutting edge as Richard's.

'That,' whispered Robin with a sad shake of her golden curls, 'looks like a people smuggler's nest egg to me.'

'Sah! *Sah!*'

Richard sprang awake and almost shouted with shock. The gaunt figure of Nahom was crouching at his bedside. His white vest seemed to glow in the moonlight. His eyes and teeth glittered eerily. He looked like something out of a zombie film. Indeed, as he blinked himself awake, Richard was half convinced he was in the grip of a nightmare. But as he came fully conscious and realized that this was real, Richard sensed no threat – only desperation.

'*Sah gat mi rubbah?*' the young man hissed urgently.

Richard sat up slowly, his mind racing. In spite of his careful movements, Robin stirred. 'What?' she mumbled, turning over. Richard found himself suddenly thankful that they had just talked when they came to bed last night. And that the air conditioning simply required them to sleep under a single Egyptian cotton sheet in matching Chinese silk pyjamas.

Both men froze as Robin moved and mumbled. Richard was pretty certain that with any luck she would just drift back to sleep. But he wasn't sure he wanted her to do so. She would have an opinion about this situation, and might well be upset if he robbed her of the chance to express it. But at least she would not be aiding and abetting whatever he did if she was still asleep when he did it. They had discussed the contents of Nahom's money belt at great length last night, and had still been undecided as to the best course of action when they came to bed, which is why they had talked themselves to sleep rather than doing anything more romantic. Her last thought voiced drowsily had been, 'It's a pity you took it from him. I mean, given our lives to live over. I'd have let him keep it and be damned.'

And here it was – the second chance. The young man was here, in the bedroom. And all he seemed to want was his rubber back.

Richard had no idea how Nahom had escaped the hospital, found his way here and broken in. But if he just gave him back the money belt and sent him on his way then they would be free and clear of the situation whether Nahom was a smuggler or a victim. He would be out of their lives and their hands would be clean. Job done.

Richard pulled back the sheet and stepped silently on to the cool marble floor. Over Nahom's moon-silvered shoulder he saw that the curtain of the master suite had been pulled back just enough for Nahom to see. The wide windows stood immediately above the French windows leading out on to the balcony – and that was the most likely way in. Security here was not the tightest. No one in their right mind was going to risk upsetting a Russian oligarch with a reputation like Max Asov had enjoyed in life – and had passed directly to his daughter with his massive fortune and enormous business empire at the moment of his death.

With Nahom close behind, Richard padded silently through to the en suite bathroom. He switched on the tiny shaving light, and that was enough for him to find the rubber tyre where it lay hidden amongst the jumble of diving gear in the bath tub. He handed it to Nahom and watched the young man give it a swift once-over. But they had closed it up pretty well – everything was back in place, wrapped in cling film and resealed with black duct tape. With a practised motion, the young man swung the belt round his hips and tied the cord tightly. He pulled out his vest so it concealed the belt and turned towards Richard. 'I t'ank. T'ank Ric'ard.'

'OK, Nahom, let's get you out of here before anyone else wakes up.'

Silently, side by side, they padded across the bedroom, leaving Robin snoring gently – a sound that Richard found deeply reassuring. They tiptoed down the marble staircase like a pair of ghosts, passing in and out of bars of moonlight. They pushed the half-open door to the dining room wide, crossed that in turn, pushed the French windows open wide enough to allow them each to step out on to the warm balcony, filled with hot, still air, the scent of flowers and the light of the low, full moon. 'I break lock. So sorry,' breathed Nahom.

As Richard stepped out he stubbed his toe on the metal clasp that had secured the last – loose – *jardinière* in place and which had now, clearly, found new employment as a jemmy to force the lock. I'll sort that out with Sasha tomorrow, thought Richard. In fact, I'll have to sort out the entire security system with him . . .

The thought was enough to take them to the gate that opened on to the lift bridge. Nahom crossed the short structure and stepped out over the safety rail. He stooped and lifted what looked like a heavy backpack from its resting place on the outer ends of the boards making up the floor of the bridge. Then, taking firm hold of the metal supports that held the lift shaft itself, he swung down them as though they were a ladder and was gone into the shadows below. Richard closed the gate, crossed the balcony, picked up the metal clasp, stepped inside and closed the French windows as best he could, then padded silently and thoughtfully back up to bed.

'You did *what*?' asked Robin, stunned.

'Gave it back and let him go. He's out of our lives and we're better off. That's what I thought you wanted.'

It was early afternoon. Richard, uncharacteristically, had been happy for Robin to sleep in, subconsciously – or perhaps semi-consciously – fearing the confrontation they were now having.

He had used the morning to talk through security with Sasha the housekeeper and some very discreet repairs had been done to the French windows while Robin was still asleep. Now, as they sat at the lunch table in the dining room, an equally discreet specialist from Sharm Security was fitting an intruder alarm to the French windows and motion sensor covering the balcony and the dining room.

'Out of our lives, perhaps – but into how many others? That money belt all but proved he's a people trafficker even if he does look all helpless and innocent. Ye Gods, Richard, how many other genuinely innocent people will he get his claws into now?'

'I know the belt looks bad, but I'm still not convinced. There has to be another explanation.'

The conversation was interrupted by a discreet knock. Sasha stepped in, closing the door behind him. 'There is a police person here who wishes to speak to you, Mister Richard. Are you willing?'

'Of course.' Richard met Robin's *I told you so* gaze. He stood up, expecting Major Ibrahim, but Sasha showed in Sergeant Sabet. 'Sergeant,' he said, masking the surprise in his voice. 'Please take a seat. Some tea or coffee? What can we do for you?'

The sergeant sat opposite Robin, who examined her with scarcely concealed interest. 'Some water, perhaps. It is approaching fifty degrees outside.'

Robin poured a glass of iced water while Richard sat down again.

Sergeant Sabet sipped, then sighed gratefully. 'The prisoner Nahom escaped from hospital last night. Major Ibrahim wondered whether he might have come here looking for help.' Her gaze drifted pointedly to the French windows.

'How on earth did he get out?' asked Richard, only to receive another one of the dark-eyed woman's steely stares. 'The hospital windows opened from the inside and the wire netting over the outside appears to have been less secure than it seemed to be. He was able to loosen some screws, push up the netting and climb through. His clothing is gone and his hospital robe was left on the bed. We have interviewed the others but no one saw anything and our guards outside the door heard nothing.'

'How would he know to come here in any case?' asked Robin.

'"Everyone knows the Villa Shahrazad,"' she answered. 'Those were the words spoken to Captain Mariner by a ward orderly yesterday morning – in front of Nahom and all the others. It is not too much of a stretch to assume he heard and understood – and acted on those words.'

'But why would he come here?' asked Richard, hoping his tone was one of innocent enquiry.

'For help, advice, money . . .' Her gaze drifted apparently aimlessly to the work being done on and around the French windows once again, and Richard felt almost certain that she had heard about the break-in. His mind raced, trying to come up with an innocent explanation. 'It's a bit of a long shot, I admit,' she continued, apparently oblivious. 'Our first thought was that he would head for one of the marinas, but apparently not. A fairly detailed search has revealed nothing. None of our people has any word of him in Sharm, but Sharm is a big place with many potential boltholes and it is early days yet. In terms of immediate enquiries, so to speak, that really only leaves the interior. That is, after all, where he was originally headed, we are certain.'

'But if that is so, then he must have been expecting to go across the Sinai in company with the other twenty-four, was it? With guides. Some kind of transport. Supplies . . .' Richard's voice tailed off.

The sergeant was looking at the French windows again. Then back at him. She knew; he was certain.

There was another discreet knock. With some relief, Richard broke eye contact, rose and crossed to the door and opened it to reveal Sharl. The cook was frowning. In a low voice, he said, 'Mister Richard, sir, I believe the kitchen was robbed last night.'

'I beg your pardon?' Richard was simply astonished. 'Are you sure?'

'Each afternoon it is my routine to check the inventory. Mr Asov liked every penny accounted for and Miss Asov his daughter has not told me to change my routines. In consequence, I have to report that half-a-dozen bottles of Hayat water, in the one and a half litre size are gone, together with several loaves of bread, beans and cheeses.'

Richard suddenly remembered the backpack Nahom had swung over his shoulder before climbing down the lift housing.

And that gave him another idea. 'Please come in, Sharl,' he said, loudly. 'There is a police sergeant here and you can report the theft directly to her.' He pushed the door wide and stepped back in, continuing to talk. 'Sergeant, it is a good thing you are here. As you will have observed, we are working on the French windows. This is because there was, in fact, an attempted break-in last night. We didn't bother reporting it, because nothing was stolen and, frankly, we weren't sure that the burglar actually got in. We have had the door repaired and as you see security alarms fitted. But now, it seems, Sharl has discovered that the kitchen was burgled. And what was stolen was just the kind of supplies we were discussing – things someone would take if they were thinking of heading across the desert and into the interior . . .'

FOUR
Market

The next three days were the hottest Richard had ever experienced, and he was used to taking Heritage Mariner supertankers in and out of the Gulf. Temperatures in the early afternoons topped fifty degrees Celsius – one hundred and thirty degrees Fahrenheit. And that was in the shade. Day after day, Sharm el-Sheikh gave Death Valley, California a good run for its money as the most scorching place on earth. Furnace-hot breezes began to stir like the breath of awakening dragons because the great desert wind of Saudi Arabia was beginning to blow. The wind named for the compass point of its origin – *shamaal*, which is Arabic for north. Just as the Arabic for desert gives its name to *sahaari*.

Villa Shahrazad was designed and built for hot weather. The dining room and the master suite above it faced west, not only to benefit from the evening sun but also for protection against the fierceness of noon. The sitting room, beside the dining room, also looked westward on to the balcony, but instead of marble flags it overlooked the cliff-edge infinity pool which swept round the southern aspect of the property, into the full blaze of the sun – for those hardy enough to risk it. But whereas the dining area's inner side was closed off by the kitchens, the sitting room had a double aspect. The heart of the villa was an open garden, shaded by the three-story building except at noon when the sun was overhead. Here too there was a pool, but a smaller one, with a waterfall feature that could be switched on and off, whose force could be varied from a tinkling trickle to a playful roar. There was room to lounge around the pool but the plants dominated. Carefully trimmed palms stooped, offering yet more shade, especially around noon. Bright pink Bougainvillea Arborea filled the garden with colour and a heady honeysuckle scent as they were supported up the walls, square openings which revealed the marble staircase climbing upward. The feature was practical as well as decorative. It was designed to make full use of traditional Moorish architecture, for the shady, central garden was almost always filled with cool air. And cool air, heavier than hot air, would flow through the sitting room in drafts and breezes that carried with them the relaxing sound of water and the honeysuckle fragrance of the bright bougainvillea flowers.

Three of the suites on the second floor, including the master suite, had double aspect balconies on one side overlooking the cliff-top balcony and the bay and on the other side overlooking the garden, as did three of the guest suites immediately above them. It took a small army of people to run the villa, but Sasha ran the house staff, pool men and gardeners with Rolls-Royce precision, while Sharl ran the kitchens and everything ancillary to them equally smoothly. The staff who lived-in were housed in the east-facing areas where the sun arrived early and hot.

Even in the face of all the carefully designed luxury of the villa, Richard and Robin spent most of the time aboard *Katerina*, hiding under the white canvas sunshade that stretched right across her top deck, sipping ice-cold drinks with lips that seemed to become parched again within ten minutes. While Captain Husan searched for the best reefs and the coolest currents – in the air as well as in the sea – the Mariners lay restlessly on deck chairs, suspicious that the near-nuclear heat was cutting through the canvas as though it were tissue and searing them unsuspectedly. Or, more often and increasingly, swimming and snorkelling in rash vests to protect themselves against the ultraviolet rays burning down on to their backs and shoulders. But even the Red Sea was tepid and the fish that usually teemed round Ras Mohammed all seemed to be seeking shade and shelter as well.

The matter of Nahom and his money belt remained unresolved between them, combining with the inescapable heat to make even the normally imperturbable Richard short-tempered and snappish. Robin simply grew, simmering, bloody minded but, unable to take her ire out on the endlessly patient and charming people who ran the cliff-top villa and the beautiful boat beneath it, she perforce saved the sharpest edge of her tongue for Richard. And somehow, the unaccustomed tension between them seemed to make any more scuba diving out of the question,

even if they had been able to forget their last adventure and
the fate of the burning man at the end of it. And even though
the deep water was the only place nearby that was anything
approaching cool.

The air conditioning in Villa Shahrazad worked overtime while
Sharl and his team in the kitchen produced ranges of cold soups,
chilled meats, cool salads and iced desserts for meal after meal
in a manner that began to tax even their ingenuity. With the stirring of the desert wind, the evenings became as stultifying as
the days, stopping Richard and Robin from making night-time
visits to the noisy, vivid, colourful, aromatic shops and bazaars
of Sharm el-Maya, the Old Town. Or availing themselves of any
of the vibrant nightlife in tourist districts of Shark's Bay's SoHo
Square and especially Naama Bay, which, like the Old Town,
was only minutes away in the Mercedes. But even though they
spent their evenings restlessly at home feeling confined – almost
imprisoned – and consequently going to bed earlier and earlier,
and even though, like snorkelling, love-making was off the agenda
for the moment, they found they were sleeping in later and later
in the mornings.

So, when Dr Zabr called at eight on the morning of the fourth
day, he woke Richard up. As the familiarly intrusive sound of
the ringtone penetrated his sleep, Richard reached for his Galaxy
on the bedside table and sat up. He cradled it between his naked
shoulder and his ear as he unscrewed the top of a bottle of water
which he also kept to hand.

'Captain Mariner?' Zabr's tone was hurried and sounded
irritable.

'What can I do for you, Doctor?' Richard sipped his tepid
water and cleared his throat as he listened, feeling the liquid
almost instantly transform itself into perspiration on his skin in
spite of the air conditioning.

'The young man you saved from drowning last week has been
returned to us by the police. He was discovered somewhere in
the desert last night, apparently. The police brought him in half
an hour ago. A Sergeant Sabet was in charge and she made the
decision to bring him here instead of to the police station. It was
a wise decision. He is not well. I am just about to assess his
condition in detail. But the finance department wishes to know

whether you are still willing to meet his expenses as you were before his escape.'

The doctor said more, but at this point Richard dropped the phone. The shock of the unexpected news combined with the sudden sinking feeling that if Nahom told the whole truth then Ibrahim – and Robin – were going to be even more pissed off with him than they were at the moment, made him seek to get a firmer hold on the slick little handset, which turned out to be as slippery as a soap bar in a hot bath. His instinctive grab to catch it emptied the water bottle over Robin, who sat up as though she had been electrocuted.

'What the bloody hell do you think you're doing?' she blazed at him. 'That was not bloody funny Richard!'

Richard retrieved the phone and pulled himself out of bed. *Sorry!* he mimed. *Accident* . . . The sheet came with him, revealing Robin in white silk pyjamas that the water had transformed into distracting pink transparency, as though she had entered a wet T-shirt contest. She rolled out of bed, leaving a sopping puddle where her bottom had been, and snatched the sheet off the floor where Richard had let it fall. She sat herself down on the dry side of the bed which he had just vacated, piled the sheet on her translucent lap and glared at him.

'Your decision?' pressed Dr Zabr, who sounded no happier than Robin looked.

'I'm sorry, Doctor,' said Richard a little breathlessly, his mind racing like a hamster in a wheel. 'I'm afraid I dropped the phone. Could you repeat that last bit?'

'Will you continue to meet this patient's bills or not? What is your decision? It will make no difference to his treatment, of course – he is an emergency case. But we have no Blue Cross or ObamaCare here. This is not the National Health Service. My accounts department is—'

'Yes, Doctor Zabr. In full. For as long as it takes. Now, tell me,' he took a deep breath, trying to steady things down, 'has he been interviewed yet?'

'Well, my admissions staff have performed an initial assessment, of course.'

'By the police? By Sergeant Sabet?'

'She may have talked to him on the way in from the desert

but I doubt if she would have gotten much information from him. My people's initial diagnosis suggests that he has been poisoned, either by a scorpion sting or a snakebite, so, combined with elements of starvation and dehydration, he won't have been making much sense.'

'Can I see him?'

'Well, visiting hours are usually after four, but if he's in a private room . . .'

'Put him in a private room, if you have one.'

'It so happens that we do have one available.'

'Fine, put him in that. Tell your finance people it's the same arrangement as last time.'

'Then of course visiting hours are more negotiable. You may come when you like. Just report to reception and they will guide you.'

'I'll be there in half an hour.'

'That's funny . . .'

'What?'

'That's just what Major Ibrahim said when I called him just now.'

Robin did not have time to forgive Richard before he dressed and left. Consequently she did not go with him. He left her still sitting angrily on the dry side of the bed. As he sat in the back of the Mercedes, feeling the welcome Arctic drafts of the air conditioning, he imagined her getting up now that he had departed. He tried not to imagine in too much detail how her silk pyjamas had been rendered see-through both above and below her waist by the accidental soaking she had received. But they hadn't fooled around for days, and he found the mental images distractingly persistent. She would probably strip off the clinging wet silk and dress in one of the towelling robes he also found so alluring. Then, knowing her, she would strip the bed, working off some of her anger and resentment as she did so. Working herself into a better mood, he hoped.

She would haul the mattress to the wide window single-handed and stand it against the glass, where the sunlight would probably have dried it before she had finished showering. If this morning was anything like the last couple, she wouldn't bother to dry her hair – she'd just open the window and let the shamaal and the sunlight dry it for her. Then she would get dressed and – he was getting jealous now – hurry down to another of Sharl's amazing breakfasts. His stomach rumbled, for he had not thought to get anything to eat on his way out.

These vaguely carnal musings were enough to fill the ride to the hospital. Sasha, as usual, insisted on chauffeuring, even though Richard was certain he had more important calls on his time. Now he turned round to look back from the driver's seat and asked, 'You want me to wait, Mister Richard?'

'No, thanks, Sasha. I'll call when I want picking up.'

As Richard strode into the hospital's reception, a familiar white SUV pulled into the car park. The major and the sergeant climbed out of the back and came towards the entrance side by side. He resisted the urge to hurry as though he was racing the police officers and Nahom was some sort of a prize. So, although he was carrying a solid-looking briefcase, the major caught up with him just as the orderly at reception directed him to the wounded man's private room. But then, seeing the police officers, he called forward another orderly to guide them all.

'Ah, Captain Mariner,' said Ibrahim as they followed the orderly and Sergeant Sabet followed them, 'I can't say I'm surprised to see you here. You seem to have forged a surprisingly close relationship with this prisoner.'

'*Very* close,' added the sergeant. 'Financially, at any rate. Are you paying for his accommodation and food again?'

'It's the Chinese, I believe,' Richard observed, 'who say that if you save someone's life you are responsible for them until they die.'

'Ah, the famous Chinese logic,' observed Ibrahim, amused. 'The inverted thinking that suggests you should pay your doctor every day you are *well*, and refuse to pay him as long as you are *ill*. I wonder how that would appeal to Doctor Zabr.'

'It's the same logic that suggests policemen should be paid only on crime-free days,' observed Richard. 'How would you like that, Major?'

'Fortunately I do not have to answer you immediately, Captain Mariner, because here we are, I believe.'

'Though,' inserted Sabet forcefully, catching up with the two men as she spoke, 'as there is almost no crime in Sharm, the major would be a rich man under your Chinese system, Captain.'

The orderly opened the door from the outside just as Doctor Zabr was about to open it from within. The four of them stood facing each other in the doorway as the orderly, sensitive to the tense atmosphere, made his escape and hurried away.

'You may talk to him, but be brief and do not rely on the accuracy of his answers,' said the doctor. 'From what we can ascertain, he has been attacked by a cobra, *naja haje haje*. He is only alive and well enough to talk because of the sergeant's swift and effective lifesaving techniques. He is on several drips as we deliver a broad-spectrum anti-venom derived from the Australian tiger snake, which has proved effective in such cases. He is fortunate. We keep it to counter the venom of sea snakes who have bitten divers, but it is equally effective against cobra venom. We are transfusing his blood. We are hydrating his eyes as well as his body. We will be putting him on a ventilator after he has talked to you, something he insists on doing at once. I warn you, however, that your time will be limited and, as I say, you may not be able to rely on the accuracy of what he has to tell you. He is feverish and occasionally seems to drift off into disturbing fantasies.'

'Well,' said the major, easing forward so that the doctor had to stand aside, 'let us see what he has to tell us before we judge its accuracy and reliability. I would like to speak to him alone, except for the sergeant.'

Richard opened his mouth to protest when Dr Zabr snapped, quite unexpectedly, 'Most of what I have just told you was addressed to Captain Mariner. It is the captain whom Nahom wishes to speak with.'

'We'll see about that,' said Ibrahim, his voice unexpectedly as steely as the expression which occasionally entered the sergeant's coffee-coloured eyes. Admitting defeat at last, Richard stood back as the room emptied and the door closed behind the police officers. Dr Zabr and his team bustled off, leaving Richard standing listlessly in the corridor, the wind taken out of his sails – a situation that lasted for less than five minutes before the door opened again. 'You'd better come in,' said the sergeant with extremely bad grace. 'He won't say a word unless you are there too.'

The room was dimly lit and blessedly cool. An air-conditioning unit hummed quietly in the background. The whole place smelt of medication, soap and antibacterial cleansers. Nahom was half sitting up in bed, supported by pillows. He looked even more skeletal than he had the last time Richard saw him. His full lips were cracked and peeling, while his high forehead was bandaged, but there were blisters at the bottom of the bandage, just above Nahom's eyebrows. His frail, skeletal body hardly seemed to lift the sheet that covered him, but his left leg lay beneath a tented section from the knee down. There were several drips attached to his arms, though his hands were still free to move. He appeared to be crying, but Richard soon realized that this was the effect of keeping his eyes hydrated. A ventilator stood beside his bed with a triangular plastic face mask convenient to his left hand, though Richard couldn't see what was in the gas bottle it was attached to. Oxygen, he supposed.

The black rubber money belt lay gaping across Nahom's thighs with its contents strewn across the sheet down towards his knees. Ibrahim's briefcase sat open and empty on a bedside chair. The major and the sergeant stood on Nahom's right, so Richard went and stood by the gas bottle on his left. Ibrahim looked down at Nahom with a frown which Richard could not quite read – irritation . . . confusion . . . enquiry . . . accusation?

'The prisoner really only speaks Arabic fluently,' said Sergeant Sabet. 'It is Eritrean Arabic, but I believe Major Ibrahim and I can understand what he is saying and make ourselves understood by him. He can manage a word or two in English, but he only spoke Arabic as we were bringing him in – not that what he said made much sense. Now you are here he will answer the major's questions and I will translate the questions and his answers into English. If you have any questions of your own which the major is happy for you to ask, I will translate your words into Arabic.'

'Thank you,' said Richard. 'That is very courteous.'

'It is the only condition under which he will speak to us,' said Ibrahim.

'Right,' said Richard. 'Please begin.' He turned all his attention to Nahom, and, although the conversation went back and

forth through the police officers, it was soon almost as though
Nahom was talking directly to him.

'My name is Nahom Selassie,' the young man said. His voice
was little more than a whisper. The sergeant's translation,
however, was brusque and forceful – the exact opposite of his
original tone. 'I live in a village near Dogali in the lowlands of
Eritrea less than thirty kilometres inland from Massawa, near the
famous Dogali Bridge. I was released from my National Service
less than a year ago to return to my family and help them on
our farm. Am I a smuggler? No, I am not a smuggler. I am a
farmer. All of my family are farmers. We grow sorghum, which
is a good crop on our small but fertile fields. However, a series
of droughts over the last few years have made things hard in our
village. My family, together with many other families, has grown
desperate as we watch our brothers and sisters, parents and children starve. But even so, I would never become a smuggler. I
hate smugglers and traffickers of all kinds. Why was I with them?
To follow the last band of smugglers who came through the Sinai
little more than a week ago. Why am I doing that? To rescue my
sister, Tsibekti, who has been kidnapped by them.'

Nahom paused, shaking, clearly overcome by emotion. His
eyes closed briefly, then opened again, their gaze focused fiercely
on Richard. Sergeant Sabet fell silent after she translated his last
heartfelt outcry. Her eyes, too, turned towards Richard, as though
she was also silently begging him to help. As much to regain the
young man's attention as to get him to state the obvious, Ibrahim
asked, 'Why must you do this, Mr Selassie? Why not go to the
authorities and ask for their help?'

As Nahom, gasping, struggled to overcome his emotion and
frame his answer, Richard thought of his own twin children, off
on summer work placements this year, though in contact by cell
or Skype a couple of times a week. What would William do if
someone kidnapped Mary, his sister, and Robin and Richard were
unable to help? He would do what Nahom was doing, he thought.
No matter what the cost or danger. And the realization was like
a knife twisting in his heart.

'Why must I do this? And I alone rather than squads of
policemen and women?' Nahom answered faintly and Sabet
translated more gently. 'Because Tsibekti left our little village

ten nights ago in the company of Bisrat, a friend of our family, who said he had contacts with smugglers – Bedouin tribesmen and various authorities who could be bribed to look the other way. He promised to find her work either in Israel or the Emirates if she would travel with him through Massawa City, down to the port and across the Red Sea to Sinai. Bisrat told us we must be silent and secret until we heard from Tsibekti that she was safely in work. To contact the authorities would simply mean that the men smuggling my sister would kill her and hide her body. Tsibekti took with her all the money our family could get together and a cell phone with which she promised to stay in touch with us. The twin of this phone here, as Tsibekti is the twin of my heart.'

Nahom at last reached into the incriminating money belt, his fingers working amongst the bundles of bank notes until he pulled free the Galaxy phone that was the only other item the belt contained. He switched it on and immediately the screen was filled with the picture of a stunningly beautiful young woman. Richard could see that hers was the feminine twin of Nahom's own face: huge dark eyes emphasized by the depth of their sockets below delicately curving brows and above hunger-sharpened cheekbones. A high, wide forehead crowned with a luxuriance of black hair hanging in lustrous waves and coils which escaped almost wilfully from beneath a modest head dress. A long, patrician nose, spread at its tip by broad nostrils. Full, finely chiselled lips, parted in a gentle smile to reveal white, even teeth and an attractive pair of dimples. A long, fine-boned jaw ending in a square, determined-looking chin. Nahom switched off the phone and, at Ibrahim's prompting, continued with his story. Though as he answered the major's questions, his eyes never left Richard's face, and their desperate glare communicated so much more than the words of the bald narrative that the sergeant ground out in English.

'At first, the journey seemed to go well and Tsibekti reported that she and Bisrat had contacted their men in Massawa docks and found their place aboard the boat. That they had crossed the sea with no incident and had landed on the Sinai at a little, unguarded bay north of El Tur. She and Bisrat were about to be met by Bedouin guides who would take them across the coastal

desert, into the mountains and north until they could spirit her
out of the Sinai through tunnels dug beneath the border, where
their associates in Israel, Jordan or Saudi would take her to
Jerusalem, Jeddah or Riyadh, which is what Bisrat had assured
us would certainly happen, as I have said. It was only on the
strength of this assurance our parents allowed Tsibekti to leave
in the first place.'

Whether because of his illness, his weakness or because of
emotional stress, Nahom's story broke off there once again and
he reached for the face mask, taking such deep gulps of oxygen
that Richard was prompted to open a bottle of water and offer
him a series of sips as soon as the mask came off. Ibrahim and
Sabet watched silently, waiting for the interrogation to resume
and for the story to proceed. Though Richard, for one, had a
shrewd idea where it was heading next, especially after his conversations with Robin, Husan, Ahmed and Mahmood.

'What happened next?' prompted Ibrahim in Arabic.

Sergeant Sabet translated both the question and the answer
into English, but her mood had changed completely. Her anger
and outrage were no longer targeted at Richard and Nahom.

'What happened next, Major? Something went terribly wrong.
Tsibekti called again almost immediately to tell us that she has
been kidnapped and is being held for ransom. The only thing
that has kept her safe so far has been the money she took with
her, which she has been able to give the brigands holding her.
But, she told us, unless we send much more money soon, she
will be raped, tortured and either murdered or sold into slavery.
And if we went to the authorities either in Egypt or at home,
she would be raped, tortured and killed as Bisrat had warned us.'

Major Ibrahim interrupted at this point, no doubt remembering
the doctor's warning that Nahom's testimony might drift into
fantasy. His tone was soft but insistent, and Sabet translated his
words that were surprisingly confrontational. 'We have
heard stories like this too often before, Mr Selassie. If we believed
them all there would have to be, somewhere up in the interior
or in the red zone of the North Sinai, a place that is little better
than a concentration camp. A place where unspeakable atrocities
happen without anyone being any the wiser. Why should we
believe you? Especially as you have told us nothing but lies until

today. Especially in the state to which you have reduced yourself now?'

Nahom took up his phone again without speaking. With trembling fingers, he touched several buttons on the screen, which abruptly sprang to life once more, but in video mode rather than still picture. He reversed it so they could all see and hear. His eyes closed and water streamed down his face. Richard no longer believed the tears all came from the hydration after the snakebite. On that thought, he switched his attention to what Nahom wanted them to see. The beautiful woman from the still picture sprang into life. But she did not look so beautiful now. She was dusty, filthy, terrified and distraught. She was screaming something Richard could not make out and someone with a phone like Nahom's was videoing it. He could see pretty clearly why her twin brother's hands were shaking as he held the small device.

Tears washed clear channels through the grit on Tsibekti's cavernous cheeks. Behind her stood a line of men, their faces masked with colourfully checked and white-fringed *keffiyehs* so that only their eyes were uncovered. The rest of their clothing was hidden beneath long white *dishdasha* robes. Behind the men stood a low, rug-covered shelter beside which knelt a camel. On the camel's back there was a sling made of similar carpet material to the roof and walls of the tent. Sticking out of it was a black tube that caught Richard's attention for a moment before he started to consider the wider view. Behind the tent rose sharp-sided mountains looking disturbingly like the pyramids at Giza. The mountains were ill-focused but it was clear that they were a striking pink with thick green bands running up their slopes where some other rock had been layered into them like the filling in a sandwich and then the whole structure shattered and stood up on its end. And in the distance, more peaks, higher, matt black in colour almost eclipsing the hard blue sky. Richard knew these mountains. They were in the interior of the Sinai Peninsula. He flicked a glance at Ibrahim. The major recognized them too.

Tsibekti's own headdress had been torn wide so that one or two coils of hair lay exposed. This in itself constituted an assault that was very close to rape, given where she was – in a public place surrounded by strange men who were not of her family. Abruptly the video picture panned down and zoomed in, showing

the young woman's rumpled and torn travelling *jilbab* as it did
so. Tsibekti's fingers were spread like spiders' legs across a
rough, pink rock. A heavy-bladed knife was resting on the first
joint of the little finger on her right hand.

The rest of the scene was almost timeless – apart from the
way it had been recorded. The mountains, the tent and the camel,
the men in their robes and headdresses, the woman in her travelling clothes, could all have come from long-past centuries. The
knife, however, was anything but old fashioned. It was a black-
bladed heavy-looking Bowie knife with SURVIVOR etched into
the blade above the blood runnel and just beneath the saw-toothed
spine. It was very modern indeed, with the black blade alone
nearly half a metre – eighteen inches – in length – a weapon as
capable of chopping off Tsibekti's head as it was of cutting off
her little finger. In a way, it was more terrifyingly threatening
than a gun would have been.

Richard didn't need to understand the words the distraught
young woman was saying to get the message. Nahom switched
the phone off. There was a short silence, then he began to speak
again. This time, as she translated, Sabet's voice was soft and
understanding. And Ibrahim asked no more questions, content to
let the boy tell his terrible tale in his own way.

'Of course, our parents are distraught. They blame themselves
for allowing Tsibekti to undertake such a dangerous journey,
though they were assured by Bisrat that it was safe, that thousands
of people had got through successfully in the past. But of course
they could not abandon their daughter. And I could not allow
anything to happen to my twin sister. Therefore, I have been
given every nakfa, Egyptian pound and US dollar the family can
beg or borrow and I have come north through Massawa into the
Red Sea and on to the Sinai to rescue her. I carry with me only
the phone I need to stay in contact with the men who are holding
my sister somewhere in the mountains of the interior so that
they can direct me to where they are and the money I need to
buy her freedom from them and bring her home again. That is
why I am here, what I am doing and why I have a belt that only
contains money and a phone.'

'You know you have been running risks that are nearly insane,
even for a soldier trained under National Service who knows

how to behave in extremes of temperature such as the Sinai shares with the lowlands of Eritrea?' said Ibrahim, and Sabet now reflected the gentle tone in which he spoke the words. 'To believe you can find one woman lost in the middle of sixty thousand square kilometres of mountain and desert, even with directions on your phone. Sixty thousand square kilometres. That is half the size of your entire homeland of Eritrea. To go into the interior alone and unprotected. Without even a weapon of any kind. If you had found these men they certainly would have killed you. I do not think you have any concept of how dangerous these criminals are, the lengths to which they will go to protect the secrecy of their movements and their absolute control over the items and people they are smuggling. They would certainly simply have taken your money and still have done whatever they wanted with your sister.'

'But what else can I do?' whispered Nahom. 'She has begged us to rescue her!'

'Leave it to us,' said Ibrahim decisively. 'We will search the interior and we will find your sister. We have the experience, the expertise and the equipment. They will not kill us – and if they try, we will kill them instead. You have seen the weapons my men carry. We have many more and we can call on the army for everything from helicopters to tanks – especially if they are foolish enough to try and smuggle her through the red zone in North Sinai.'

Sergeant Sabet continued speaking on her own behalf after Ibrahim stopped, then she translated what she said to Nahom for Richard's benefit. 'You have been very lucky. You were told not to contact the authorities but chance has made the authorities contact you. This is very fortunate. As you recover, we will search. And when you are well enough, we will take you up to our main police station on El Benouk Road, where you will be reunited with your sister, both of you safe and sound. And we will be able to send you both home again, *inshallah*, with no harm done.'

Ibrahim added something and Sabet translated, 'As long as you are careful not to break any more of our laws in the meantime.'

*   *   *

'What laws has he broken?' demanded Robin as Richard finished telling her what Ibrahim's interview with Nahom had revealed. It was half an hour after the conclusion of the interview, when the three of them had left Nahom gasping into his respirator, so overcome that he hadn't even had the strength to protest when Ibrahim swept the money belt and its contents, including the phone, into his briefcase.

Sasha had not been called to pick Richard up. He had ridden home in Ibrahim's SUV as Villa Shahrazad was on the way to El Benouk. The major made further use of this act of courtesy by talking matters through with Richard and insisting very forcefully that his involvement with Nahom and his sister should go no further than paying for the poor man's hospital bills if he felt the urge to do so. It seemed clear to both Ibrahim and Sabet that Nahom wanted Richard, the man to whom he owed his life, to replace him in the search for the kidnapped woman. Exercising more Chinese logic, Richard suspected they might be correct. After all, time was of the essence and even Nahom would have to admit that he was not strong enough to go out into the desert again for a while. Richard had remained calculatedly noncommittal, and by the time he was dropped at the Villa Shahrazad an air of tension between the visitor and the authorities had returned.

Now, ensconced securely in the cool, shady dining room, Richard finished peeling a hard-boiled egg and turned his attention to a big, ripe tomato. 'Attempting to enter the country illegally,' he said. 'Let's start there.'

'But he didn't actually do so, did he?' countered Robin, pouring a cup of strong, black coffee and sliding it towards him through the remnants of her own breakfast. 'I mean, *we* brought him in – him and the others who made it to Sharm.'

'Good point. And I think Ibrahim recognizes that. But Nahom is an illegal alien as far as the authorities are concerned. And he did escape from police custody, damaging hospital property as he did so.' He sipped his coffee, buttered a piece of toast and began to pile boiled egg and sliced tomato on it.

Robin passed the salt and pepper amenably enough to show that this morning's angry words were all forgotten. 'They won't charge him with anything so petty, surely?'

'No,' he answered, taking a bite and chewing deliberately before he completed his thought. 'I don't suppose they will.' He sipped his coffee. 'But Ibrahim clearly doesn't want any more shenanigans like running off alone into the desert, no matter how strong his motive may be.'

'But you think they're going to pull out all the stops looking for this poor Tsibekti girl?'

'She's another illegal alien, of course. And she *did* enter the country illegally. But I think that's by the by as far as Ibrahim's concerned. He'll be going after the smugglers because they have broken an enormous number of Egyptian laws, and if he rescues her that will be all to the good. It's not going to be his primary aim, though, because there's another element I'm pretty sure Ibrahim noticed, though Sabet might not have done. And I'm not sure Nahom would have noticed it, even after his National Service training.'

'What's that?'

Richard reached for the salt cellar and ground a couple of turns on to the top of his egg and tomato. 'The camel,' he said.

'The camel? The one in the video clip? What's so strange about a camel in the middle of the Sinai?'

'Nothing. It's just that it was carrying something that was sticking out of a sling they had rigged across its back. It looked to me like the business end of a QW1 Vanguard shoulder-launched missile system. It's the kind of thing that used to be smuggled into Palestine before the Israelis closed the tunnels between Rafa and Gaza in 2014.'

'So you don't think they're just smuggling people?'

'No. They're smuggling weapons as well. Even if it wasn't a Vanguard, I'm pretty certain that it was some kind of MANPAD system. We saw enough of them when we got caught up in that situation in Africa – the kidnapping of those orphan girls by the Army of Christ the Infant. I mean, I know well enough what the damn things look like. God knows what else is packed on to that camel – and any others they have with them. Drugs, maybe. Anything there's a ready market for, I suppose.'

'These are not nice people, lover.'

'No, they're not. I wonder how we can find out more about them.'

'Why would you want to do that? You're not thinking of going up against them yourself, are you?'

'No, I'm not,' he said with more certainty than he felt. 'I'd be even further out of my depth than Nahom; certainly if I tried to go in there unsupported – without a guide and supplies. And wheels. Preferably attached to a very robust Land Rover. Still and all, I'd be fascinated to know what really goes on in the interior.'

'Where would you start looking?' she asked, intrigued in spite of herself.

'There's no place like home. I bet Sasha and Sharl know a thing or two about what goes on in the secret alleys and back rooms of Sharm. And if they don't know what goes on out in the desert then I'll bet they know someone who does.'

'You going to ask them? Straight out? Just like that?'

'Not both at once. One at a time, maybe . . .'

As soon as he finished breakfast, Richard and Robin went to Sasha's office, which was on the north side of the villa, beside the main entrance to the building. Its windows overlooked beautifully maintained lawns and flower beds which sat astride a long drive leading in from Al Kahazzan road, past a tall but sadly ineffectual security gate. Sasha welcomed them into his domain with his usual courtesy and no sooner had they sat down than he was offering them cold drinks. Sensitive to the customs and tradition that demanded all guests be offered refreshments, they accepted gratefully.

As soon as they were settled, Richard plunged into the topic which had brought them here in the first place. Sasha heard him out courteously, and then answered regretfully, 'I'm afraid I know nothing that could be of help to you in this matter, Mister Richard. Of course, you must ask Sharl if that is your wish, but were I in your position, wishing to learn what you wish to learn, I would ask Captain Husan. Such is his reputation that most of the house boys believe he spent much of his youth as a smuggler in any case, though on the sea rather than in the interior. And of contraband rather than of weapons or people. However, if he does not know what you want to learn himself, I am sure he will know someone who does.'

Richard was still kicking himself for not starting out with

Husan when, after tea and cakes in the kitchen, Sharl repeated almost word for word what Sasha had said in his office.

'We might not have learned anything new from our chat with Sharl the chef,' said Robin as they headed past the infinity pool towards the balcony and the lift to the beach, the private marina, *Katerina* and her ex-smuggler captain, 'but it was worth it just for those cakes!'

'Keeping you fat and happy is my main mission in life,' said Richard.

She thumped him on the shoulder, but it was more of a love-pat than a serious assault. Things were looking up at last, he thought.

Like Sasha and Sharl, Husan offered them refreshments as soon as they were seated in *Katerina*'s main cabin. Glasses of blood-red chilled *karakadey* hibiscus juice. Robin particularly loved it, for it was the icy, sweeter, more intense cousin of the hibiscus tea that had replaced Earl Grey in her affections while she was in Egypt. She even liked the way it put a kind of lipstick effect on her mouth and turned her tongue bright ruby.

'Now,' rumbled Husan when they were all settled, 'what is it you require of me? Are we to start scuba diving again? Shall I call Ahmed?'

'Thank you, no,' answered Richard. 'This time we want to ask your advice about something entirely different.'

'Something to do with the land rather than the sea,' added Robin. 'Is there any more of this delicious drink?'

Half an hour later, after a very detailed discussion indeed, Husan sat back, thoughtfully tapping the side of his empty glass with the nail of his right index finger, his eyes veiled. 'One condition,' he said at last.

'What condition?' asked Richard.

'Swear to me that you are not thinking of going after these smugglers yourself. Even though there is a young woman in terrible danger and even though your life has become entwined with that of her brother. It would be death to pursue these people with anything less than the army that Major Ibrahim plans to call upon. Swear to me that you are not considering doing this foolish thing.'

'Very well. If you insist, then I swear,' said Richard.

Husan nodded once, his mind made up. 'Very well. Then I have just the man who will be able to give all the details you could ever wish to know about the smugglers, their practices and their secret pathways. It is my cousin, Saiid. I will try and make a rendezvous with him tonight in the Old Market.'

Five of them entered the Old Market just before midnight. Richard and Robin with their guide, Husan, were also followed by Mahmud and Ahmed. As soon as they passed under the great square archway with its imposing pharaonic figures apparently stolen from the pyramids and the tombs of the kings, they were swept into the heaving bustle that made the place so timelessly attractive, so edgily exciting, so redolent with that heady promise of risks an inch or two outside their comfort zone. Richard had known the old souk in Manama on Bahrain Island in the past – a souk which had existed there for centuries – and he would have been hard put to tell the difference, even though the Old Market in Sharm was less than fifty years old. Husan, Mahmood and Ahmed insisted on accompanying Richard and Robin, not because they feared any danger, but apparently because they too enjoyed the heaving excitement of the tourist-packed streets and alleys, alive with vendors calling passers-by into their shops, stalls, bazaars and restaurants. And the way the contents of the shops and stalls overflowed exuberantly on to the pavements, the dazzling colours brightened by a fairyland of lanterns which added their smoky aroma to the overwhelming odour of the place.

The market itself was squashed hard up against a low pink granite cliff whose leading edge was scored with steps and pathways, caverns hollowed into restaurants, all illuminated, like the market streets, with an amazing array of electric lights and glowing lanterns. Halfway up this cliff was a restaurant whose nether regions reached right back into the living rock. And it was here, Husan said, that Saiid would be waiting to talk to them. But they had to get through the market to reach the cliff and the restaurant halfway up it.

Richard and Robin had been here before, and as seasoned travellers were more than capable of holding their own against the most insistent of salesmen. Richard's only polished and perfect phrase in Arabic was *La aa shukran*, which roughly translated as *I don't want it, thank you.* The only real precaution that they had taken was that Robin was responsible for carrying the credit and debit cards. Richard had left his wallet undisturbed in the drawer where he had shoved it after transferring it out of the towelling dressing gown when he had settled up with the hospital. Robin's cards were in her purse, safely zipped into the handbag she carried tightly under her arm. But with the three local men surrounding them, there was no trouble at all. The salesmen in their checked shirts and jeans, their open keffiyas and dishdasha robes, their sandals, flip-flops and Nike trainers, looked at the tight little unit hurrying past and stepped back silently. The only thing that slowed their progress, in fact, was the way in which both Richard and Robin were entranced by shop after shop, stall after stall.

The Manama Souk on Bahrain Island had had specialist areas, Richard recalled – the street of the goldsmiths, the street of the pearl sellers, the street of jewels. Areas specializing in rugs, clothing, leather goods, foodstuffs, herbs and spices. Each had their own particular look and smell. From the heady fragrance of the Street of Herbs and Spices to the eye-watering odour of the vats filled with animal hides and camel urine on the Street of the Tanners. He could see no particular order here, however, and discern no particular patterns of odour. Shops bright with fragrant, citrus-smelling fruit and everything from piles of melons to pyramids of pomegranates stood cheek by jowl with blood-redolent butchers in whose windows hung sections of halal lamb, beef, chicken, camel and, for all he knew, horse. Beneath these lay bright platters of liver, kidney, heart, tongue . . . 'What,' whispered Robin. 'No sheeps' heads? No eyeballs?'

Ahmed leaned forward as she slowed. 'Sheeps' heads inside,' he said. 'You wish to buy one?'

By the time Robin explained she was not serious, they had reached a particularly fragrant fish shop. Richard lingered hungrily outside the window, looking at a range of fish he had last seen on their scuba dives all laid out on beds of crushed ice. He liked his fish suppers but they had both been warned by Husan that they should eat little at dinnertime because Saiid wished to entertain them as well as giving them the benefit of his wisdom. There were solid, steely-sided tuna, both whole and in steaks laid out among multicoloured unicorn and squirrel fish. Firm, silver-scaled trevallys, red-finned wrasse, fat copper sea bream, grey and green eels. There were flat-faced, blue-sided parrotfish which Richard thought were inedible; napoleonfish with bulging golden foreheads. And, he was particularly glad to see, several big bellicose titan triggerfish almost rhomboid in shape, all multi-coloured with hard, sharp beaks rather than mouths. There were squid, cuttlefish, octopi, prawns, shrimps, grey-green lobsters. And oysters. Barrels and kegs of oysters, which put him in mind of his plans for bedtime now that Robin was in a more amenable frame of mind.

'Come on,' she snapped, bustling past him, 'Stop gawping like a haddock. There's a handbag and leathergoods shop I want to look in over here.'

And so they worked their way through the raucous, heaving bustle, grateful that the desert wind had dropped but still glad of the ice-cold air-conditioned breezes that wafted from the open doors behind the tall racks of goods which all but blocked the pavement. The sounds, like the smells, were overwhelming: the cries of the vendors and restaurant owners praising their wares. The conversations of excited tourists, calling directions and suggestions to each other in a dizzying range of languages and accents. The snapping of still cameras. The whirring of videos. The grumbling of camels that wandered, seemingly masterless, through the throng. The honking of car horns as drivers tried to ease their way through those streets that were not pedestrian only.

The leather shop was succeeded by a hat shop which stood beside a perfume shop, then there was a bazaar selling gold and jewellery, and watches that pretended to be by Breitling, Tag Heur, Omega, Seiko, Rolex. Next in line was a textile shop selling everything from scarves with labels suggesting they were from Gucci, Prada, Armani, Lauren and a host of others to carpets purporting to be genuine Arbadil, Bakhtiari, Isfahan and Kashanl, which stood beside a shop selling a range of tourist memorabilia including model camels, pharaonic crockery, hookahs, camel-skin lampshades and statues of the ancient Egyptian gods. After that there was a wall illustrated with pictures of Cleopatra, which did the legendary queen, her fashion sense, followers, accoutrements and barges very little justice. And that in turn stood beside a spice shop which doubled as an apothecary – for every spice, essence or tincture they sold was not only a matter of odour and colour but also, according to the notices in the window, of health and well-being.

Even the signs were bewildering. Amici, Al Kazzan, El Gezira Vodafone. HD Bank and ATM. Hammad Sports. But the brightest sign of all was the one comprised of tall letters spelling out EL KHADIWY that stood just beneath the low, bright moon at the crest of the cliff they were hurrying towards. Even as they approached through all the distracting bustle of street entertainers who congregated here at the heart of the market, swallowing swords, juggling with fire, performing incredible feats with ropes or beds of nails and charming cobras just like the one that had so nearly killed Nahom, so the colours of the big letters changed, from blue to green, to yellow, to red.

Side by side they ran up the carpeted stone steps past the black and gold statues of Anubis that guarded their way and up on to the bare rock balcony that led back into the cliff itself, where the rock roof closed claustrophobically lower and lower while the shadows grew darker and darker. Just when Richard thought he was going to have to fold himself in half or smack his head on the ceiling, they arrived at the innermost table. It was lit by a beautifully coloured lamp made of camel skin – like many of the lamps in the market outside. The dim, multicoloured light showed that the only occupant of a table for four was a grey-bearded man wearing a plain white turban in place of the more general keffiyah. He rose to greet them, just able to stand erect beneath the sloping red rock roof, for he was physically identical to his cousin, Husan. As he did so, Richard noted that he was wearing the almost universal white cotton dishdasha robe, identical to those worn by the men in the video clip of Nahom's kidnapped sister. Seeing that there were only four settings at the table, Richard glanced around as their host was courteously clearing his throat. And was surprised to realize that, somewhere along the recently trodden way, Mahmood and Ahmed had vanished.

'You are welcome, Mister Richard and Mistress Robin,' said the white-robed man in sonorous English. 'I am Saiid, cousin to Husan. I understand you wish to know about matters in the

interior and even up in the Red Zone. Please be seated.' Saiid
gestured, and, looking down, Richard realized that they were to
sit cross-legged on carpets and cushions in the Bedouin style,
which at least explained why a table could be placed so far back
in the restaurant. But Saiid continued, smoothly, as he crossed
his legs and sank to the floor, 'I have ordered food. And as we
eat, we will talk.'

FIVE

Sahaari

Saiid leaned forward. In the weird light from the camel-skin lamp his eyes looked strange, seemingly glassy. And, thought Richard, their colour was unusual too: pale, almost hazel, with flecks of blue and darker brown like agates, their colour enhanced by the dark skin of his cheekbones, the heaviness of his eyelids and the granite grey sweep of his eyebrows. His beard, too, was unusual. It was of medium length and straight-haired, almost bristling. On the sides of his face in front of his ears and down along the line of his jaw it was white, but beneath the beak of his nose and on the breadth of his chin it was as grey as his eyebrows. And it was parted. There was a vertical parting running straight down from his nose to a cleft in his chin which matched his clean-shaven cousin Husan's. Beard and moustache had both been brushed to the right on the right side of his face and to the left on the left side. The effect was arresting, especially as the moustache was long enough to have upward-curling points at each end. The whole effect was almost as striking as those strange, light eyes and the way they twinkled amid a maze of wrinkles as Saiid smiled, seeing Richard and Robin studying him with such interest. 'Is this then the first time you have met a true *rajul bin sahaari*, a man of the desert?'

Both Richard and Robin sat back, embarrassed. Saiid's smile grew wider. 'Do not be concerned,' he said gently. 'You are here to learn. And if I am to teach you, you must begin by learning to trust me.'

'Of course we trust you,' said Richard. 'We have Husan's word on that. And the question of trust is not crucial at the moment. We really just want to know about the Bedouin, the interior, and anything you think would be relevant in the current situation. Who might be holding this young woman Tsibekti, Bisrat and the others. Where they might be being held at the moment. How accessible such a place might be – and what chances the authorities might have of getting there to rescue the hostages. Anything you might know about the local tribesmen's secret smugglers' pathways to this place and away from it. I've promised Husan that I have no intention of actually trying to go in and rescue Tsibekti or Bisrat, so we won't be relying on your information in any life-or-death situations. But we are . . . *I* am fascinated to know about what really has gone – *still goes* – on up in the heart of the Sinai. In the Amber and Red Zones as defined by the British Foreign and Commonwealth Office.'

The conversation was interrupted by the arrival of glasses of hibiscus tea, mint tea and Hayat sparkling water. 'I have taken the liberty of ordering for all of us,' said Saiid. 'Perhaps you will come to trust my taste in food and drink as well as in matters concerning the interior. In fact, you might say that you will trust me to guide you through the *saharri* desert and the *gebel* mountains which stand behind it along the *wadi* – dry river valleys that run between them after I have guided you through the courses of the meal I have selected for you.'

As they sipped their drinks, the first courses began to appear. Richard had no idea where the restaurant kitchens were, but the food arrived piping hot and in mouth-watering variety. The first courses were small but intensely full-flavoured. Saiid introduced each of them, switching from talk of the desert to culinary explanations mid-sentence. There was a *sayyadiah* of local prawns in a piquant spicy tomato sauce sprinkled with cumin seeds, poppy seeds and finely chopped coriander leaves, served on a fried flatbread, which was succeeded by little cups without handles filled with half-a-dozen sips of *sorba ads*, a thick, spicy lentil soup. With the first of these courses there was a silver filigree bowl filled with freshly made breads. Saiid said, 'We call bread *aysh*, which means life.' But succeeding the soup, another solid silver basin arrived piled with freshly fried crispy falafel that were light as clouds and tasted of broad beans and chick peas, fresh parsley and coriander leaves, ground coriander seeds and cumin. They were sprinkled with sesame seeds and served with thick, buttery sesame-flavoured tahini dip.

'So,' intoned Saiid as they nibbled and sipped their way through this prelude to the feast, 'you want to know if there is a secret location somewhere in the interior where unfortunate people such as your friend's sister can be held for ransom. That is the heart of the matter, is it not? The routes towards such a place and the pathways north from it towards the borders with Gaza, Israel, Jordan and Saudi are incidental at the moment. Whether or not such secret pathways exist is of limited interest beside the knowledge of whether the woman you are seeking can be held securely there, who would be holding her and where such a prison could be.'

'We have heard of such places in Saudi,' said Richard, putting down his empty cup of sorba ads and reaching for a little more of the bread of life. 'There have been programmes on British television as well as on Sky and Al Jazeera, among others. Some of them are still up on YouTube. But is it possible that the same sort of thing could be happening here?'

'Wherever there are smugglers and traffickers, such things are possible,' answered Saiid. 'No. More than possible: *likely*. Perhaps even inevitable. We are not dealing here with the sort of smugglers popular in children's stories of times long past and romantic adventures.'

'I see what you mean,' Richard said thoughtfully, reaching for a falafel. 'We really live in a much more cynical, ruthless and violent world.'

After a pause to allow more general conversation and further sharpening of their appetites, a basin full of rice arrived as a precursor to the courses of their main meal. This was *kosheree*: steamed white rice mixed with green and black lentils, topped with dark threads of fried rice noodle and garnished with crispy deep-fried onion. Together with the rice, the waiter brought a bowl of spicy tomato sauce. Hard on his heels came colleagues carrying lamb *fattah*: tender, full-flavoured shanks braised in onions, butter and a glaze of honey. Alongside the fattah came Red Sea snapper. 'This is how we prepare Nile perch,' Saiid explained. 'But the Nile is a long way from here and it works equally as well with the snapper. The fish have been marinated in lemon and lime, coriander and dill, cumin and nutmeg, then barbecued until the skin is dark and crispy but the flesh is soft and fragrant. The spiced mixed vegetables that accompany them complete the main course. I have ordered these dishes because they overlap in many ways. It does not matter which combination you choose to explore, the effect will still be authentic and delicious.'

He was right, and conversation came and went during the next half hour or so as each of them tried different combinations of rice, sauce, lamb, fish, vegetables and breads. But soon enough they got back down to business and the conversation started properly again as the empty plates, platters, basins and bowls were removed. 'The Bedouin are lords of this desert as the Berber, the Riff and the Tuareg are lords of the great deserts west of the Nile, the *Reg* desert mountains and the *Erg* great sand sea. All of them have been forced to adapt their traditional ways by the changing conditions of the new centuries. They have always traded – and smuggled, if you will. But as the modern world has caught up with them, increasing numbers have been forced off the land which they grazed and herded over but never *owned*. At least, not according to the laws passed in Cairo. The past few decades have been difficult for the Bedouin. Even the establishment of the new resorts such as Sharm and Dahab has brought new troubles. They were moved off land they thought was theirs. They were forced to face the destruction of their traditional values as well as of their livelihoods. Bedouins living in the Sinai didn't benefit much from employment in the new holiday destinations. Sudanese and Egyptian workers were brought here as construction labourers instead. When the tourist industry started to boom, local Bedouins increasingly moved into new service positions such as cab drivers, tour guides, campground or cafe managers. However, the competition is very high, and many Sinai Bedouins are still unemployed. Since there are not enough employment opportunities, Tarabin Bedouins as well as other Bedouin tribes living along the border between Egypt and Israel are involved in inter-border smuggling of drugs and weapons, as well as the infiltration of prostitutes and African labour workers, such as Tsibekti's companion Bisrat hoped to be. All this is common knowledge. Any Bedouins who held desirable coastal property have lost control of their land as it was sold by the government to hotel operators all along the coast between Taba and Sharm. The successive governments in Cairo did not see the land as belonging to Bedouin tribes, who, as I said, only had grazing and herding rights over it, but rather as a state property. In the summer 1999, the army bulldozed the only Bedouin-run tourist areas north of Nuweiba and replaced them with the system that had been so successful in Sharm.

'On the other hand, the political problems of the last few years promised to bring more freedom to the Sinai Bedouins. But since they were deeply involved in weapon smuggling into Gaza after a number of terror attacks on the Egypt–Israel border, and increasingly against the police and soldiers trying to keep control in the dangerous northern areas, the government has started much more active military operations in the Red Zone of North Sinai. Underground tunnels leading from Egypt to Gaza that were used as smuggling channels and gave profit to the Bedouin families on the Egyptian side, as well as the Palestinians on the other side of the border, have been closed by both our government and the Israelis, especially during the conflict of 2014. The army in the Red Zone has delivered a threatening message to the Bedouin: *cooperate with state troops and officials or face our full force.* And that is also the message of the even more powerfully armed and equipped Israelis if you smuggle arms into Gaza. But some of the hardiest and most desperate see no alternative. They are too proud to serve, to drive taxis, to wander the tourist beaches offering rides on their camels. They know the old trade routes and the secret places – knowledge passed down from generation to generation. The non-Bedouins, even those in the Sinai, have no such knowledge. *Al sahaari* – the desert, is a hard mistress but she can offer much to those who know her and are willing to take risks. And that is the situation as it stands at the moment. Many Bedouin live in the cities, earning their living in service positions. Much like in England, eh? Where your economy depends on service industries?' Saiid gave a knowing wink, then continued, 'But there is still a minority who use their ancient skills and knowledge. Not to herd sheep or goats, or horses and camels, but to smuggle people, weapons and anything else that will turn a profit and keep their families from starving.'

The intense conversation about the Bedouin, lords of the *sahaari,* was interrupted by dessert. '*Mahalbiya* – milk pudding,

is something of an acquired taste,' said Saiid. 'Though they do
a particularly fine one here flavoured with rosewater and
cardamom seeds, sprinkled with pistachios and sultanas. I
thought, however, you would prefer *ataif* – sweet pancakes stuffed
with mixed nuts and coconut deep fried and dipped in honey.
And the chef's masterpiece, *omm ali*. To call *omm ali* bread and
butter pudding, as I have seen in even the best hotels, does it a
great disservice. The sweet bread is prepared with fresh cream,
full milk, sultanas and walnuts. It is topped with puff pastry
pieces and served with yet more cream. If your hearts can
stand it, your tongues will think they have attained *ferdoos*
– paradise.'

After all their tongues had visited paradise, the waiters brought
them cups of thick, foamy coffee flavoured with cardamom. As
they sipped this, Saiid continued his explanation. 'The pathways
into the mountains are not dictated by whim or by chance, of
course. They are dictated by water, as is almost everything here.
I say almost, because there are routes also dictated by history,
by commerce, by religion.

'There are ways across the Sinai that have existed since the
pharaohs ruled Egypt. They lead to mines where men have dug
for gold, copper and turquoise since before recorded time. One
of the earliest names for this place is Land of Turquoise.
According to the Christian Bible and the Jewish Torah as well
as the Holy Qur'an, there are routes followed by the children of
Israel as they escaped from the pharaohs. Routes that led the
prophet Musa, blessings be upon him, whom you call Moses, to
converse with the one true God. There are routes that lead the
faithful on their Hajj and have done so for more than a thousand
years. There are hidden roads that have led defensive armies to
long-deserted fortresses where they could stand against rapacious
crusaders.

'All these, as well as those which follow the waterways, are
known to the Bedouin. But as your friend Nahom has learned,
following paths to water is not easy. The uninitiated might suppose
it is simply a question of going from one oasis to another, or
following a course dictated by the wadis. This is not so. To begin
with, there are very few oases, and where they exist, townships

tend to have grown up around them. And smugglers, of course, wish to avoid towns. But they are few and far between, particularly in the mountains of the interior. Mountains that are often all but impassable. And that, too, is important because, although there is sand desert along the coast, which we may cross these days with a range of vehicles from four-by-fours to quad bikes, the mountains are closed against such modes of transport.

'There is, say, sixty kilometres between the oasis at El Tor, where your friend believes his sister to have come ashore, and the oasis at Abu Zenima, which is the next one north along the coast. Sixty kilometres – a journey of little more than an hour in a car. Nothing. However, consider this. The oasis of Feiran is about the same distance from El Tor. Sixty kilometres or so. But it is in the mountains to the north-east, in behind Gebel Serbal, whose peak is more than two thousand metres high. This sixty-kilometre trek cannot so easily be made by car. The last ten kilometres, at least, must be made on foot. So a journey of little more than an hour becomes a trek of at least six hours. And the next oasis north of Feiran, Ain Akhbar, is a mere thirty kilometres further but that pathway is all in the mountains. On foot, that is a long day's march. Not that anyone would travel right through the day, but still, *thirty* kilometres on foot, in a place where *three* can be the difference between life and death.

'There is one road through the southern mountains. Only one – though it has sidetracks every now and then. It links El Tor on the west coast to Ras Abu Galum, just north of Dahab on the east coast. It follows Wadi Feiran for the most part. It is there – at least partly – because it passes close by two of the most holy sites on earth: the Monastery of Saint Catherine where Musa, peace be upon him, saw the burning bush and was directed to return to Egypt. And Mount Sinai itself, where the Ten Commandments were delivered to him.

'In fact, there are really only three roads across the Sinai. The first is the one I have just mentioned. The second is the one that joins Suez to Taba, and passes through Nekhel. Nekhel is in the heart of the Sinai and the roadway is the border between the South Sinai and the North Sinai – between the Amber Zone and the Red Zone. Then there is the coast road joining Quantara Sharq on the canal with Rafa on the border of Palestine.'

'You mean there are no roads running north/south?' asked Richard.

'None that go the length of the Sinai through the interior. There is a coast road linking Sharm with Dahab, Neweiba and Taba in the east, then running north along the Israeli border to Rafa. And there is another linking Sharm with Suez and Port Said in the west. But no roads run northwards though the mountains in the south or northward across the great desert plateau or the Gebel Al Tib mountain ranges in the centre. There is one road north from Nekhel to El Arish on the Mediterranean coast, but that crosses the great desert which is like the Great Sand Sea of the Sahara, and the dunes often sweep across and bury it.'

'*Dunes*,' said Richard, to whom this was something of a revelation, even though he had captained ships passing through the Suez Canal which ran alongside it.

'Dunes twenty to thirty metres high that drift with the wind like waves on the ocean.' Saiid nodded.

'So, anyone smuggling – or being smuggled – across the Sinai from south-west to north-east – from El Tur, say, to Taba and the Israeli border, faces a flat coastal desert backed by all but impenetrable mountains more than two thousand metres high, followed by another trackless desert plateau that has only one road running east–west across it and another range of mountains sitting behind it also reaching more than a thousand metres in height, then they get faced with your own equivalent of the Great Sand Sea with dunes that can reach thirty metres or a hundred feet. With what, a dozen recorded oases, which smugglers would want to avoid in any case. All this in temperatures that regularly top fifty degrees Celsius in the shade. And, once you get across the road past Nekhel, it's not just the Gebel Al Tib and the dunes, it's being trapped between Hezbollah or al-Qaeda and the Egyptian army as you sneak up towards Gaza and a warm welcome in all sorts of ways from either the Israelis or the Palestinians, depending on which tunnels you are hoping to sneak through.

'*And*, what with one thing and another, you'll probably have to do most of this five hundred kilometre journey on foot because there are no roads or any access even for four-by-fours. Furthermore, there are no obvious pathways, while the only people who really know their way around are the Bedouin, and especially those Bedouin who refuse to cave in to economic, social and political pressure and settle in the cities. Those Bedouin who have been forced to turn to smuggling, in fact, or watch their families starve.'

'That's about it,' said Saiid. His face crinkled into another wide smile. 'I'm pleased to see you were paying attention. I was afraid the food might have distracted you.'

'But there are ways through,' said Richard, the rising inflection of his tone making it clear that this was a question rather than a statement. 'Daunting and deadly as it sounds, even before we start to include the resident fauna like scorpions and half a dozen sorts of venomous snakes such as the one that bit Nahom; there must be ways through, otherwise there would be no smuggling or trafficking. That stands to reason.'

'You are right, Mister Richard, there are ways through.' Saiid nodded in reply. 'Though I have to observe that you are a little naive. The market is always there – people who are starving in Africa will always want to try for a better life, no matter what the risks. I suspect that smugglers could take hundreds, perhaps thousands, into the interior and just dump them there – and still get more hopeful men and women to come. Certainly, all you need to do is look at the death toll in the Mediterranean of people desperate to get from Africa to Europe through Italy. Two hundred more were drowned last week; thousands drown every year – and yet they still come in their thousands, paying upwards of ten thousand American dollars each. And I am sure they would still come here to the Sinai even if no one ever got through . . .'

'Because the traffickers have people on the ground, in Eritrea, Sudan and Somalia, selling the hope of a better life like confidence tricksters,' said Robin quietly, her tone flattened by the horror of what they were discussing.

'That is so,' agreed Saiid. 'Like your banks in Britain selling Payment Protection Insurance that they knew to be worthless, perhaps. It is making a profit that is important.'

'But they do get through,' said Richard, his inflection rising again. 'People do get through to Israel, Saudi and the Emirates.'

'They do. Because the smugglers and traffickers can make

more profit that way. You can't sell on a corpse, not even for spare part surgery, though I am sure they would try. While their victims are still alive there is more money to be made, as your desperate friend Nahom would seem to prove.'

'But if there are ways through, then why don't the authorities find them and close them?' asked Robin.

'In some countries that would be because the authorities too can make a handsome profit from the trade. But here it is more complex than that. The ways through the Sinai are known only to those who use them regularly and repeatedly. Nature and even history conspire to outwit the authorities. The pathways are at once ancient and yet ever-changing. They can vary depending on who has gone before and what decisions they have made along the way. They can move, appear or vanish with the passing of each of the seasons, within the seasons, and even with a change in the weather. Not even our weather here in the Sinai – indeed, a change in the weather nearby can be enough. You will have noticed, for example, that the great north wind, the shamaal, has been blowing in Saudi during the last few days. The result here in Sharm has been extremely hot winds day and night. This will mean that several of the more popular routes will have been closed – those that rely on the smaller pools of water, which are fatally transient. Puddles that form from dew when the nights are much colder than the days and collect in depressions in the rocks. Streams that come and go mere inches below the beds of wadis that are apparently dry. Water that can be found within the plump leaves of some varieties of desert plants. Little groves of watermelon that ripen or wither depending on the height of the sun. If Nahom's sister is with a group following such a route, they will have gone to ground, literally, in caves and caverns such as this.' Saiid gestured to the low-ceilinged cavern they were sitting in. 'Our word in Arabic for cavern is *magaara*. Such places are cool and provide shelter. They will not move until the nights cool down again, and the temporary water supplies are restored.'

Intrigued, Richard said, 'Have you any idea where on earth they might be?'

'You have heard, perhaps, of The Wilderness of Sin?'

Richard regularly acted as a church warden when he was at

home in England, so he knew his Bible well. 'That's mentioned in the Book of Exodus,' he said. 'The Wilderness of Sin is one of the locations that Moses – sorry, Musa – led the Children of Israel through on his way to Mount Sinai and the Ten Commandments.'

'It's where God sent manna to rain from the sky, isn't it?' added Robin.

'Like many places mentioned in the early books of the Bible, the Wilderness of Sin is real,' explained Saiid. 'Though I'm not sure whether you can still get manna there. It is an area in the mountains inland from the oasis of Abu Zenima that we have already mentioned.'

'Sixty kilometres north of El Tor and the secret cove where Tsibekti and Bisrat came ashore,' said Richard, his memory as sharp as ever. 'It's taken them ten days to cover, what, a hundred and fifty kilometres?' he added incredulously.

'Travelling at night, in secret, on foot.' Saiid shrugged. 'It is not so inconceivable, but I would suspect that they will have reached the wilderness within four or five days of setting out. It is a place where water can be both found and carried – the Oasis of Ain Akhdar is not too far, so if the transient water supplies dry up, a little ingenuity and some plastic jerrycans will keep everyone hydrated. And more. Although this trade is almost timelessly ancient – does not the Bible once again talk of Joseph being sold into slavery by his jealous brothers? – it is also modern and adaptable. In the township near Ain Akhdar there are facilities the smugglers find useful. Internet access. Wi-Fi. ATM machines. You do realize, don't you, that Nahom could simply have come carrying his phone and a credit card, and that would have been sufficient? But the main strength of the Wilderness of Sin, from the smugglers' point of view, remains the fact that the mountains there are full of caverns or *magaarat*, so concealment is easy as well. I have even heard talk of gold and copper mines in the area. And, I believe, a ruined fort. The whole place is a maze. And is, therefore, supposed to be a popular resting place.'

'So why don't the authorities . . .' Robin began.

'The Wilderness of Sin has an area of nearly a thousand square kilometres.'

'That makes it half the size of West Sussex, back home,'

observed Richard. 'Remember the Sinai as a whole is bigger than Belgium; in fact, it's damn near the size of Belgium and Holland combined.'

'And, as we have already said,' emphasized Saiid, 'this area half the size of your West Sussex is a three-dimensional maze of mountains two thousand metres high, wadis that wind crazily all over the place, thousands of magaarat, half of which have never been fully explored, mine workings and ruins which were probably ancient when the prophet Musa, peace be upon him, led the Israelites through.'

'Why would Tsibekti still be there?' wondered Robin. 'Wouldn't they want to move on? Especially if there is a shortage of water because of the shamaal?'

'Look at it from the smugglers' point of view,' suggested Saiid. 'The moment they got Tsibekti to call home, they had to stop and wait. There is no point in getting Nahom – or whoever – to come rushing to her rescue laden with yet more money if they've moved on so far that he can't catch up with them. So they want to stay somewhere close to the coast. They're not in any rush. They have water – and probably food. As long as their merchandise stays alive and fairly healthy their investment is secure. And consider, Tsibekti came in through El Tur. As far as I know – which is what you have told me – Nahom was coming in through the same way. The Wilderness of Sin is the closest safe place to that particular section of the coast – therefore it is the logical place to wait. Nahom believes they were going to guide him to his sister using the phone. That is a standard ploy, but of course it is yet another lie. Actually, I am sure at least one of the others on that boat was working for the smugglers and would have found a way to guide him into the wilderness.'

'He didn't have a guide last time he tried,' Robin observed.

'And he was starting a hundred kilometres too far south,' agreed Saiid.

'You think they'll try to come and get him?' asked Richard. 'I didn't count the money in his money belt but it looked like a fair amount. Well worth putting a little effort into.'

'But only if they know he's got it,' inserted Husan, who had been sitting silently all this time.

'They must know he's got something,' observed Richard

thoughtfully. 'If they had people on the boat, and I agree they must have, then they'd have signalled ahead, surely? It would just have needed a quick phone call. Because what would be the point of him coming if he didn't have the ransom with him?'

'There are several things to consider, then,' said Saiid. 'Whether the smugglers' associate on the boat made sure he stayed with Nahom if Nahom was the main target. Whether that person or people are still with him, or rather with Major Ibrahim in custody and waiting for him to come up from hospital. Whether they can arrange to get him out of jail and as far as the Wilderness of Sin, if that's where Tsibekti and the others are. And, indeed, whether Nahom was the only person aboard who was bringing ransom money.'

'If there were others,' said Richard thoughtfully, 'then they're either in prison in Hurgada or in prison in Sharm – and whatever they were carrying is in the hands of the authorities, like Nahom's money belt.'

'But where does that leave poor Tsibekti – and anyone else who's with her and in the same boat as she is?' asked Robin.

'Up the wadi without a paddle,' answered Richard with unintentional brutality.

Richard's plans to parlay the fact that Robin was no longer angry with him and the thoughts prompted by the barrel full of oysters into a night of romance all came to nothing. Even in the face of a low, romantic moon just a night or two past its fullest, of a sky scattered with stars like candle flames flickering in the lingering heat haze, neither of them could rouse themselves from the depression that the conclusion of their talk with Saiid had engendered. Instead of doing what he had planned, they lay side by side in the silvery, air-conditioned darkness, each wakeful, wrapped in their individual thoughts until Robin exploded, 'Dammit, Richard! We must be able to do *something*!'

'I don't see what. We have no power or influence here. Major Ibrahim and Sergeant Sabet seem capable, and I'm sure they're doing their best. Anything we're likely to do will simply get in their way and be more of a hindrance than a help. And, of course, I gave my word to Husan that we wouldn't go off after Tsibekti and her kidnappers as a condition of him introducing us to cousin

Saiid in the first place. So I'm afraid that, one way or another, we're painted right into a corner. As far as I can see, all we can do is keep paying Nahom's hospital bills and hope he recovers quickly.'

'So that's it?' she answered, frustration making her sound even angrier than she was. 'We just sit here and let those dreadful men do what they want to that poor girl, then chop off her fingers, cut her throat and leave her dead in a ditch?'

'A wadi.'

'Oh, for heaven's sake, Richard! Ditch, wadi, *gebel*, cave or *magaara*, the poor girl will still be raped, tortured, mutilated and bloody well left for dead, won't she?'

That was where the conversation ended. Sleep did not come swiftly or easily for either of them, but it came eventually, and it lasted through the night.

So when Sergeant Sabet led a raid on the Villa Shahrazad just after dawn the next morning, it came as a complete surprise. The first thing Richard knew about it was when a distraught Sasha knocked on the bedroom door with unaccustomed forcefulness. He jumped awake, heart thumping, surfacing from a dream that would have shocked the bloodthirsty Macbeth. 'Come in,' he called, having glanced across at Robin, who had not stirred. The bedsheet covered her almost as completely as the robes favoured by the most conservative of Muslims. Sasha came in. 'Mister Richard,' he said, his voice shaking. 'It is the police. They believe the illegal alien Nahom Selassie is hiding here. They have paperwork.'

Search warrants, or their Egyptian equivalent, thought Richard, glancing down at Robin once again. He considered shaking her awake, but decided at once that he could not even consider doing that in front of either Sasha or Sergeant Sabet and her men.

'They wish to search the entire villa, and of course they want to speak to you and Mistress Robin.'

'Right. Thanks for the warning, Sasha. We'll get dressed and be down as soon as possible.'

Sasha left the room and closed the door almost silently.

At this point Richard did shake Robin awake, almost as brutally as he had dismissed Tsibekti up her wadi without a paddle. And he was right to do so, for under normal circumstances she would not actually surface fully until she had been presented with at least one cup of tea. At the third shake, she sat up in just the same way that she did yesterday when he'd soaked her. But providentially in a better mood.

'What?' she asked, less confrontationally than twenty-four-hours earlier.

'Nahom's gone again,' he said.

'So?' Reading between the lines, he understood she was wondering *what in heaven's name has that got to do with me?*

'They think he's here. There's a whole bunch of policemen wanting to search the villa and cross-examine us.'

'*Now?*' Her gaze darted round the room, looking for an outfit suitable for a cross examination which she could get dressed in within the next few minutes.

''Fraid so,' he rumbled and rolled out of bed. The decision was easy for him – slacks and a shirt, both readied before he tucked down last night. Sandals and he was off.

Under normal circumstances, he would have stayed with Robin as she orientated and clothed herself. But his interest had been piqued by the intellectual leap he had made – not that it was a large one. If Sabet was looking for Nahom then Nahom had vanished again. Now that was something he wanted a lot more information about. Especially after the dinner conversation with Saiid last night.

Richard ran down the stairs so quickly that he caught up with Sasha, who seemed to be glad of his company as they walked down the last few steps to the ground floor. Sergeant Sabet, dressed in the spotless white uniform and headdress that was becoming all too familiar to him, was waiting for Richard in the reception hall, and opened her mouth as soon as she saw him. But he spoke before she could get a word out.

'So,' he said, 'Nahom has disappeared again.' His tone was carefully balanced. There was simple enquiry. No accusation of police inefficiency.

'The hospital contacted us this morning,' she said flatly. 'They said he had made an impressive recovery and so he could be transferred to our care. They put him in an ambulance and sent it to El Benouk Road. But it never arrived. We found it in the Old Town near the market. There was no sign of the driver or the orderly accompanying the patient.'

'The guard?'

'There was no guard. They had all returned to base. We believed Selassie was too weak to escape unaided and we needed men to help with the others at El Benouk Road.'

Richard raised an eyebrow but made no comment.

In the brief moment of silence, the bustle throughout the villa established the speed and efficiency with which Sabet's colleagues were searching. 'What makes you think he's here?'

'It's where he came before. I'm not accusing you or Captain Mrs Mariner of helping him. But last time he ran he came here to steal supplies. Maybe he will do so again.'

'You're right. That's a good point. May I offer you a cup of coffee or tea while your men search?'

'Thank you, no.'

At that point Robin arrived. Like Richard, she was dressed in light, casual clothes, and looked to have brushed her hair with her fingers. 'They're going through the bedroom now,' she said.

'What? Do they think he's hiding under the bed?' asked Richard, amused at the thought.

'Heaven knows,' said Robin. 'Is there any tea going?'

'I expect Sharl will have some on the go. I mean, the whole house is up and about now,' said Richard, still amused. 'Go and check in the kitchen. I'll stay here with the sergeant.'

Robin vanished.

'What do you think he's planning to do?' Richard asked. 'Major Ibrahim has his phone and his money. Short of wandering into the middle of the desert and shouting her name, he's never going to find her. And even if he does, how's he going to buy her freedom?'

Sergeant Sabet was still shaking her head when the officer searching their room came down the stairs, clutching something that he handed over to her, speaking in impenetrable Egyptian as he did so. It was at this point that Richard noticed they were both wearing latex gloves. 'Hey,' he said as Sabet took what the officer gave her and the policeman fell silent. 'That's my wallet.'

'When did you last use it?'

'A couple of days ago. I used it to set up payment for Nahom in the hospital on the first occasion he was taken in. That was the last time.'

'Where do you normally keep it?' asked Sabet.

'In the drawer of my bedside table,' he answered.

'Not a particularly secure location, I'm afraid. It was found under the bed, up against the wall,' she said as she opened it.

And as she did so, Richard could see that it was empty.

All his credit cards were gone.

'It has to be Nahom,' Richard said to Robin a few minutes later. 'I don't know whether to laugh or cry! Light-fingered little sod!'

'Be fair, he was desperate,' said Robin soothingly. 'He probably found the wallet when he was searching for his money belt, before he was reduced to waking you and asking for it, and took the cards for insurance. *Then* he woke you up, and you got the belt for him but he still hung on to them just in case. Remember you didn't realize he'd rifled the kitchen till the next morning either!'

This conversation was happening in the villa's study as Richard waited to get through to Sentinel on the phone so that he could cancel all his cards while Sergeant Sabet went to report the latest news to Major Ibrahim.

'Anyway,' Robin added bracingly, 'he can't do much without the PIN numbers, can he? And he won't have those.'

'No,' said Richard grimly. 'But Doctor Zabr needed the PIN for the AmEx to set things up in the hospital. If the orderly who's vanished with Nahom got sight of it as I keyed it in, then we might be in trouble, because I'd say it was a fair bet that the ward orderly who was so happy to show me to the finance office and the driver who has vanished with him are working for the smugglers, so if they are following any kind of a plan, getting the PIN might well have become part of it. Like Saiid said last night at dinner, these smugglers are tech savvy. If there's a scam with a card they'll likely know about it.'

'What's the limit on the AmEx again?' she enquired.

'It's the Heritage Mariner roving business account so it's one hundred thousand dollars.'

'Insured . . .'

'Against all eventualities. With Lloyds of London, the same as the Heritage Mariner fleet.'

'That's a relief.'

'I'd still like to get it back and have a word or two with young mister Selassie.'

'I bet you would! Thank heaven I've still got the holiday emergency account card we took out with us last night in case I saw anything irresistible in the market. That has a limit of ten thousand pounds sterling, so we won't starve in the meantime.'

'We wouldn't in any case. I can get funds wired to the HSBC bank up in Naama Bay. In fact, I'll do that as soon as I've finished here . . . Hello? Hello, Sentinel? This is Richard Mariner of Heritage Mariner here. I'd like you to put a stop on all my credit and debit cards please. Yes, they've been stolen. Yes, I have reported it to the local police. Of course. The third letter of my security code word is . . .'

Little more than an hour later, Richard stepped out of the lift at the foot of the villa's private cliff and turned sharp right towards the private marina and *Katerina*. There was a spring in his step that came from the uplifting feeling that he had dealt swiftly and efficiently with a potentially nasty situation. All his card accounts were closed – but there had not been time to do a forensic check on whether any cash had vanished from them under suspicious circumstances, though it was going to be a tricky job by the look of things to differentiate between the legitimate charges from the hospital and anything else paid out in Sharm and its environs. An effectively limitless line of credit had been opened at the HSBC bank on Malek al Bahrein in Naama Bay, and Robin was on her way over in the Mercedes to complete the necessary paperwork on the promise that new cards would be couriered over to the Villa Shahrazad at the earliest opportunity.

As Richard jumped aboard *Katerina*, Husan came out of the bridge and ran down the exterior companionways to meet him. They stood side by side on the deck for an instant, shaking hands in the full blaze of the sun. Then went through into the shaded lower cabin and Husan poured cold drinks while they talked. Richard briefly explained the situation both with regard to Nahom's second disappearance – possibly with a couple of companions this time – and his missing credit cards. 'I'm going after him,' he said in conclusion. 'Do you think Saiid would be willing to help?'

'After *him*?' Husan probed, Richard's earlier promise unspoken between them.

'Him, not *her*. I've no intention of breaking my word to you, Husan. But you must admit, things are different now.'

'In several ways.' The captain nodded. He took a reflective sip of his Pepsi Max. 'If Nahom has used your cards already, then he is likely to be carrying a large amount of your money. What is the limit on your AmEx – the one you're worried about?'

'One hundred thousand dollars.'

'A *day*?'

'It's a business card. A Centurion. I've been using it at home and abroad for years. That's the upper limit. I've been on to Sentinel and closed all the card accounts, of course.'

'But he's had it how many days?'

'Four, by my count. But I really don't think he'd have used it until Major Ibrahim confiscated his money belt. He may not even have had a chance to use it since, depending on who he's with and where they're taking him.'

'If he has used it, then he will probably be safe enough if whoever is with him wants to take him to the others. In the Wilderness of Sin or wherever. On the other hand, if he hasn't used it yet then he and his sister are, of course, dead.'

Richard sat for a moment, stunned into silence by the simple truth that Husan had stated. He had acted on automatic pilot, without thinking about the implications of his actions. Of course, Husan was right. If Nahom hadn't got the money already then the moment he put any of the cards into an ATM the machine would refuse payment and would in all likelihood confiscate the plastic altogether. His call to Sentinel had quite possibly signed the death warrants of both twins. And, from what Nahom had told and shown Ibrahim, Sabet and Richard himself in his second hospital room, neither of the twins would have an easy or a quiet death.

'I've got to find him, or do my level best at least!' he said. 'Christ, what a mess! Do you think Saiid would help?'

'We can only ask. I'll get him on my cell phone now.'

Saiid's battered, white-painted long wheelbase Land Rover Defender sat in the drive outside Villa Shahrazad as Richard,

Sharl and Sasha carried out the last of the equipment and provisions Saiid suggested they might need – mostly water. There was a fridge in the back that ran off the battery power. Richard packed as much water into this as he could. It was still mid-morning and the sun had yet to attain its full fierceness. The shamaal had died and the day was calm, almost breathless. 'What I propose is this,' said Saiid as Richard stepped down out of the back and swung the door shut behind him. The Bedouin guide leaned forward across the big, square bonnet, pushing the end of his red-squared keffiyeh back over one shoulder and smoothing a map on to the cool metal as he did so. 'If I was correct in my suppositions over dinner yesterday evening, then they will be in the Wilderness of Sin. Nahom and whoever is with him will almost certainly be driving up the west coast road towards El Tur and Abu Zenima, where they will turn east and go into the mountains either on the road that crosses the whole peninsula to Dahab, or they will be trying the northern road here that stops in the mountains at Bir Nasib. What will happen then, either way I would suggest, is that they will leave their transport in the hands of the driver, go on foot to contact the others and either relieve Nahom of the money he took from your account before you closed it, or they will try to use an ATM at Ain Akhdar and find the cards are worthless. We could follow them, but we would need to be very fortunate indeed to catch them. Especially as I noticed when I drove in that Major Ibrahim is keeping a close eye on you. There is a police car parked immediately outside the gate. If we headed off towards El Tur, that would ring alarm bells and he might even stop us and search us – something I would prefer did not happen. His suspicions would be aroused primarily because there is little at El Tur to attract a legitimate tourist. There are reefs for diving – but if you were visiting them you would take *Katerina*, not the Land Rover.

'But look. Here is an alternative, which at least has a tincture of legitimacy about it. If we go east and take the coast road up past Dahab, then we can swing west on to the road that runs across to El Tur. That road is there because tourists in their thousands visit the Monastery of Saint Catherine here. And, if Ibrahim or his men ask, that is what we will say we are doing. But see, if we keep going west, the road goes over the watershed here at the Wadia Pass, then runs down into the Wadi Feiran. The Wilderness of Sin will therefore be below us, on our right hands, to the north. There are tracks and pathways running down into it that the Land Rover might just be able to handle. Approaching from that direction might well allow us a broad view of the wilderness. And anyone coming northward and eastward could well run straight into us.'

'That's all very well,' said Richard. 'But how long will it take us to do all that?'

'If we leave now we will be in Dahab before noon; at Saint Catherine by early afternoon and in the Wilderness of Sin perhaps an hour later still. If we have found no sign by the time we begin to lose the light – which happens later there, of course, because it is on a high, west-facing slope – we will come back down on to the road north of El Tur here and be back in Sharm an hour or so later, just in time for dinner. And at dinner we will plan tomorrow's exploration. Perhaps to Gebel Musa, the Mountain of Moses – Mount Sinai itself – or perhaps up as far as Nekhel, at the heart of the Sinai. Always passing through places where men such as those we seek can most often be found.'

'Right,' said Richard. 'That all sounds good. Just let me pick up one or two last things and say goodbye to Robin, then I'll be with you.'

As he spoke, he turned and ran back into the villa. Robin was all alone in Sasha's office, looking out across the flower beds to the Land Rover parked on the drive. Richard was still in the light linen trousers and white cotton shirt he had put on to greet Sergeant Sabet earlier. But he had swapped his sandals for high-sided desert boots and he now took the sleeveless fishing jacket Robin was holding for him. Its pockets were filled with necessaries such as ID papers, visas, sunglasses, cell phone, wallet – filled with a bundle of dollars, some Egyptian pounds and one of her cards – sun-block and so forth. He swung it on, then took the blue-checked keffiyeh scarf she held out next. Folding it swiftly and expertly, he slipped it over his head and secured it. Then he leaned down and hugged her. 'It's all right,' he said. 'We have this all planned. It'll be like something between *Beau Geste* and *Lawrence of Arabia*.' He felt her begin to turn her face up for a farewell kiss, but then she stiffened.

'Look!' she whispered in his ear. 'More like Bruce Willis than Beau Geste, I'd say.'

He swung round and looked where she was pointing. The office window gave a clear view of the Land Rover and the three men clustered round it – Saiid and the two other men who would accompany Richard on his search, Ahmed the dive master and Mahmood, Husan's lieutenant. Unaware that they were being watched, they were busily packing stuff into a compartment under the bench seat across the rear of the vehicle. He couldn't be absolutely certain, but he was a bit of a boy toy buff. It looked to him as though Mahmood was just putting a British Enfield SA-80 assault rifle safely out of sight. Ahmed was waiting to conceal his Turkish MKEK MPT-76 Mehmetçik-2 automatic, while Saiid was holding out an Israeli 7.62 Galil ACE model 32 and waiting for Mahmood to take that and hide it with the others; an armoury that showed how sensible Robin's decision to stay here had been.

Richard looked down at Robin's pale face and grinned. 'That's a relief,' he said. 'I was worried we were going to have to go up against these people armed with nothing but our natural charm and a winning smile.'

SIX

Sin

R ichard had never experienced anything quite like the weight of the noonday sun in the high *gebels* – the mountains above St Catherine and Sin. Glad of the keffiyeh covering his head and the sleeveless gilet on his shoulders that protected him against the burning load of the heat, he stood in what little shade the Land Rover offered. Outside that blessed pool of relative coolness, the heat radiating up from the rocky ground hurt the bottoms of his feet even through the thick crepe soles of his desert boots, just as the sun's rays roasted the top of his head, his shoulders and the backs of his hands. Every time he touched the Defender's bodywork, he was grateful for the fact that it was painted white. Had it been any colour other than cool, reflective white, he would have blistered whichever piece of skin rubbed up against it.

On the other hand, he had to be careful when he handled the burning black barrels of Saiid's incredibly powerful Zeiss Victory 8 X42 T*FL binoculars as he pointed them down towards the monastery that looked more like a medieval fortress than a place of worship. Somehow he had expected it to be on one of the mountain peaks nearby – a high defensive position, like a real crusader castle. Nearer to heaven into the bargain. But it was down on a valley floor. On the bed of a wide, dry wadi, in fact. Which, now that he thought about it, was logical. The place had been built around a bush. It had been constructed especially to protect the bush and to give hardy anchorites a place in which they could worship the deity who placed the bush there, made it appear to burn, and changed the life of the prophet Musa and indeed the history of his people because of it. So it was logical enough that the bush – which still miraculously flourished there – should grow right down on the bed of the apparently dry wadi, pushing its thirsty roots into the water table hidden metres beneath

the burning desert. It was that kind of thinking, after all, which
allowed the men they were hunting to follow the hidden pathways
on the far side of the high pass of the watershed, down in the
Wilderness of Sin.

But, to be fair, Richard thought, a certain amount of human
interference was involved in the divine protection of the undying
holy bramble bush, for there were all sorts of plants and even
trees growing around the imposing red walls of the monastery,
and they had clearly been irrigated. Their primary purpose seemed
to be to offer brief but welcome shade to the congregations of
pilgrims wandering, awestruck, through the oldest continuously
functioning place of worship in the Christian world. He found
himself just as awestruck as the pilgrims. However, he was
considering not the monastery or its plant-life, but the colossal
desolation of the sharp-peaked, red-flanked mountains with which
the place was surrounded, their rough slopes seemingly clawed
by gargantuan ancestors of the wild leopards that once roamed
the place.

But in fact, although he knew the wadi was dry, the power
radiating from the sun and the rocks it heated twisted the air
itself, so that from here the whole valley seemed to be filled with
crystal-clear water – a huge, trembling lake on which the monastery, the vegetation around it and the tourists within it all seemed
to be floating. Richard had seen mirages before, but never
anything like this. It was as though the furnace heat of the huge
white ball at the top of the hard blue sky was able to twist the
very fabric of reality. Or, at the very least, was powerful enough
to make this part of the earth, already seemingly at red heat,
tremble on the verge of melting.

'Richard!' Saiid's voice interrupted his reverie. He lowered
his binoculars. Saiid was offering him a paper plate on which a
split pita was filled with rapidly wilting salad and what looked
like the delicious *Tamiya* falafels he enjoyed so much last night.
He dropped the Zeiss glasses to hang from his neck by their
strap and took the plate and the bottle of iced water Saiid was
also offering. As he did so, Saiid continued, speaking quietly, 'It
looks as though the police car that followed us from Sharm has
given up the chase and gone home.'

'That's good. So it was well worth stopping here after all.

What about the tail we thought we'd picked up on the way past Dahab?'

'No sign. We're in the clear. When we've finished here we'll go up through the Watia Pass then try some of the back roads down into the wilderness.'

Richard nodded his agreement and pulled his keffiyeh away from his mouth. Using the Defender's bonnet as a table, he ate the delicious food hungrily and followed every second or third mouthful with a couple of sips from the small half-litre bottle of chilled Hayat water, feeling the liquid being translated into sweat all over his body even as he swallowed it.

'In half an hour or so you'll be able to look down on a Wilderness of Sin instead of a valley of prayer,' Saiid joked cheerfully.

Richard smiled and nodded, his mouth too full of pita and falafel to answer. He was well aware that the word 'Sin' in the name of the area was supposed to refer to the moon-goddess Zin; not to the breaking of any of the Commandments. But it was still an amusing notion. And, given the mission they were on, amusing notions were few and far between.

'Will anything be moving in heat like this?' he asked, swallowing the last of his lunch and his water.

'The sun will be heading west by the time we get to the best position,' Saiid assured him. 'We need to be high up, with an unrestricted view, but we also need to be west of the wilderness so that we can look down with the sun behind us and anyone looking up towards us will have the glare in their eyes. And, of course, beyond the watershed, all the valleys open to the west, so we'll be looking into them from the best angle.'

'And you know such a place?'

'I do.'

'Let's go then.'

Robin leaned forward in the chair and looked across Major Ibrahim's fastidiously tidy desk. Even though the day outside was blazingly hot beneath the noon sun, in here the atmosphere was cool – as cool as the glass of water the major had poured for her the instant she sat down. The air-conditioning unit murmured softly in the background. The hornets clustered along the lines of shade on top of the mesh frames outside. It was as though the air conditioning was giving the swarming insects a voice. 'Richard has gone to the monastery of Saint Catherine,' she said, raising her voice above the persistent hum. She was, frankly, a little surprised that her request to talk to someone about security in the mountains should have taken her from the police station's reception to the major's office so rapidly. Surely a man in his position would have more to do than to discuss terrorist fears with passing tourists. Except, she suspected, that he was actually hoping to get some further information out of her about precisely what her errant husband was really up to. Particularly as Sabet's report about the theft of Richard's cards was on the desk in front of him. It was written in Arabic script and was utterly impenetrable to her, of course. But he had marked off one or two details as he checked them through with her.

'Why the sudden interest in matters of religion?' asked Ibrahim now, pushing the theft report aside, resting his elbows on the edge of his desk and steepling his forearms. His right elbow brushed against an old-fashioned mahogany-covered intercom box, the sort of thing that cell phones seemed to have replaced. 'Is he hoping for divine intervention in the matter of his stolen cards?'

'It's not sudden,' answered Robin. 'And it has nothing to do with his cards. Richard is a church warden at home in England – on the rare occasions we're actually there for any length of time. He couldn't be here on the Sinai and not go to one, maybe both of the holiest sites nearby. So he's at Saint Catherine's monastery – or on his way there – now. And he'll be trying to visit Gebel Musa itself, maybe, later on. Though I am aware that the actual position of the biblical Mount Sinai is a matter of some discussion. And so is he. I just wanted some reassurance that he's going to be safe out there beyond the Sharm security cordon.'

Ibrahim looked at her in silence for a moment. She met his gaze squarely, genuinely wanting reassurance. Sharm was the only area of the entire peninsula that was currently a Green Zone under the ruling of the British Foreign and Commonwealth Office. Green Zone rating meant the British government considered it

safe for all sorts of visits and visitors. Richard was out in the
Amber Zone – where the British officials advised visits only in
the case of an emergency. And he was heading towards the North
Sinai Red Zone which they advised all British travellers to avoid
at all costs because of the apparent lawlessness of the place –
even in the face of the Egyptian Army – and the danger of kidnap
by Bedouin, or terrorists fond of decapitation, or of suicide attack
either by individuals or by vehicles.

Ibrahim looked away first, unwilling to reveal that he had had
Saiid's Land Rover followed into the Amber Zone – even though
she would possibly find the idea of a police escort reassuring.
Except for the fact that historically it was the police and army
who were the terrorists' main targets.

'If, as you say, he and his guide have gone via the Dahab
route, then he should be perfectly safe,' he said at last. 'There
have been terrorist attacks in South Sinai, but not for a long time
now. And none anywhere near where you say he has gone. It is
well over ten years since there was any terrorist activity in Dahab,
though there was some unrest amongst the local Bedouins a few
years back because one of their number was being held in the
Dahab police station. It all came to nothing. However, there was
an incident in El Tor in May 2014. A guard manning a security
point there was killed. That is probably why Captain Mariner
and his guides chose to go east instead of west. But there has
been no repetition of violence in El Tor.'

'I thought some tourists were killed going to Saint Catherine
. . .' Robin's tone was truly worried. The sight of the guns in
Saiid's Land Rover had not reassured her that Richard and his
guides would be safe at all. It was bad enough that he had
gone haring off after Nahom and the stolen credit cards, but
even the smugglers seemed less worrying than the possibility
that he might find himself face-to-face with tribes of Bedouin
keen to follow the Somali technique of kidnap for ransom,
groups of well-armed Jihadists willing to chop the heads off
foreigners and put the executions on YouTube or to blow themselves up for their beliefs. Or, indeed, with platoons of nervous,
trigger-happy soldiers with orders to shoot first and ask questions later.

'In February 2014. Indeed, a tragic incident.' Ibrahim nodded.

'The victims were members of a religious group. But they had already visited the monastery. They were waiting at Taba to cross the border into Israel when the atrocity occurred. Two men and a woman from South Korea died along with the Egyptian bus driver. And, of course, the bomber himself, who was also, apparently, Egyptian. Responsibility was claimed by a terrorist group called Ansar Beit al-Maqdis, who have been active in the North Sinai. Their spokesman said the attack would be the first of a series and indeed more soldiers have been killed in terrorist incidents since then. However, if Captain Mariner has gone to Saint Catherine as you say, then he would have turned off the Sharm to Taba highway long before he got to Nuweiba, let alone Taba and the Israeli border.'

Robin nodded, satisfied. On the terrorist front, at least. 'Will that be all?' asked Ibrahim. But just as he did so, a phone started ringing. He frowned, looking around in mild confusion. The ringing phone clearly did not belong to him. 'It's not mine,' said Robin.

'Nor mine,' confirmed Ibrahim. He sat back from the desk, unlocked a drawer and slid it open. The ringing got louder. 'It's the cell phone I confiscated from Nahom Selassie,' he said. 'I must have switched it on accidentally as I put it away.' He lifted the phone out of the drawer carefully and showed it to Robin. The screen was filled with a picture of Tsibekti. 'His sister is calling.'

'Or her kidnappers are.' She nodded. 'Should you answer it?'

'I don't know.' He frowned.

'Maybe safer not to, unless you are fluent in Eritrean Arabic.'

'No. Anyone listening would know at once. My accent . . .'

'You can still get through if you're quick, though,' she said. 'You must have the better part of a dozen Eritreans in custody here.'

'So I do. That is a very good thought.' He pressed a button on the mahogany intercom box on his desk. 'Sergeant Sabet,' he said. 'I need one of the Eritrean prisoners in here at once.'

'Preferably one who knows Nahom, or comes from his village,' added Robin.

But by the time Sergeant Sabet escorted the man Robin recognized as the Eritrean she had brought to the surface herself and announced, 'The prisoner Aman Kifle says he can help, Major,' Nahom's phone was quiet once again.

Tsibekti's picture, and the chance of contacting her, had gone.

As Saiid's Land Rover ground up the final incline and into the Watia Pass, Richard looked around, awestruck. The mountain slopes rose almost vertically on either side, to jagged peaks hundreds of feet higher than the narrow, precipitous roadway. Against the blue-steel dome of the sky, they looked almost black. Lower slopes were terracotta red, vertically banded with serpentine green. They were ridged with jagged valleys, as though the rock walls themselves were cracking open with the bludgeoning heat.

The Land Rover lurched over the watershed and on to the western downslope. The enormous V between the peaks was suddenly filled with the tyrannical white ball of the afternoon sun. Richard pulled his keffiyeh tighter and settled his sunglasses so that they covered the slit between his forehead and nose. There was a fan on the dashboard but all it seemed to be doing was circulating incredibly hot air, like some mechanism in a blast furnace. Richard was at that stage where he felt he needed protection, even if it meant suffocation.

'Not long now,' called Saiid as he shifted gear.

The mountain pass opened briefly into a simmering vision of red peaks dancing and wavering like the fires of hell. And, far away, beyond the farthest of them a still, steady line the colour of royal-blue ink reached from north to south. It took Richard an instant to recognize it as the sea. The Gulf of Suez, in fact, which he had sailed more times than he could readily remember, cocooned in the air-conditioned security of his command bridge, blissfully unaware of the colossal nuclear energy being unleashed by the sun upon the place he was passing. No sooner had the dazzling vista appeared before Richard's steaming eyes than it was gone again as the black slopes closed like curtains. 'Not long now,' repeated Saiid.

He was as good as his word. Richard was still trying to blink the tears away when the Land Rover swung hard right. The blinding blaze of the west-facing road was replaced by a narrow, shady track running northwards, parallel to the distant coast. Richard understood at once why Saiid favoured the Land Rover

– and why the vehicle was so battered. What they were driving down seemed little better than a camel track, littered with stones and occasional boulders. The slope steepened until Richard began to wonder whether they would ever be able to get back up it again, should they need to. But after ten more minutes or so, Saiid swung left and the path began to level out. They were following a gorge that appeared to be little more than a steep-sided cleft in the living rock of the mountain side. The sky was a thin band high above, the sun nowhere near as overpowering as it had been up at the watershed. The temperature in the lurching vehicle cooled, and Richard pulled his damp keffiyeh away from his perspiring face. Then he removed his sunglasses and slipped them into the breast pocket of his gilet. The fan on the dashboard was suddenly effective, chilling his face and throat as it dried the sweat which had gathered there. He looked across at Saiid, but his face was closed, his concentration absolute. Richard could well understand why. A second later the front left tyre hit a boulder and the whole vehicle jumped sideways, the door beside Richard crashing into the black stone wall of the canyon. Now was clearly not a good time for a chat.

The Land Rover continued to rumble and buck its way westward for half an hour before Saiid suddenly swung hard right again. After ten or so minutes, the walls of the canyon vanished. The Defender came to a juddering halt. Richard found himself looking down across the three-dimensional maze that Saiid had described last evening at dinner. The Wilderness of Sin. But he was high above it, looking back eastwards, with the sun, as Saiid had promised, westering behind him. The camel track that Saiid had been following turned south-westwards again and vanished into what appeared to be a tiny crack in a beetling black cliff at the western edge of the rocky outcrop. But here, just for a few tens of metres, the weird geology of the place dictated a flat-topped balcony thrusting out of the north-eastern face of the three thousand foot peak of Mount Serabit.

'Everybody out!' called Saiid. 'I need to hide the Defender. It stands out against the rocks too clearly. Even someone looking up into the sun could probably make out a white Land Rover parked in front of a black cliff.'

The three of them piled out into the sweltering afternoon and

Saiid drove the Defender slowly and carefully into the gorge at the foot of the black rock wall. Richard could see why he drove so slowly and carefully: one thing that would stand out more clearly than a white Land Rover was a big cloud of red dust. Even as the Defender ground away, Richard was walking to the edge of the natural balcony. The sun was above and behind his right shoulder, but he was not casting a long shadow yet. Even so, the fearsome heat of midday was past. He left the tails of his keffiyeh dangling and did not bother with his sunglasses. At the edge of the natural balcony stood several battered red boulders. Richard crossed to one of these and used it as a table to steady his elbows as he brought Saiid's binoculars to his eyes. With the magnification set to maximum, he swept across the panorama in front of him, simply staggered by the amount of detail he could make out. True, as Saiid had said, the Wilderness of Sin was a maze. Jagged peaks fell away from the distant line of the watershed. Between and among them, dry wadis writhed like the tracks of gigantic snakes. Interlocking spurs showed where forceful young torrents raged as soon as any rain fell. Red sand slopes showed where the outwash came, patterned like the root systems of enormous trees.

In the sides of the steep-walled valleys there were the black dots of cave mouths; the black portals of mine shafts. On the one hand, because of his position high and to the west, all of the valleys – and the pathways they contained, seemed to open before him, giving the impression that there was nothing he could not observe. That no one moving down there could possibly escape his gaze. And yet, everything he could see seemed to swell and waver, like an undersea reef examined from above the waves, for there was still sufficient power in the sun and the super-heated landscape to make the air writhe into a heat haze that rendered even the clearest vision deceptive.

'See anything?' asked Saiid, coming to stand beside Richard.

'Not yet. You were right, though. This is an amazing observation point.'

Saiid made a movement of his upper body which Richard felt rather than understood, until his guide spoke. He'd been checking his watch. 'Half past three,' he said. 'If they're down there, they'll be moving about within half an hour or so.'

'I thought you said they'd stay still and wait for Nahom,' said Richard, mentally breaking the vista in front of him into squares and beginning to move the binoculars regularly across each one.

'That was then. This is now. And the difference is that they *have* Nahom. Or rather, at least one of their associates has him.'

'So we can assume that whoever is with Nahom knows the route and will be able to catch up more easily. Therefore there's no need to hang around any longer,' said Richard, his tone thoughtful.

'So they're likely to be on the move again,' rumbled Ahmed. 'Perhaps a call from the sister to motivate him a little further and then they'll be off.'

'Yes,' said Richard, not entirely convinced. 'Surely they'd only call Nahom if whoever is with him doesn't realize his phone was confiscated along with his money and belt. Otherwise they'd just end up speaking to Major Ibrahim or Sergeant Sabet. If they've switched the phone on, of course. And there's no guarantee that they will have done that.'

'It's all in the hands of Allah,' rumbled Ahmed. 'Such things are beyond our reckoning so they should not concern us.'

'At least we have chosen the best moment to spot them,' added Mahmood, his tone bracingly positive.

'And we're in the best position to do so,' added Saiid.

'The best except for in a helicopter,' suggested Richard.

'No,' Saiid corrected him gently. 'If we were in a helicopter we would never spot them. They would hear us coming and go to ground at once. What gives us the edge is not just our position but also our silence.'

Nahom Selassie sat in the back seat of the battered little Nasr-built Egyptian version of the venerable Fiat 128, covered in sweat and shaking, almost deafened by the screaming of the motor. His condition was nothing to do with the exhaustion and dehydration – or even the snake bite – which had put him in hospital so recently. Both the perspiration and the uncontrollable jumping of his limbs came primarily from his mental confusion. He didn't know whether he was elated or terrified; whether his actions were daring or criminal. Whether he was a hero riding to save his beloved sister or a victim heading towards an agonizing death and a shallow grave. But at least this time it looked as though he was really getting somewhere. For the first time since the boat hit the reef, in fact, and he had become entangled in the anchor rope. That memory made him shudder more. But in truth he was not nearly as weak and ill as he appeared to be. His body was naturally long and lean. Starvation had made it skeletal, but his muscles were strong as whip-cord. He was from the coastal plain of Eritrea and was therefore acclimatized to temperatures that could touch fifty degrees Celsius. Furthermore, like the majority of Eritreans his age, he had been forced to do some years of National Service, and the tough requirements of the army still lingered in the depth of his chest, the strength of his muscles and his ability to think quickly and clearly under pressure. Doing a little play-acting and pretending to be much less well than he truly was, while strengthening his contact with Ali, the hospital orderly, had really begun to pay dividends.

Ali was in the threadbare, sagging front passenger seat now, though he was clearly the leader of this section of the enterprise. He was a lean and angular mongoose of a man with a false grin and shifty eyes. He had been working as a ward orderly in the hospital and that was where first contact had been made after Nahom's return. It had been Ali who'd guided the Englishman Mariner to the finance office and – almost without thinking – made a mental note of the PIN number reflected in the convex mirror which revealed what the Englishman's fingers were typing into the terminal.

Ali had sidled up to Nahom in his private room almost exactly a day ago and whispered that he might be able to help the young man with his mission. He had introduced the other man as Tariq as they bundled Nahom out of the ambulance and into the yellow vehicle in the Old Town a couple of hours earlier, both praising Allah who had seen fit to ensure the prisoner was transferred without an armed guard. Tariq, built like a hippopotamus, was the ambulance driver. They both, obviously, worked for the men who were holding Tsibekti. Ali had cut all ties with the hospital as far as Nahom could see – there would be no going back for him. But Tariq was in two minds and seemed to have evolved a plan that might allow him to go back to work if things went wrong here or wherever they were heading for.

Tariq was driving the Nasr now as though he had flashing lights and a siren. That in itself was a terrifying experience, not really ameliorated by the wall of religious icons and texts that cluttered the dashboard or hung from the rear-view mirror, or even by the copy of the Holy Qur'an that was wedged in a glove compartment too small to hold it. In fact, the rear-view mirror's main function seemed to be as a hook on which to hang things, for Tariq never seemed to look in it. If he wanted to know what was behind him he tended to glance back over his shoulder or, occasionally, to twist right round as far as his bulk allowed and study the road behind with narrow, pig-like eyes. But it was Ali who was turned around in the passenger seat now with no thought of wearing a seatbelt. He was waving his phone at Nahom and shouting angrily.

'What a fool I am,' bellowed Ali over the screeching of the elderly eleven hundred cc engine as it tried to pull the battered old body along at one hundred kilometres per hour – a feat it had hardly been capable of even on the first day it was bought. And that was many years and owners ago now. 'I have the wit to look into the fish-eye mirror for the PIN number of the English crusader's American Express card but not the wit to charge my cell phone! Look at it! Dead as Tutankhamen! Tariq, where is yours?'

'I left it in the ambulance. After we are finished with this run I will go back to Sharm and report to the police. I will tell them I was hit in the head and have no memory. Then I will ask for my job back. Leaving my cell behind makes this story look more true.'

'That is very cunning, Tariq. Good luck with it. Nahom? Where is yours?'

Nahom's mind raced. Would he be more or less likely to be killed if he admitted his phone was with his money and his money belt in the hands of the police? *More likely*, he calculated. Tell them as little as possible, he thought. 'I can't get a signal,' he said. Which was true, after a fashion. And, to be fair, it was quite believable. They had left Sharm behind a good while ago, easing their way through the security point by the skin of their teeth. El Tor was still a long way ahead. The road was quite busy, mostly with buses and trucks – many of them on the run between Sharm and Cairo. But on one side of it, the rust-coloured desert stretched away to the flat blue line of the sea. On the other it stretched away to the jagged red line of the mountains. Apart from occasional stunted bushes of acacia and camel thorn, often draped in plastic bags blown there by the relentless wind, there was nothing to be seen. Certainly neither real palm trees nor the impossibly tall, straight ones constructed by the phone company to house their cell phone aerials.

'They will be trying to contact us!' snarled Ali. 'I had just begun to report in when the battery went flat.'

'Will we stop in El Tor and go to an ATM machine there?' asked Nahom, who had been terrified that the theft would be discovered and the cards cancelled long before he got the money, almost as much as he was consumed with guilt at having stolen from the man who had saved his life. But it wasn't for himself, he kept repeating. It was for Tsibekti. Desperate situations required desperate actions. Allah would surely understand that.

'We will if we get the chance,' confirmed Ali. 'And if the security at the checkpoint outside town isn't too tight. A guard was blown up here in 2014. They've been a bit jumpy ever since. We'll certainly try, though. At El Tor there will be somewhere I can charge my phone. Somewhere you can get a signal as well as the money.'

'Perhaps,' suggested Nahom cunningly, 'you could charge your phone and make contact while I get the money. That would be quicker all round.'

'And,' added Tariq, turning round in his seat like Ali to show a great, gap-toothed grin, 'we can use some of the English crusader's money to buy a good big meal! There are some really good restaurants in the *souq* behind the El Mecca Hotel.'

'If you do that,' snarled Ali, 'you had better hope that the others don't find out. Or they'll find another way to make your story of having been hit in the head look more believable!'

'*Inshallah,*' shrugged Tariq. If God wills. He gave Nahom another gap-toothed grin and a big conspiratorial wink.

So Nahom, in the back seat, was the only one in the Nasr actually looking at the road ahead when the goat apparently appeared from nowhere and nonchalantly ambled into the carriageway in front of them.

*   *   *

'You will need to pretend to be Nahom. Can you do this?' asked Robin.

'I can,' answered Aman Kifle confidently. 'Tsibekti and Nahom are my cousins. Bisrat is my brother. We live in the same village. We grew up together. I had always hoped one day Tsibekti would be my wife. That is why I came with Nahom. That is why I nearly drowned trying to free him from the anchor when the boat ran on to the reef and sank.'

For a frustrated lover recovering from a near-death experience whose bride had been kidnapped by a band of rapacious murderers, Aman sounded disturbingly cheerful to Robin. There was something about the cocksure young man that really grated with her. Unlike Richard with his Chinese proverbs, she felt no further responsibility for the person whose life she had saved.

'Do you know of any passwords or codes the kidnappers might use to confirm Nahom's identity?' asked Robin, suddenly, her head full of vague memories of Hollywood blockbusters and TV police series.

'Nahom talked of the famous landmark near our village. The bridge at Dogali.'

'She will recognize your voice,' added Ibrahim with a frown. 'What good will a password be then?'

'She will, but no one else would. What will these Bedouin know to tell one Eritrean voice from another? It is the Bedouin who will want the password. Tsibekti will surely just pass messages and say what they tell her to. But Tsibekti is quick-thinking and determined. When I begin to speak with her I will make her understand what is going on without giving anything away. It will be like a game.'

'That's a strange game, Kifle,' snapped Sergeant Sabet, clearly as unimpressed by the glib, overconfident young man as Robin.

'You have never played it, Sergeant? Perhaps you do not come from a large family. Or you have never wished to discuss things with a sister or a cousin in front of parents and older relatives but still being secret about the truth of what you are saying. I thought all teenagers had such a code. Tsibekti, Nahom, Bisrat and I certainly did.'

Sergeant Sabet sniffed her disapproval. Robin caught her eye and smiled in sisterly sympathy. Sabet's frown deepened. She, also, apparently, disapproved of this intimacy.

'Is that water?' asked Aman, blissfully unaware of the byplay his breezy confidence was engendering, eyeing Robin's untouched glass as he spoke.

'Here.' She passed it to him, hoping the action did not upset any of Ibrahim's notions of hospitality. Sabet's frown had made it clear that she was only still in the room by the skin of her teeth. One false move and she would be out on her ear.

'What you may not be aware of,' rumbled Ibrahim, 'is the prisoner Selassie's current situation. On his way here from the hospital, he has escaped or been abducted. Two men are missing with him. A hospital orderly named Ali Haykal and an ambulance driver called Tariq Fathi. He has no money – though I suggest it would be unwise for this information to be made public.'

'However,' interrupted Sabet, 'he almost certainly has the credit cards belonging to Captain Mariner. Those will make a very acceptable alternative if they can access the funds at a bank or an ATM. Do we know what sort of funds they could access?'

'The American Express card will deliver ten thousand US dollars a day up to a limit of one hundred thousand dollars,' said Robin. And was surprised by the sudden silence that surrounded her. 'Or it would,' she added, 'except that Richard has blocked it.'

'These men, Ali and Tariq,' said Aman, after a moment, 'are they part of the gang holding Tsibekti?'

'We must assume they are,' answered Ibrahim.

'Then they may have notified their friends of what is going on.'

'A risk we'll have to take,' decided Ibrahim.

'Not that *we're* actually taking it,' observed Robin drily. 'Nahom and Tsibekti are.'

Sabet opened her mouth to snap a riposte, but the instant she did so, Nahom's phone began to ring again and Tsibekti's picture filled the screen.

Ibrahim nodded. Aman picked up the phone.

Robin understood only four Arabic words of the conversation that Aman Kifle had with whoever was at the far end of the connection. These were: *Dogali*, *Tsibekti* and *Nahom*, which all arrived in the early part of the animated Arabic exchange. And,

right at the end, *Nekhel*, which was said first in a rising, inter-
rogative tone, then repeated flatly and forcefully. But in the
middle, again more than once, the even more familiar English,
'American Express.'

There were other, half-familiar words that simply got lost in
the rapid conversation, but almost from the word go Robin was
out of her depth, with no chance whatsoever of following what
Aman was saying in his disguise as Nahom either to Tsibekti or
to her captors.

But then, as abruptly as the conversation had begun, it stopped.

Aman put the phone back down on Ibrahim's desk gently, as
though it were delicate or dangerous. Or both. The round-cornered
oblong of the screen was blank. The little machine was silent.
The air conditioning buzzed, giving a sinister voice to the frustrated hornets roasting outside. All three of the Arab speakers
looked at each other thoughtfully – perhaps, thought Robin, even
calculatingly.

'What was all that about?' she asked.

'Perhaps Mr Kifle will explain to all of us,' suggested Ibrahim.
'Although I taped the conversation, of course, I only got his side
of the exchange.'

'And we do need to get some idea of where the kidnappers
are, and what they plan to do next,' added Sabet. 'Particularly
because the major called in one of our shiny new American
Apache attack helicopters to take a look at the Wilderness of Sin
this afternoon.'

'There!' said Richard. 'Can you see it? Just beneath the peak of
Gebel Foqa. In those caves on the lower slopes?' He pushed his
elbows down almost painfully on the hot, rough top of the boulder
he was using as a table to steady the Zeiss binoculars.

'Yes,' answered Mahmood. 'I see it. A movement . . .
Something . . .'

Although Richard was using Saiid's top-of-the-range binoculars, the others were also well equipped, for they knew what
their mission would entail and had kitted themselves out accord-
ingly. They were looking through a range of Leicas, Orions and
Lugers – the cost of which added together would have come to
a good deal less than the Zeiss Victory 8X42 T*FL binoculars

he was holding. He zoomed in to maximum magnification as the tiny figures began to emerge from the black-mouthed caverns low on the mountainside into the first promise of evening shadows. The super-heated atmosphere was weirdly helpful to the four men spying from above. The air itself seemed to act like an extra lens, making the mountainside and everything on it seem larger. To Richard, in fact, it seemed as though he was watching a group of people quite nearby walking down a brick-red slope towards a crystal lake. But as they approached the surface of the mercury-silver illusion, they twisted weirdly, like aliens in a Sci-Fi movie, and became inhuman, then invisible, swallowed by the vagaries of the superheated air.

He moved the binoculars up fractionally once again, seeking sufficient detail to identify Tsibekti at least. But the best he could do was to detect a couple of figures whose robes were black, as opposed to the dazzling white preferred by the Bedouin. But then they started leading the camels out into the sunlight and he became distracted by a vision that seemed to come straight out of a painting by Salvador Dali.

'Is there any way we can be sure that those are the people we're after?' he asked Saiid.

'There won't be very many other travellers out here in the Wilderness of Sin,' he answered. 'But you're right. The only way we'd ever be one hundred percent is to get close enough to identify Tsibekti.'

'Or get hold of one of the others and ask a few pointed questions,' suggested Ahmed.

'They're too far away,' said Saiid. 'We'd be lucky to catch them.'

'But they seem so close.'

'They also,' observed Mahmood, 'seem to be stretching out like rubber and vanishing into a lake of mercury. You can't rely on what you think you see.'

'There's no way we can get to them in time, is there?' asked Richard, the tone of his voice showing that he already suspected the answer.

'No,' confirmed Saiid. 'But at least we know where they are – and we have a pretty good idea where they're going in the short term.'

'North-east,' suggested Richard.

'North-east,' confirmed Saiid.

'So, what's our next move?' wondered Ahmed. 'Do we drive down the next set of goat-tracks and try to follow them? Try to capture one or two? Rescue Tsibekti? What?'

'It's Nahom we have to watch out for,' said Richard. 'We need to keep an eye on these people until we're sure Nahom's not joining them, then, if he doesn't appear, we need to see if there's any way we can get to him before he tries to use my AmEx card.'

'How will we know if he joins the party?' wondered Mahmood.

'I suppose if anyone new turns up, we'll have to assume that's him,' answered Richard.

The caves were empty now. All the black-and-white-clad figures and all the camels had wavered, disturbingly elongated, into the great still lake which did not exist, and were no doubt making their way invisibly towards their next secret path.

Then it struck Richard. 'Saiid,' he said. 'They're moving. Moving, not waiting. Does that mean they've heard from Nahom, do you think?'

Saiid nodded, transferring the gesture to Richard through the contact between their shoulders. 'Looks like it,' he said. 'Looks like they've made another rendezvous.'

'Off-hand,' said Richard, 'I'd say that was good news for Tsibekti. And good news for her must mean good news for Nahom. If anything had gone wrong so far, I guess there'd be a body or two left behind, here or wherever.'

'That seems logical,' Saiid agreed.

'Except,' added Richard darkly, 'that we can't see what they're up to down in the *wadi* because of the heat haze. They could be slaughtering everyone left and right down there and we'd be none the wiser.'

'No!' called Ahmed. 'Look. They are coming out of the haze now as they turn north towards the Forest of Pillars. They seem to be moving quickly. There isn't much shelter down there.'

'Lucky the afternoon's beginning to cool down,' said Richard.

'It is up here,' said Saiid. 'I'm not so sure about down there.'

'But at least,' added Ahmed, 'the Forest of Pillars opens on to an area that can be reached by vehicles. Well, four by fours.'

'And where would they go?' asked Richard.

'Due north,' answered Ahmed. 'They'd come due south and then go back due north. It's the only way.'

'And what's due north of the Forest of Pillars?' asked Richard.

But before any of the others could answer him, a deep *thrumming* sound suddenly came pulsing through the air. It did not fade up from near-silence – it was suddenly there, almost loud enough to drown conversation. Certainly loud enough to distract them all from what they were discussing.

'What on earth?' said Richard.

But Saiid and the others knew well enough what the sound was. 'Mister Richard,' said Saiid. 'We should return to the Land Rover now. Quickly, please. We should not be here. And even though we are not the primary targets, we do not wish to be seen.'

Richard, however, set the binoculars to a wider focus and began to sweep the sky rather than the ground. After a moment or two, a black shape buzzed across his vision. He focused on it and the big blurred blob resolved itself into an American Apache attack helicopter.

As he pulled the menacing black shape into focus, it began to fire a combination of thirty-millimetre M230E1 Chain Gun and Hydra 70 general-purpose unguided rockets into the valley they had just been observing.

Tsibekti Selassie had never been so terrified in all her life, though the events of this morning ran what was happening this afternoon a close second.

'Run!' screamed Bisrat. 'Tsibekti, *run!*'

She could only hear what he was saying over the terrible rattle of gunfire and the deeper concussions of the explosions behind them, over the thundering whirl of the helicopter above them, because he was right behind her, also running for his life across the stony red ground that shook as though they were trapped in an earthquake.

But it was not just the danger, the overwhelming noise and the nearness of death that frightened the young Eritrean. It was the fact that the men who, for the last few days, had reduced her to a quivering wreck were all equally terrified now. Perhaps more so, as they all ran across the juddering floor of the wadi, screaming and howling, followed by their camels, who added their own brays of fear to the disorientating storm of sound.

The day had got off to a disturbing start, for the leader of the smugglers had suddenly appeared beside her clutching two cell phones – his and hers. He had brandished his at her, snarling in his barbarous Arabic, 'Your brother is on his way now – my men are with him. Contact him again. I want him to know exactly what will happen if he delays or fails to pay up!'

Trembling with fear, but wondering at the same time why the great Bedouin bully had not made things clear himself – it must have been a very short call indeed – she took her own phone and dialled.

For the first time in several days it did not go straight to Nahom's voicemail. It rang. And rang. And rang. At last she gave the phone back to her looming captor. 'No answer,' she said.

'We will wait ten minutes then try again,' he snarled.

While they waited, he paced around the huge cave they had all been hidden in for three days now, waiting for the contact that had obviously just been made. Waiting, in effect, for Nahom and his money. Perhaps for other brothers with yet more money – there was a good number of young men and women being trafficked from a range of East African coastal countries. But no one talked to anyone else, except for the Bedouin traffickers, who talked to whoever they liked. And on occasion did more than merely talk.

'Again!' snarled the leader.

Tsibekti dialled. Three rings. Connection was made and things got worse, for Tsibekti knew at once she was not talking to Nahom. She was talking to an Eritrean at least, but the strange voice sounded more like Bisrat's brother Aman than anyone else.

'Give me the phone,' ordered the leader roughly, and she had no choice but to hand it over. Then, in the grip of too much tension to sit still and await her fate, she went to the back of the cave and joined the other women while the Bedouin spat his threats and orders into her phone, apparently unaware that he was speaking to the wrong man.

Five minutes later, he swaggered over to her. 'Count yourself lucky your brother is so quick-thinking,' he said. 'He brings not only money but American Express. All we need is an ATM machine and he will add ten thousand dollars to your price! It is fortunate for you that I have arranged to meet at a place where there are many such machines.' And he swaggered off, pushing her phone back into the folds of his robe.

And that was that.

Until the helicopter appeared from nowhere just as they had all left the safety of the cavern and started raining *Jahannam* – Hell and destruction – down upon them.

Tsibekti glanced over her shoulder, trying to gain some sort of control. There was a wall of fire between the panicked crowd and the caves in which they had hidden from the midday heat. It began to occur to her that perhaps the helicopter's fire was not being directed at them, but simply being placed between them and their latest refuge. Like the vast majority of young Eritreans and her brother, Nahom, Tsibekti had served a stint in the army. Bisrat and Aman, with the cunning for which the Kifle family were well known in her village, had managed to avoid their National Service. But that gave Tsibekti an edge, for she had been prepared and trained to go under fire. She had never done so, as chance would have it, but she had been trained; she knew how to behave. In fact, it gave her a considerable edge, because, like Bisrat, the Bedouin traffickers who had been holding her captive for the better part of ten days had clearly not done National Service either.

Tsibekti's mind whirled. Could she maybe form a unit of like-minded Eritrean captives who had seen service? Or were they too lost and scattered among the other nationalities that were being smuggled along with them – the Ethiopians, the Sudanese, the Somalis, the couple from Djibouti?

The thought had to be put to the back of her mind for the moment, however. For the leader of the smugglers, who she had named Al-Ayn or 'evil eye', proved the least cowardly and quickest-thinking of them all. 'This way!' he called. 'To the Forest of Pillars! Quickly!'

The others of his band knew what he was talking about – unlike their captives. They started to herd the frightened and confused Ethiopians, Somalis and Eritreans towards the valley leading north out of the wadi.

Tsibekti followed helplessly with Bisrat, as usual, close behind her. And, behind Bisrat, the camel herders trying to keep their strings of terrified animals under control, all too well aware that if a stray shot set off what the camels were carrying in the slings made out of carpet that hung against their ribs on either side, then the explosion would likely decimate the smugglers and their victims – and very likely blow the chopper out of the sky into the bargain.

Tsibekti found herself in a narrow, steep-sided offshoot of the main wadi, running northward. The height of the walls was a protection in itself, but it was clear that Al-Ayn had bigger things in mind, for he kept running and they all followed him like sheep and goats, herded by his increasingly confident band of men. After ten minutes or so, the narrow cleft opened out. The walls fell back and their slope eased off. In spite of the fact that they were in an exposed position once again, Al-Ayn slowed his pace and his men did likewise. Tsibekti looked around, trying to work out why the smugglers were suddenly so confident that they were safe. And she found herself at the southern edge of a forest. But a forest like no forest she had ever seen.

Filling the centre of the valley stood a forest of tree trunks. Some stood erect, while others leaned over and still others lay as though they had been felled. There were no branches or leaves, only tree trunks. She could see – and, when she moved forward, she could feel – the rough bark with which they were covered. But the bark was cool – especially on the shadowed sides. And it was disturbingly unyielding, for these trees were petrified. Literally. As though by the spell of some evil *djinn* thousands of years in the past, the tree trunks had all been turned into black stone.

'This is a national treasure,' called Al-Ayn in his barbarous Bedouin accent. 'A famous tourist destination. They dare not fire upon us here in the Forest of Pillars.'

And, as though the men in the helicopter heard his words, the black machine turned and swooped back the way it had come, dragging the clattering pulse of its rotors behind it.

'Even so,' called Al-Ayn, 'we march on.' One of the camel handlers brought his travelling camel up and the beast knelt. Al-Ayn climbed aboard and prodded the beast to its feet before he continued to address them from high above their heads. 'It is important to move swiftly now.' His evil eyes swept across the men and women he was trafficking northward. 'Anyone who cannot keep up with us will die.'

They all knew his threat was real. They had all seen stragglers executed more than once already. So they all crowded together and shuffled off in the wake of his camel's slow and stately pace, into the black stone forest as the sun began to lose even its afternoon fierceness and the western sky above their right shoulders became as pink as the rocks beneath their feet. Paying no heed to Bisrat who stuck to her like a leech, Tsibekti worked her way through the crowd of prisoners until she was near enough the front to catch a word or two that the overconfident Al-Ayn was saying. And it was not that difficult. He was the only one riding at the moment, so he had to call his conversation down to the men walking beside him.

'I have arranged it . . . We will make good speed . . . all night . . . at Gebel el Igma by dawn . . . Pick up there . . . Straight run north . . . To Nekhel . . . No, they'll never catch us, even with their accursed helicopters . . . The pilots are all city boys from Cairo. They know nothing of the Sinai . . . I'll wager they only discovered us by chance or by the direction of some evil djinn . . . They'll never find us again . . . Yes, we'll all meet up at Nekhel . . . Collect the money and go on from there . . . Nekhel . . . I have arranged it.'

SEVEN
Nekhel

'*Run!*' shouted Saiid, his voice just audible over the combined thunder of the Apache's rotors and its armaments.

'Wait!' answered Richard, steadying his elbows on the boulder and he focused the Zeiss binoculars on the valley below and the thick red cloud kicked up by the barrage. Beyond the billowing sand grains he could still make out the crowd of people and camels running northward into the mouth of another narrow valley. When the helicopter opened fire he had expected to see carnage on the ground, but there were no bodies left behind the fleeing men, women and animals. He frowned, his mind racing. After his discussion with Saiid about helicopters he was simply flabbergasted that the Apache had managed to sneak up on them all without giving warning of its approach. And now that it was here, he was damned if he could work out what on earth it was up to.

'We can't afford to be seen here,' emphasized Saiid, already moving towards the Land Rover where it stood concealed in the opening of the cleft in the cliff. 'Especially if they're shooting the smugglers and their victims! Massacring defenceless people whose only crime is to be smuggled or trafficked. Witnesses to anything like that aren't likely to live for long.'

'But they're not!' called Richard. 'They're not shooting *at* them. They're shooting *behind* them, closing off their route back to the caves.'

'What's the point of that?' wondered Ahmed, hesitating between Saiid and Richard.

'No idea,' shrugged Richard. 'Perhaps they're trying to herd them somewhere. Chase them into the open then land and arrest them.'

'Well, that won't work,' said Ahmed. 'They've just driven them into the one place they can't follow them – certainly not with gunfire. The Forest of Pillars. It's too important a historical site to risk anything. They can't hope to land a chopper there either, come to that. It's a forest of petrified tree trunks. The smugglers and their victims will just get lost among them. Unreachable from the air.'

'The chopper pilots clearly don't know the area,' insisted Mahmood. 'They've just driven the smugglers into the one place that ensures they're going to get away!'

'Looks like that's what's happened, all right,' decided Richard, straightening. 'So we'd better do what Saiid suggests. We don't want to be the booby prize for some pissed-off policeman who's just realized he's screwed up his main mission.'

They walked across to the Land Rover as quickly as possible without seeming suspicious or behaving in any way that might attract the chopper pilot's attention. The crack in the tall black cliff face seemed narrow from a distance but as Richard approached it he realized that it was actually quite wide. Certainly there was no difficulty in opening the Land Rover's doors on each side and climbing easily into their seats.

'Where do we go from here?' asked Richard as Saiid eased the big Defender into motion.

'Ultimately, home,' answered Saiid.

'Ultimately?' asked Richard.

'We have to go via El Tor,' explained Saiid. 'We won't stop there. But this track will take us down on to the main Sharm to Suez road just north of El Tor, then we'll turn left and head south. It'll take a couple of hours, but we should be back in time for *maghrib* – evening prayers.'

'And for dinner,' added Richard. 'I hope you'll all join us. It may not be up with what we had at the restaurant, but Sharl is an excellent chef . . .'

'So,' said Saiid. 'The all-important question. Did you see Nahom Selassie?'

'No,' answered Richard. 'And, thanks to your incredible binoculars, I got a close look at everyone down there, even allowing for the heat haze and the dust. One or two had their keffiyehs wrapped around their faces but they were all camel handlers. And the guy who looked like the leader wore his up too, but he had a cast in one eye. No. I'm as certain as I can be that Nahom was not down there.'

'So, the boy and your cards are safe for the time-being,' rumbled Mahmood.

'That's the way it looks. I wish there was something more we could do to help his sister, Tsibekti, though. I got a good look at her and I'd give my right arm to go down there and get her out.'

'Be careful what you ask for,' warned Saiid, glancing nervously out of the window beside him. 'The djinn of this place have a wicked sense of humour. They might just make your wish come true.'

The track wound down between high rock walls until it opened into the Wadi Feiran and joined the main road heading westwards there. Once again, Richard found himself looking straight into the white-hot fireball of the westering sun, but it was mid-afternoon now and some of its power was waning. He put his sunglasses back on, but the fan on the dashboard managed to keep him cool enough so that he did not feel the need to resort to wrapping his keffiyeh round his mouth and nose. After an hour or so they came to a T-junction with the road they were following at the top of the T, reaching straight on towards the vibrant blue of the Gulf of Suez. It was just possible to see the far shore, but Richard found all of his attention captured by the succession of tankers and container ships running north and south, to and from the canal like freight cars on a train.

Saiid swung right and headed south down the spine of the T. 'El Tor is halfway home from here,' he said.

They drove on in silence for a while. Then Richard said, 'It's a pity we have no idea what vehicle Nahom might be in. I mean, with them heading north to El Tor or wherever and us heading south, we could easily pass them and never know. Look at that battered old Fiat there. It looks as though it's been in some kind of an accident. He could be in that. It's heading in the right direction.'

'There's nothing unusual about battered cars down here,' said Ahmed. 'Some men are very dangerous drivers indeed, talking on their phones, driving with one hand, believing if they crash it is the will of God – inshallah – and there is nothing they can do about it, other than to pack their dashboards with religious artefacts and keep a copy of the Holy Qur'an in their glove box.'

'It was on this road a couple of years ago,' added Mahmood, his voice sad, 'that a couple of tourist coaches collided. More than thirty people killed. What a tragedy! Even if it was the will of God!'

The four of them fell silent after that and Saiid pushed his foot to the floor. The Defender's speed on the open, nearly deserted highway rose to the better part of one hundred kilometres per hour. And it would have rolled on at that speed all the way to Sharm had Richard not called out, suddenly, 'Saiid! Stop! It looks as though there was an accident here! Those skid marks come right across the central reservation. And that's the front bumper of the Fiat we passed a while ago, I'll bet. And what are those birds over there hovering just behind that sand ridge?'

'*Rachama*,' said Saiid, moving his foot on to the Defender's brake pedal. 'Vultures.'

''*Andak!*' shouted Nahom. *Watch out!* He could hardly believe his eyes. A goat! In the middle of a six-lane highway! '*Maa'ez* – goat!'

In spite of his bulk and apparent sloth, Tariq reacted quickly. He swerved to his left even before he started to turn around and learn what he needed to watch out for. The word '*Goat!*' had not yet filtered into his consciousness. The car skidded on down the road as the wheels fought to pull it left. But the tarmac was almost melting in the vicious afternoon heat, the brakes needed some urgent work and the tyres were all bald. The Fiat went into a skid that almost immediately became a spin. By the time Tariq and Ali were front-facing they were looking at the central reservation and the goat was near the car's rear door, so they never really saw it at all.

Had the goat's reactions been as swift as Tariq's, the crash might still have been avoided. But instead of leaping backwards, the animal froze. Already swinging towards the central reservation, the Fiat's rear offside door hit it sideways on. The goat's head smashed the rear window at the same time as the door frame and the car's roof immediately above the window shattered the goat's skull. The animal never knew what hit it. Its forequarter slammed into the door hard enough to dent it, and the shock threw Nahom to his right, so that he went headfirst into the spray of window glass, blood and brain matter that came through the offside rear door. His head actually hit the ruin of the goat's skull hard enough to stun him. When the car jumped over the low wall of the central reservation, Nahom was thrown helplessly one way as the body of the goat flew the other.

The Fiat hit the opposite carriage way still moving at the better part of fifty kilometres per hour. Providentially, the road was empty. Miraculously, the bald tyres did not burst, but they left thick black tracks across the carriageway. The shock was enough to smash the front bumper loose, however. As Tariq fought to regain control, Ali shouted a series of prayers so rapidly he did not seem to breathe in throughout the whole incident. He hung on to the dashboard with one hand and the conveniently placed Qur'an with the other. As the Fiat jumped off the blacktop and into the desert beside it, the bumper came loose altogether and fell free to lie half on and half off the road at the end of the tell-tale skid marks. The headlights shattered, spraying shards of glass on to the tarmac and the sand. The shock stopped the eleven hundred cc engine as effectively as the collision had stopped the goat's heart.

Nahom was thrown back against the undamaged rear door, which burst open and allowed him to spew out on to the rough red grit. On his way out he smacked the back of his head on the doorframe, so that when he hit the ground he was deeply unconscious. He rolled away across the sand as though all his bones had been shattered, leaving a good deal of skin behind, and he ended up on his face, lacerated arms akimbo and his legs spread. The door which had swung wide swung shut again, the noise of its closing lost in the general thunder of the near-disaster just before the motor died. Then there was just the shuddering rumble of the car's chassis bottoming on dune after dune.

Tariq finally brought the Fiat to a stop in a cloud of coarse red dust. He and Ali sat silently for a while, waiting for their pulses to slow, their hands to stop shaking, their breathing to return to normal. The sand grains whispered against the windscreen and the roof as they settled. 'Allah smiled on us today for certain, blessings and peace be upon him,' observed Ali as he reluctantly released his death grip on the Holy Qur'an.

'He did,' agreed Tariq, feelingly. 'What do you think, Nahom?' And he turned round to look back at his passenger.

But the back seat was empty.

'Ali,' said Tariq, his voice quiet with puzzlement at yet another near-miraculous occurrence amongst so many, 'Nahom's gone.'

'What do you mean, he's gone?' Ali began to turn, only to discover that whiplash had stiffened his neck and shoulders.

'He may have been thrown out through the window,' Tariq continued dreamily. 'It's broken. And there's a lot of blood . . .'

'*What?*' Ali swung right round at last. His eyes seemed to bulge as they swept across the glass-strewn shambles of the blood-soaked back seat. '*Besmillah!*' he whispered. 'What has happened?' He tore his door open and staggered out on to the sand. Stumbling on shaking legs, he followed the tyre tracks back towards the road. And there, a good ten metres from the tarmac, lay Nahom. Ali could tell at a glance that he was dead. He had worked for some time as a hospital orderly and counted himself as well qualified as many of the doctors. He certainly believed he knew death when he saw it. Perhaps Tariq was right, he thought. Perhaps Nahom had come out through the window. Certainly, he was covered in glass. His clothes were torn and his skin caked with red grit, through which blood was oozing listlessly. Lifelessly. The back of his head had a huge welt across it that was crusted with congealing blood. And, Ali realized with a sickening lurch, it was also leaking grey-pink brain matter. He sank to his knees beside the unmoving body, thinking that he had never seen so much blood in all his life. The still air stank of it, and beneath the metallic stench was another one that was almost like cheese. Ali realized that the cheese smell was probably Nahom's brains. His stomach heaved again.

'*Wald il qahbaa!*' said Tariq, coming up behind him. 'Son of a bitch, that is one dead *bala'a il a'air.*'

'He won't be the only dead cocksucker when we get to Nekhel empty-handed!' snarled Ali.

'It's not him we needed anyway,' observed Tariq. 'Just the cards he stole. You know the PIN and all.'

'Shit! You're right!' said Ali, his voice rising with revelation. 'We can still complete the mission. Though there's no way we can risk the security point at El Tor with the back seat looking like that. They're not so picky at Nekhel; we'll catch up with the others and an ATM there. And maybe get a piece of that hot bitch, his sister, for our good work, eh?'

'I'd like that,' said Tariq. 'You think there's a chance?'

'We might have to join a queue, especially if she's as hot as she's supposed to be.'

'I wouldn't mind that,' said Tariq. 'Be an easier ride if she's broken in first. Nice and smooth – and no fighting back. Where are the cards?'

'They're in his back pocket.'

'Which looks to be the only bit of him not covered in blood and brains. And flies,' observed Tariq, looking at the creatures which were already swarming over Nahom's body. 'Where do they come from? It's a mystery.'

As Tariq was discussing philosophy and flies, Ali was reaching into Nahom's back pocket, and pulling the cards free with shaking hands. 'Right,' he said. 'Now let's just pray that Allah will allow the engine to start and the Fiat will get us safely to Nekhel.'

'Think we ought to bury him?' asked Tariq.

'With what? We don't have a shovel, even if we had the time or the inclination. And think about it. As things stand it looks like an accident. A traffic accident. If we bury him then it'll look like a crime scene. No, let's get in the car and get on our way as quickly as we can.'

'What did we hit, though?' wondered Tariq. 'Should we go and check?'

'He said something about a goat,' answered Ali.

'Oh,' said Tariq. 'That's what he said! *Goat!*' He shook his head in simple wonder. The pair of them looked across the empty roadway but, like Nahom, the goat was sprawled invisibly behind a low roadside dune, well out of sight.

After a moment, Ali turned back to look at the battered Fiat and was violently sick on the sand. As he straightened, wiping his mouth with the back of his hand, a shadow flitted across the ground beside him and he looked up to see the first vulture circling, its arrival as mysterious as that of the flies.

Major Ibrahim glared at Sergeant Sabet with such naked rage in his dark eyes that the usually imperturbable young woman blenched. Had her habitually charming and patient boss's all-too-obvious anger been directed at her, she would have felt positively faint. But fortunately it was aimed at someone much further away than the young woman seated on the far side of his immaculate desk in the gathering dusk of his east-facing office. Much higher in the air. And flying westwards, seemingly oblivious to the outrage he had caused.

'What did this *imbecile* think he was doing?' Ibrahim demanded, his voice shaking, the fine nostrils of his narrow, aquiline nose flaring, his pencil-thin moustache bristling.

Sabet opened her mouth to answer, too disorientated to realize that the question was rhetorical.

'I sent him out to scout for them. To report to me if he got wind of them. *Not* to open fire on them and herd them along the route they were probably planning on taking in any case! And what is the end result of all this grandstanding?' The tip of his tongue brushed over his finely chiselled lips, collecting a little saliva released by the vehemence of his anger.

Again, Sabet drew breath to answer.

But again, he prevented her, his frown thunderous, his long, elegant finger pointing directly at her. 'He's heading back to Borg-el-Arab airfield in Alexandria where he will no doubt report *job well done* to some other city-bred moron of a commander there who has no idea of what is really needed down here on the Sinai and what has actually been done to our investigation. And they'll just put him back on traffic watch or crowd control and leave us high and dry!'

'They wouldn't use an Apache for traffic duties, would they?' asked Sabet, sidetracked. Fortunately he didn't seem to hear her.

'There's no point in trying to get to the Wilderness of Sin now, of course,' he raged on. 'The traffickers will have gone up through the Forest of Pillars expecting to be met at the northern edge of the gebel by trucks that can get up and down across the el-Tib plateau, and they'll be in Nekhel before *dhuhr* – midday prayers!' He closed his long eyes as if mentally following the one section of the smuggling route that was at least to a certain extent predicable, given that the section of desert the trucks could traverse was several hundred kilometres wide. Sabet noticed for the first time in their lengthy association how long and thick his eyelashes were.

Ibrahim stood, unable to contain his outrage. He began to pace from side to side of the room, from one window to another. The thick-piled hornets shifted as he approached, as though they too could sense his fury. But he did not stop talking. 'It's too late to get a unit up to Nekhel now. Even if I could get something organized, we'd have to drive all night and get there sometime in the small hours between the *fajr* and sunrise prayers. That's if we got a police convoy through into the Northern Zone without rousing any hostility, or alerting anyone capable of warning the smugglers to change their route or go into hiding as we approach. In any case, by the time we got there they'll all be in innocent-looking untraceable trucks and ready to head out for Taba or Rafa depending on which way their victims are being smuggled across the border! The best I can do is alert my opposite number up there, Captain Fawzi, and hope he can get some news of them before they pass through.'

'It depends on which border they're heading for, too,' added Sabet.

'You're right.' He nodded, pausing in his pacing. 'They could be going into Gaza from Rafa, into Israel from any point between Taba and Rafa. Or into Jordan after another short boat ride from Taba, or into Saudi after a slightly longer one. *Bismillah*, they could even take them north of Rafa to El Arish on the Mediterranean coast and try for Turkey, Greece or Italy!'

'We could try to get the army to close the road east of Nekhel if you don't think Captain Fawzi will be able to stop them in Nekhel itself,' suggested Sabet, shifting in her chair, wondering whether she too should be pacing the room like a leopard in a cage that was too small to contain it. 'The North Sinai is their jurisdiction.'

'They're too busy mopping up the consequences of the last confrontation between Gaza and Jerusalem, tracking the locations of the sixteen Jihadist camps that are supposed to be hidden somewhere out there, trying to release the seven police officers kidnapped last month from our most recent attempt to close that road – and attempting to discover who has blown up the gas line to Israel *again*! Not to mention the likelihood of soldiers manning roadblocks turning themselves into sitting targets for Ansar Bayt al-Maqdis, and anyone else ISIS, al-Qaeda or Hamas is running up there, just as our police and security people have done in the recent past. More than thirty dead in the last suicide car-bombing!'

Sabet opened her mouth to protest at this all-too-depressing list.

But Ibrahim continued, unaware. 'I've been on to the army liaison people, and we'd get no help from them. And you can see their point. Why worry about a few dozen illegal immigrants when they have something close to a border war going on? In the middle of a desert that keeps moving like a slow-motion ocean, complete with thirty metre dunes tens of kilometres long with a rate of travel you can measure in kilometres per hour. No reliable oases. Quicksand. Snakes and scorpions . . .'

Sabet closed her mouth and sat back, looking up at the frowning man. She had never seen Ibrahim this depressed before. Or this insensitive. Ansar Bayt al-Maqdis terrorists had claimed responsibility for the improvised explosive device that had killed her husband, police Captain Husani, and left her widowed and childless five years earlier, the year before she joined the force in his place. Since which time she had been without a man, in spite of the very proper offer made by Husani's younger brother to take her as his second wife and look after her. An offer she had rejected with, perhaps, more forceful language than was absolutely necessary. And the price of her rudeness had been loneliness. With a frisson of shock, she realized she had never looked at Ibrahim as a man before. As a lean, hawk-faced, dark-haired, very desirable man. 'It is late, Major,' she observed gently. 'If, as you say, there is nothing to be done, then perhaps you should go home.'

He looked at his watch and his eyebrows rose in surprise when he saw what time it was. 'So should you,' he said, turning to face her, his eyes still distant, his gaze distracted by his own thoughts. 'It is almost time for maghrib, and I note that you have had nothing to eat today.'

'At home I have a fattah of lamb with rice ready to be heated,' she said. 'I shall be glad to see it, I must admit. But what about you, sir?'

Ibrahim's distracted gaze slowly focused on her, for the question marked a new level of intimacy in their formally professional relationship. Sabet knew as well as everyone else in the El Benouk station that Major Ibrahim's existence was as close as his religion allowed to the monastic lifestyle favoured by ancient Christians at St Catherine's Monastery. He had no family other than the force. He had no parents living; no wife or child. Some joked that he had no home other than the El Benouk station. And that he digested nothing but old case files. Which at least explained his long, lean body – if not the breadth of his shoulders or the depth of his chest.

'As you may know, I live at the top of Ras Um Sid,' he said, surprising her with the familiarity and the revelation. 'I reserve a table at the restaurant called Sadiki up there. Their baba ghanoush is particularly good because they cook the aubergines on an open fire for an especially smoky taste. A bowl of that with a plate of bread is usually more than enough for me. But their salads are also excellent.'

Sabet looked in something akin to awe at a man who apparently subsisted on little more than bread and aubergine dip. At least it explained the body that hardly filled his perfectly pressed uniform, she thought. And then, irreverently, she began to wonder precisely where on Ras Um Sid he laid his darkly handsome head. A memory stirred. Somewhere on El Fanar, was it? Husani had been dead five years. How much loneliness was one woman supposed to put up with? She shook herself, suddenly, shocked that her thoughts had drifted into such dangerous areas.

She opened her mouth to say something – she had no idea what – but she was prevented by a firm official knock at the door.

'*Aji*,' he called – *come*.

The door opened and the sergeant manning the reception desk this shift came in. 'There is a phone call,' he said. 'It has come through to the central switchboard but I thought you would want to know about it immediately.'

'*N'aam?*' snapped Ibrahim. *Yes?*

'It is from Captain Mariner,' explained the sergeant. 'He says he has found the escaped prisoner Nahom Selassie and will be bringing him in at once. There was some kind of a traffic accident on the road to El Tor, apparently, and the prisoner Selassie was left for dead at the side of the road. He will take him directly to the hospital. They will be there in an hour or so.'

Ibrahim's eyes rolled upwards. 'Very well,' he said. 'I will wait and meet him there.'

The brown eyes swept round to Sergeant Sabet. 'I will have to forego my baba ghanoush, by the look of things,' he said. He would have added more, but she forestalled him, driven by motivations too deep for her to fathom into a suggestion that was somewhere between impertinence and unprofessional conduct.

'Then I will forego my fattah. But we need not be at the hospital for an hour. Is there a restaurant nearby where we might get something to eat?'

He looked at her for a moment and she was suddenly breathless with fear that she had stepped over some line that should never be crossed with him. But then he gave a fleeting smile. 'There is the Columbus,' he said. 'Their fish tagine is excellent. But we will have to share a private booth, I'm afraid – or both of our reputations will be ruined.' Then he stopped and froze for a moment, as he thought the matter through. 'Better still,' he decided. 'I will call them and have them deliver the food here. That way our reputations will remain inviolate.'

'And when we have eaten,' she added, 'we will be conveniently placed to drive down to the hospital and see whether the cat-like Nahom Selassie has used up all of his lives at last.'

'Is he dead?' asked Mahmood. 'He certainly looks dead. *They* clearly thought so . . .' He gestured to the vultures they had scared off with their arrival, which now circled as low in the sky as they dared, keeping their beady eyes on the blood-soaked body.

'Looks can be deceiving,' answered Richard, waving the clouds of swarming flies away as he knelt over the prostrate figure. 'They certainly are in this case. He's bruised and battered and that's a nasty welt on the back of his head. But almost none of the blood is his, as far as I can see – and those are not his brains either because his skull is as solid as a bowling ball. His pulse is strong and his eyes react to light when I pull the lids back.'

'Mister Richard!' came Saiid's voice from the far side of the carriageway, borne across the empty road on the evening breeze. 'There's a dead goat here. They must have hit it.'

'What does its head look like?' called Richard.

'Smashed open,' answered Saiid.

'Brains?' he demanded.

'Gone,' Saiid confirmed.

'*The times have been*,' said Richard, speaking to himself, ironically misquoting Macbeth once more, '*that when the brains were out the goat would die . . .*' He rolled Nahom on to his back and pulled his torso up into a sitting position. '*But now they rise again . . .*' He held his hand out and Ahmed passed him a bottle of cold water from the Defender's icebox. Richard let it trickle over Nahom's battered face and head. The eyes flickered. The young man sucked in a massive breath and came back to consciousness like a reanimated corpse.

'You're going to have to find some way of getting around Sinai, Nahom,' said Richard cheerfully, 'other than in ambulances . . .'

Nahom's eyes slowly focused on him. 'There was goat . . .' he mumbled.

'We know,' Richard assured him. 'You seem to be covered in a good deal of its blood and most of its brains.' He hesitated. 'Though I have to say, this particular bloody goat seems to have been much brainier than the average.'

Nahom shook his head gingerly, clearly having no idea what Richard was talking about. The way he moved made Richard ask, 'Is your neck OK? *Neck?*' he gestured.

Nahom shrugged and rolled his head. Richard was close enough to hear the vertebrae crackling as the column moved – but there seemed to be no serious damage. 'Think you can stand?' he asked.

The pair of them rose unsteadily together, and once they were upright, the vultures winged silently away to join their companions circling low above the dead goat.

The back seat of the Defender was a bench seat. They gently wedged Nahom between Mahmood and Ahmed, then Richard swung back into the front passenger seat and Saiid climbed into the driving seat. They all strapped in. Saiid eased them back on to the road and headed back southwards, pushing the speed up towards one hundred kilometres per hour once again. As soon as Richard sighted the first unnaturally tall, straight palm tree, he pulled out his cell phone, dialled the number for the Sharm el-Sheikh police, and reported in.

By this time, Nahom had consumed a couple of bottles of cool water and was beginning to look a little more with it. 'Where were you going?' asked Richard. 'Before you hit the goat?'

'Nekhel,' answered Nahom.

'Nekhel,' echoed Richard. 'That's a name that keeps coming up. Tell me all about Nekhel, Saiid.'

'Nekhel is the heart of the Sinai,' answered Saiid. His voice became almost dreamy. 'It has stood there since the age of the Pharaohs. It was part of the province of Du Mafkat in Ancient Egypt, and a fortress was built there long before the prophet Musa saw the burning bush at Saint Catherine and led his people to Mount Sinai and to freedom.

'Sixteen hundred years before the birth of the prophet Isa, whom you Christians call Jesus, the Pharaohs built the way of Shur across Sinai to Beersheba and on to Jerusalem, and the way of Shur passed through Nekhel, whose power, importance and fortifications were strengthened beyond measure. In succeeding years towards properly recorded history, Nekhel was always part of the Egyptian Empire, even after the Pharaohs fell from power and Cleopatra loved first Caesar, then Antony of Rome and handed the power of the land to the Roman Emperor Augustus. It was the ancient capital of the entire Sinai province of Egypt because of its strategic location at the exact centre of the peninsula. The region provided the Egyptian Empire, then the Roman Empire with minerals, turquoise, gold and copper. As you know, there are well-preserved ruins of mines and temples all around there. In those days, Sinai was known as The Land of Turquoise and Nekhel stood at its heart.

'Nekhel slowly fell out of favour and importance, becoming little more than an isolated desert waypoint after the collapse of the Roman Empire. But then, in the days of the Prophet, blessings and peace be upon him, the town began to prosper once again. Nekhel found itself located on the new Hajj route as the faithful came up out of Africa through Sinai towards Mecca. It became once again the capital of Sinai – the main rest and trade destination for Muslims during Hajj season. Thus it was rebuilt as an even more imposing citadel guarding the oasis called the Well of the Sultan, built by Sultan Al-Ashraf Qansuh al-Ghawri for the pilgrims coming north and south.

'These were the days of peace on the Sinai before Richard I became the crusader king of England. By that time, in the twelfth Christian century, crusade after crusade had attacked the lands of Islam. Consequently, several Sultans had built forts and castles in Nekhel to defend Egypt from Crusaders coming out of the west and south along the Red Sea. Nekhel's importance was further enhanced as it played a central role as a military base in defeating succeeding Crusades and freeing numerous provinces of the Islamic Caliphate. It has featured as a part of every war in the nearby area ever since. And the toll of this led the town itself to shrink even as the forts grew ever larger.

'Early in your Christian nineteenth century, the fort was a great building with stone walls but the city had waned in size and importance. There was a large reservoir of water for the pilgrims filled from a brackish well. The fort's garrison consisted of about fifty soldiers and the building was used as a magazine to provision the Egyptian Army. Even though the route was still regularly used by pilgrims, the road was supposedly infested with *dabba* – hyenas, which fed on the dead camels which had fallen by the wayside. Packs were known to have attacked solitary travellers and infested the outskirts of the town which were now largely abandoned. The residents of Nekhel would not leave the centre of town at night for fear of attack and kept dogs to frighten off the scavengers.

'By the beginning of your twentieth century there was little more than a square fort on absolutely barren ground built as a place to provide Hajj pilgrims with water, but little shelter. The fort was manned by an officer and ten soldiers; there was little more than a village around the fort consisting of fifteen to twenty houses inhabited by ex-soldiers and their families. All food was transported from Gaza or Suez though the villagers cultivated small patches of ground with corn and maize when the nearby Wadi el-Arish flooded. This did not occur every year and the wadi dried up very quickly. Some of the villagers also kept camels. It took the Cairo pilgrims three days to reach Nekhel from Suez and another three days to reach Aqaba. There was little for them in Nekhel any more. At about this time, therefore, the pilgrimage switched its route to one along the shores of the Gulf of Suez and Nekhel went into almost terminal decline. The fortress was blown up by the Turkish army during the First World War. Two British cavalry columns with three aeroplanes, commanded by Colonel William Grant, approached Nekhel in 1917 to find that it had been abandoned. This was the last British action in their Sinai campaign against the Turks, in spite of the famous involvement of the man you know as Lawrence of Arabia, who crossed the Sinai north of Nekhel at about the same time and nearly died among the sand dunes of the Great Sand Sea there.

'During the Second World War, there was no action in the Sinai and Nekhel had no military significance, therefore. But on the evening of the thirtieth of October, 1956 by the Christian calendar, during Israel's Sinai campaign, Nekhel was captured by the 202nd Paratroop Brigade of the Israeli Army under the command of Colonel Ariel Sharon, who used the ruined fort as a base, re-emphasizing its military importance. Little more than ten years later, in the 1967 war, Nekhel fell to the Israeli Defence Force's 14th Armoured Brigade, a force belonging to General Ariel Sharon's 38th Division. In the battle the Egyptians lost sixty tanks, over 100 guns and 300 other vehicles. It was these actions at Nekhel that cemented Sharon's reputation and led to his election as Prime Minister of Israel. Ironically enough, they also led to the rebirth of both the city and the fortification – as their strategic importance could no longer be overlooked by the government in Cairo.

'Nowadays, Nekhel is a township on the boundary where South Sinai becomes North Sinai. It is border country, where one law stops and another starts. Where the police are no longer so fully in charge and have handed control over to the army because what happens north of Nekhel is not so much acts of illegality as acts of outright war. There is an international peacekeeping post close by and a brand-new landing strip has been constructed there to keep the place supplied.

'But Nekhel itself is the last bastion. It is where, sometimes, given the right circumstances, people can meet in peace who would otherwise find themselves in conflict. Where negotiation can prevent annihilation, where bargains can be struck before throats are cut. There is still something lingering there of the Well of the Sultan and of the ancient Bedouin laws of hospitality;

a chance for life shared in the face of death. Shared with all who come, equally, without fear or favour. If we can catch Nahom's sister and her fellow travellers at Nekhel, we might have a chance. If we miss them there, the chance may well be lost.'

'Nahom says if you let him wash he will be fine,' translated Mahmood. 'He has hurt his head and scraped his knees and elbows. He is covered in bruises but most of the blood and all of the brains are not his. They belong to the goat. He reminds you that he has been a serving soldier and is well trained in self-preservation, as is Tsibekti. Do not underestimate their strength and fortitude. He also says the cards are gone. Ali and Tariq must have taken them.'

'The cards are not important,' said Richard. 'I have put a stop on them.'

While Mahmood translated this for Nahom, Saiid pushed the Defender at top speed south towards Sharm. 'In any case,' he said to Richard over the quiet hum of conversation in the back and the rumble of the big engine hard at work, 'It is not we who will decide about Nahom's ablutions. It is Major Ibrahim . . .'

He would have said more, but he was interrupted by an exclamation of surprise and anger from the rear seat, followed by an impenetrable stream of Eritrean Arabic. 'He says,' translated Mahmood, 'if the cards are worthless then it is more important than ever that he retrieves the money belt and gets it to the kidnappers before they visit any further violence on Tsibekti.'

'That too will be for Major Ibrahim to decide,' observed Saiid.

The Defender was waved through the security checkpoint at the junction of the road south to Ras Mohammed National Park, at the next one as they headed north towards Sharm and, indeed, through the internal checkpoints along the approach road to the Old Town, the Travco Pier and the hospital that stood beside it. The only things that slowed their progress, in fact, were the regular humps in the road that Richard thought of as 'sleeping policemen'. The man responsible for this relatively swift and trouble-free passage was standing waiting for them in the reception with Sergeant Sabet beside him. And, unexpectedly, Aman Kifle, looking perky and self-important.

'Nahom's not as bad as he looks,' said Richard as he and

Mahmood led the blood-covered runaway back into the chilly brightness of the hospital lighting. 'He says he just needs a wash and brush-up then he'll be good to go.'

'To go where?' demanded Ibrahim at once.

'Wherever you want,' shrugged Richard. 'Left to his own devices, he'd be off to Nekhel. The cards he stole are worthless, so his sister is back in all sorts of deadly danger. He says the men who helped him escape and then left him for dead will be heading there as fast as they can – given that they probably won't dare stop at any checkpoints or go into any towns along the way. They'll have to take a fairly circuitous route, therefore, and that will slow them down, for all the good it'll do.'

Suddenly Nahom himself was in full flow, his words tumbling over each other, his tone reeling between begging and demanding, reason and outrage.

'He's putting it to the major,' translated Mahmood, 'that the girl's only hope now is the money belt. They must give him back the money belt and the phone. These are the only things standing between Tsibekti and a terrible death.'

The major answered more calmly and reasonably than Richard supposed he would. Mahmood continued his half-whispered translation: 'The major says they have the phone here. The kidnappers have been calling on it and Aman Kifle has been answering as though he was Nahom. The money belt is in his office up on El Benouk. If he thought it would help the situation he would indeed return it. But there is no way to get to Nekhel before the smugglers now. The race is lost. There is nothing to be done.'

'Especially,' added Richard, raising his voice, 'if you have been in contact with the smugglers within the last hour or so Aman. Because if you have, as soon as they catch up and report in, Tariq and Ali are going to tell them they've been talking to a dead man.'

'They will be bound to catch up at Nekhel,' added Nahom desperately in English, 'by morning prayers tomorrow.'

'I understand,' said Ibrahim in the same language. 'But we are not djinn. We have no magic carpets. We cannot fly there . . .'

'No,' said Richard. 'But . . . Wait a minute . . .' He pulled his phone from his pocket and speed-dialled Robin. As soon as she answered, he said, 'Robin, can you give me the number of that tour company who were offering to fly us from Sharm to Cairo at any time we wanted to go and see the pyramids?'

Five minutes later, he was on to the number Robin had given him as the others watched, open-mouthed. 'Hello? Is that SharmTours? Excellent. Your English is very good. Really? University of London? My name is Richard Mariner. My wife and I were enquiring about a day trip to Cairo by plane. We're on your database . . . Wonderful. I was wondering whether I could make one or two changes. Price is no object . . . That's right. OK, well, what I have in mind is . . .'

Fifteen minutes later still, he broke the connection and looked around them all. 'You probably got all the details anyway, but I'll run through what we've agreed would be possible if you gave the go-ahead, Major. Pick-up time would be four-thirty a.m. tomorrow and we'd all go out to the International Airport. Obviously, you could make your own way there if you decided to come. We – and whoever else you wanted to bring, within reason – would go aboard an eight-seater jet. A Cessna Citation, the largest mid-range they have. That would be Robin, myself, Nahom and Aman. You, your sergeant if you wished to bring her and two other police personnel. We would depart Sharm at five thirty a.m. – or earlier if you could get us clearance. Cairo is a forty-five minute hop so the new landing strip at Nekhel would only take half an hour. We'd be there by dawn. And the plane would wait to bring us home if the mission's a success. What do you say?'

The Cessna canted to the left as it entered its short final approach to the new landing strip at Nekhel. The Pratt and Witney turbofans eased back a fraction. Robin leaned across Richard and both of them pressed their faces close to the window like children at a toy store. It was just dawn on the ground, though it had been full day for a while up here, and the beams of the rising sun threw everything below them into incredibly sharp relief in the clear desert air. The township of Nekhel sprawled along the brutal black line of the main Suez to Taba highway. The ancient fort sat behind and above it like something out of *Beau Geste*, clinging to the foothills of the Gebel El Tih. The compound which housed the International Peacekeepers stood a little to the west, and the airstrip lay in between. All of it was nestled against the incline of the gebel. The mountains rose, red and majestic, to the north, their east-facing slopes a startling terracotta, their valleys and west-facing slopes an impenetrable black. From up here, at least, there was no sign of life or even of vegetation. For a disorientating moment, Richard thought that he might as well be looking down on the planet Mars.

To the south, seeming to start and end with the black ribbon of the six-lane highway, lay the great flat plateau of El-Tib, which they had flown over in the darkness just before dawn. Now it was revealed by the pitiless sun as a great, flat expanse, clearly almost as wide as the Sinai itself, and the better part of a hundred and fifty kilometres deep. The angle of the sun's rays made every track and trail, every boulder, rock and stone stand out, each one seeming to cast a long, west-pointing shadow. And once again there was nothing moving – nothing growing. The Cessna tilted the other way and the panorama slid out of view. 'I can see why you were worried you would never track the smugglers across that, Major,' said Richard. 'There must be as many ways across it as there are across the English Channel, and that's about a fifth of the size.'

'If I may continue your comparison,' said the major, 'it's not so much the size of the plateau as the lack of safe ports on the northern side. If the people we are following need any kind of rest or refreshment, there are only two safe havens available to them: Nekhel and El-Thamad.'

'But,' added Sabet, 'with a little planning and foresight, they can be met anywhere along the Nekhel to Taba road there and be put into trucks to be spirited away – and we would never catch them.'

Nahom spoke forcefully, and Aman, who had replaced Mahmood as translator, explained, 'Nahom says that almost everyone involved, from the leader of the smugglers to Ali and Tariq, all say they are to meet up at Nekhel. All we have to do is to get there ahead of them.'

'And we also have to meet up with the men from Nekhel police station,' added Ibrahim. 'I have only two of my men aboard and we will need many more than that.'

'That's true,' said Richard. 'I . . .' His mind raced as he tried to work out a way to reveal that he had a good idea of the size of the group without letting slip that he had escaped from the police watchers' scrutiny by pretending he was stopping at St Catherine, that he had lied to Ibrahim and had seen the helicopter attack while spying on the men and women they were pursuing now. 'I believe, from Saiid, that this is rumoured to be a large group. At least twenty, perhaps thirty. Counting victims and camel handlers.'

'That is not unusual,' nodded Ibrahim. 'And they are likely to be heavily armed.'

'Independently of any heavy arms that they might be smuggling,' agreed Richard. A thought struck him. 'Do you think they would use any weapons they were smuggling against us? I mean, if there were things like shoulder-launched missiles?'

'It is only a few years,' answered Ibrahim, 'since somebody just outside Nekhel – somebody, I must say, who is still at large – launched a missile at the army base at Sheikh Zuweid of North Sinai. Similar rockets may have been fired from close by here towards Gaza. Everything from SAM7 shoulder-fired anti-aircraft systems to massive GRAD multiple-launch rocket systems have been confiscated or destroyed up here. At least one helicopter has been brought down with a rocket.'

'I wish you'd told us that before . . .' said Robin.

'I am talking of some years in the past. And besides, this is a civilian plane; the targets are usually military or security personnel and equipment. No. If you wish to worry about anyone, worry about the patrol I ordered to be sent out from Nekhel as we were waiting to board this plane at Sharm. It has gone west from Nekhel along the road that leads to the crossroads with the highway down to Ras Sudr and El Tor, hoping to run into the battered Fiat and the two who left Mr Selassie for dead but brought your cards along.'

'Were you going to . . . what's the word . . . *arrest* these men?' asked Nahom, his voice full of righteous indignation.

'No. We were going to follow them to their rendezvous,' answered Ibrahim.

'And if you do not find them?' asked Aman.

'Then you two will get the phone back and the money belt – and we will stake you out like goats at a leopard hunt. If we cannot find a way to get to them, perhaps they will give themselves away when they come after you. Nekhel exists as a place like the old Wild West in American movies. It is full of well-armed and ruthless men who thrive on the generation of rumour and the sale of information. And on the more ancient businesses of theft and murder. I would not be surprised if word of our arrival is already out – someone will have heard the jet engines passing overhead. And in any case, I had to alert a lot of locals to our plans last night. Some of the men I talked with I would hesitate to trust. And that lack of trust – and the information I gave out – was all carefully calculated. All I would have to do is let you two out into the town, apparently alone and unobserved, and the local predators would come sniffing around. Then it wouldn't be long before our particular man-eaters got to hear about you and came by to collect their ill-gotten gains. Then, snap! My trap would close on them.' As he said 'snap!' he closed his hands together, claw-fingered, turning the long, artistic digits into a kind of man-trap. 'What did you think?' he continued, his tone changing to give more than a hint of the anger and frustration he was feeling. 'That I would bend and break the rules simply so two illegal alien siblings could be reunited? No! Those idiots from Cairo in their helicopter with its rockets and its guns have come into my jurisdiction and made me look small and powerless. If I do not apprehend these people they will boast that they found the fugitives with no trouble and yet the local force could not follow up their good work! I will not allow this. Just be grateful that in this one instance your wishes have coincided with my own.'

There was a short silence, under which it was just possible to hear the pilot discussing the upcoming landing with the tower at Nekhel airstrip. Richard nodded grimly to himself. The major's plan was logical if ruthless; his motivation clear and understandable. Even if he had not been so keen on saving face in front of his superiors and competitors in Cairo, Richard shrewdly suspected that he would wish to save face in front of Sergeant Sabet, who was suddenly looking at him with something much warmer than mere professionalism in her wide brown eyes. And finally he had no doubt that Nahom would be a willing part of it, no matter why it had all been put in train; no matter what the risks or likely outcome, considering what the alternative might involve for Tsibekti.

Richard's suspicions were confirmed at once. Nahom went into a short but energetic conversation with Aman, who shrugged fatalistically at the end and said, '*Inshallah*. Nahom says we have his phone. The men holding Tsibekti have hers. He will simply phone them and say he is here and waiting with the money belt. They will come. Then you may spring your trap; but only when we are sure Tsibekti will come safely home.'

'You know, of course . . .' the major suddenly became more expansive, '. . . that in the days when leopards roamed freely through these mountains, the local villagers would tether a goat right in the back of a cave and keep watch. When a leopard went in for the kill, they would roll a boulder over the cave mouth and seal them in together. It is said that up in the hills where nobody much goes you can still find caves with the scattered bones of goats and the skeletons of leopards that starved to death after that one last meal. But you have to roll the boulders aside first.'

'Nowadays, however,' added Sabet brusquely, 'if you roll the boulder away from a cave mouth you are more likely to find a jihadist arms dump than a dead leopard.'

She had no sooner finished speaking than the seatbelt lights came on and the pilot's voice over the intercom warned them that they were just about to land.

There were several groups of people waiting to meet them as they stepped into the cool morning. Richard glanced around as he stepped down the steps from the cabin and strode across the apron. The sun was quite high already, the mountains to the north as red and threatening as those around the Wilderness of Sin, but Nekhel was more than four hundred metres above sea level, and although the temperature would likely approach forty degrees Celsius at midday, the recently departed night had been almost chilly. He could afford these distracting thoughts because for once he was very much a supernumary here – he and Robin allowed along merely because he had chartered the plane. The major would clearly have preferred to bring more men and leave the tourists back in Sharm. But he could not do so – another element he found almost as irritating as the helicopter's thoughtless actions yesterday.

Ibrahim strode on ahead with Sabet at his shoulder and his two policemen immediately behind them. A short, tubby man saluted punctiliously, his uniform jacket straining across his paunch. 'That'll be Captain Fawzi, Ibrahim's opposite number in the Nekhel police,' muttered Robin as she caught up with Richard. 'Let's hope he's got the men Ibrahim ordered. The major is suddenly a scary individual.'

'He's certainly not a happy bunny,' agreed Richard. 'And I guess the forbidding looking group of individuals in fatigues further back are the local army brass come to check out this invasion of their turf,' he added.

'And the two crestfallen boys over there who look like naughty students outside the headteacher's door will be the two sent down to the crossroads commissioned to track Nahom's friends, Ali and Tariq . . .' observed Robin.

'. . . only to return empty-handed,' completed Richard. 'Yes, I think you're right.'

'Well,' said Aman cheerfully as he and Nahom caught up with them, 'at least they made it back alive.'

'Let's hope you and Nahom manage to do the same,' said Robin. 'It looks like you've just gone from being the hunters to being the bait.'

Richard remembered Saiid's warning words. The djinn of the Sinai had a wicked sense of humour. They had just granted Nahom's wish.

Ibrahim, Sabet and the other policemen joined them. There were no introductions. No conversation at all, in fact. In a stormy silence, Richard, Robin and the two Eritreans were led to a pair of two-ton military-style green-painted trucks and handed up into the canvas-covered rear sections. There were no seats as such – simply benches running front-to-back. Richard and Robin sat, surrounded by policemen in one – Aman and Nahom were put in the other. Ibrahim, Sabet and the local police chief climbed into the front of the truck carrying the English couple, beside the driver. Tailgates slammed up. Engines coughed and the trucks juddered forward.

It took twenty minutes to reach the outskirts of Nekhel. By

the time the trucks rolled into town, life was stirring. There was sufficient traffic to slow their progress. Pavements which had been empty as the Cessna swooped over them were beginning to bustle. Looking back through the open section above the tail-gate, Richard marvelled at how swiftly Nekhel was coming to life under the red beams of the still-rising sun. But, he knew, there would be little or no activity between eleven and one because the heat would be too much to work through – unless there was air conditioning. Or unless, he thought wryly, Noël Coward was right – and you were a mad dog or an Englishman.

Richard half expected the trucks to pull up outside a police station, though he had little idea what Nekhel's equivalent to the building on El Benouk would look like. But no. They came to a stop in the middle of a large square and everyone piled out. 'It's the market,' said Robin.

Nahom and Aman joined them. 'The Nekhel souk,' agreed Aman. 'A famous place. It once supplied the faithful on Hajj. They don't come this way any longer but it is still important. And it is market day. Everyone comes here.'

Richard and Robin looked around, caught between bemusement and wonder. For, indeed, the edges of the square were bright and busy with shops opening and stalls being set up. The two police trucks were almost immediately lost in a jam of trucks, cars, carts, bikes pulling laden trailers or carrying bulging sacks, and even camel trains as the farmers from outlying smallholdings and Bedouin nomads from even farther afield brought their wares in for sale. The shopkeepers and stallholders were all men, dressed in a range of costume from simple cotton dishdasha robes and *taqiyah* caps to full Bedouin dress with heavy white cotton *tobs* under *kibr* gowns and sleeveless striped *aba* robes. White keffiyehs were held in place with black camel-hair *igals* – for the most part closed so that only the eyes could be seen. On the other hand, the shoppers were almost all women, modestly dressed in *abaya* robes and either *niquab* or full burqa headdresses.

The noise and the smell were overwhelming. Exciting. Irresistibly romantic. Everything from the essence of camel – with the complaining braying to accompany it – to the elusive scents of saffron, cumin, turmeric and cardamom. And, early though it was, the mouth-watering aromas of the street vendors cooking both sweet and savoury breakfasts. Everything from sweet *belila*, barley and cinnamon porridge to fiery chicken and goat kebabs. Accompanied by the calls of the cooks, stall holders and shop-keepers touting their wares.

Suddenly Ibrahim was beside them with Sabet at his shoulder. The gathering crowd of retailers and shoppers kept clear of the uniforms, creating a little space where they could stand easily and talk clearly. 'Right,' he said to Nahom, 'I will return your phone and money belt. It has been arranged that you will both go over there to the spice stall. The local police have already set up a secure cordon, though the men on watch are of course well-hidden. We will make a show of getting back in our trucks and pulling away. Captain and Mrs Mariner, I see no reason why you cannot make use of the time by doing a little shopping. It is, as they say, a once-in-a-lifetime opportunity. Tourists are something of a rarity here. I would strongly urge you, however, to cover your hair and face, Mrs Mariner. The summer dress you are wearing is quite well suited to this place but the local people are unused to seeing any woman's hair, let alone hair that is *dahab* – gold.'

'I brought a scarf on purpose,' said Robin, and in a moment she was as modestly covered as the other women around her; or nearly so, for many of them were in full burqas. Even so, she reminded Richard of an ill-disguised character from the TV series *Homeland*.

'Good,' said Ibrahim. 'We will go now. But if you stay in this general area, you will be safely under our eyes at all times.'

'Everywhere but the spice shop,' observed Richard drily, looking across at Aman and Nahom lingering conspicuously outside the colourful cliff of wares, phone in hand, as the police climbed back into their two-ton trucks and roared away. 'I rather think we're being set up as a distraction.'

'What?' said Robin. 'Just another couple of goats tethered at the back of a cave, waiting for a hungry leopard, you mean?'

They were no sooner alone than a gang of small boys descended on them – more like piranhas than leopards, thought Richard. They were calling in a range of accents and languages until they worked out that English was the most effective. 'You come, *effendi*. You see my father's shop. It is cheaper than Walmart. Cheaper than Asda, I promise . . .'

But both Richard and Robin were well trained in handling such matters – not least by their visits to the Old Market in Sharm and the bustling commercial heart of Dahab. So they remained courteous but unwavering as they wandered around the stalls, intoning '*La aa shukran*' as though it was some kind of mantra as they made a pantomime of looking for something worth haggling over but tried to keep an eye on the spice shop at the same time.

Time sped by, for the market was nothing if not distractingly exciting. There were none of the touristy shops they were used to in Sharm. Instead, as in Dahab, there was an over-abundance of spice stalls, vegetable stalls, butchers' stalls – selling mostly chicken, goat and camel. Then there were the more familiar products which they discovered in a modest supermarket at the heart of the market. A dark, cool cavern with sliding doors to keep the air conditioning in and high-piled shelves full of Western produce. Coke and Pepsi, Fanta, Sprite – all in cans and bottles. Tonic, soda and ginger ale by Schweppes. Lipton's and Twining's teas. Oreos. Twinkies. Hershey bars. Cadbury's. They wandered, unmolested, around the aisles, letting the air conditioning cool them down.

But as they stepped, empty-handed, back out into the bustling square, they found themselves confronted by a tall figure in Bedouin dress. An anonymous man wearing a heavy white keffiyeh that masked his face. Two brown eyes stared angrily at them. The tall stranger pulled the tail of his keffiyeh aside to reveal Major Ibrahim's familiar frown. 'Did you see them?' he demanded.

'See who?' asked Richard.

'Nahom Salassie and Aman Kifle,' snapped Ibrahim. 'The pair of them have disappeared.'

EIGHT

Dune

'Disappeared?' echoed Richard. 'How on earth . . .'

'I don't know,' snarled Ibrahim. 'But I certainly intend to find out.'

'As long as it doesn't distract you from the main point of your investigation; catching the smugglers and rescuing that poor girl,' warned Robin.

'Although,' allowed Richard, 'finding out how the pair of them disappeared might well *be* the whole point of the investigation if they were *helped* to disappear. And if the people who helped them are on the one hand associated with the smugglers or on the other hand something to do with the local authorities who were supposed to be keeping them under close observation.'

'Precisely,' snapped Ibrahim. 'Though even if it was simple inefficiency, it will still need to be rooted out!' He looked around, eyes narrow, as though the whole of the market was packed with smugglers and terrorists.

'Then again,' hazarded Robin, 'it might be that Captain Fawzi and his men were simply outsmarted. That there was an element in the situation here that they weren't really prepared for.'

'What do you mean?' asked Ibrahim, his frown shifting subtly from outrage to enquiry.

'I assume they were briefed in the belief that the two subjects – Nahom and Aman – were going to cooperate with the stake-out,' Robin explained. 'But what if one or both of them actually wanted to join the smugglers? It's not an unimaginable scenario, is it? And I'm sure it must have crossed your mind as well as mine. Aman and his brother Bisrat could easily be the smugglers' front men in Eritrea – we agreed that the smugglers need apparently disinterested people to talk potential victims into taking the fatal journey . . .'

'Or,' added Richard, picking up on her train of thought, 'Nahom might well have preferred to rely on himself rather than on the authorities. With all due respect, Major, so far in this affair, and in spite of our best efforts, we have done nothing to actually help him. In fact, all we have done is put hurdle after hurdle in his path.'

'Which,' added Robin, 'he may simply see as one barrier after another designed to stop him rescuing Tsibekti.'

'He would need to be mad to think this,' snapped Ibrahim.

'Mad,' allowed Robin. 'Or desperate.'

'Either way, and no matter what the truth of the matter turns out to be,' said Richard shortly, 'we need to get after him as fast as possible.'

He saw that Ibrahim was hesitating, clearly tempted.

'Before the trail goes cold,' he added.

Ibrahim frowned. 'The trail will not go cold,' he snapped. 'It leads from here to Taba. One road. One trail.'

'Then let's get to it,' said Richard, already looking around for a means of transport. Then he realized. The jet that had whisked them here from Sharm was useless now. It could follow and overfly the fleeing smugglers, but there was nowhere for it to land between here and Taba International Airport at the far end of the trail. There was no time to summon up more helicopters – even assuming Ibrahim was inclined to trust the over-enthusiastic flyboys again. Any meaningful pursuit in the immediate future must be on the ground – and along that one roadway whose black tarmac width separated the potentially dangerous Amber Zone from the possibly deadly Red Zone.

'You need to move your trucks, Major,' he said. 'The faster you hit the road the better your chances will be.'

'I can see that!' snapped Ibrahim. 'That much is obvious. But the trucks are not mine, are they? They belong to the local command. I will need to negotiate their use. I will also need to ask Captain Fawzi to fill them with his best men. Unfortunately, these are the same men who have already allowed our two goats to slip through their fingers and into the clutches of the leopards.'

'But we still have a chance to roll the boulder over the cave mouth,' insisted Richard. 'If we can move quickly enough.'

'*We*,' snapped Ibrahim. 'There is no *we*. There are the men of my Sharm command and the men of Captain Fawzi's Nekhel command. I must return to Sharm, and I suspect that the pilot of your Cessna will be keen to do so too. Myself and my sergeant, yourself and Mrs Mariner will all be aboard when the plane lifts off.'

There was a short silence after Ibrahim said this. Suddenly a breath of oven-hot wind blew past them, laden with sand grains, hissing out of the north and blowing purposefully southwards. Under the abrupt, threatening weight of it, the whole of the market seemed to still for a moment. A woman in a black abaya robe and a full burqa headdress appeared at Ibrahim's shoulder. The only parts of her body visible were her dark chocolate eyes.

'Is that going to work?' asked Richard. 'One truck with your men among some more locals and another completely full of Captain Fawzi's men. Nobody from your command in charge. Nobody to report back to you what is going on. You don't fully trust them, in any case – they might well have allowed your two little goats to escape. I can see very clearly that you are wondering whether someone up here is actually working with the smugglers.'

'He is right,' said the burqa-clad woman in Sergeant Sabet's decisive voice. 'Send me with them, Major. I can take command of our men – of the entire expedition if needs be. Our men will obey me and will whip the Nekhel men into line if necessary. I will look after them and report back to you.'

'That is a tempting suggestion, Sergeant. But you know very well that I would hesitate to send you on such a mission unsupported. You may well be able to command our men, and I have no doubt they would be able to keep the local contingent in check. But I would still be concerned if there was no one actually there to watch your back.'

'Then allow Captain Mariner to accompany me if you yourself cannot,' Sergeant Sabet suggested in her forthright way. 'He has proved himself more than capable of handling a range of dangerous situations. We are only here because of his quick-thinking about the jet. The men we are pursuing are only alive because of him. This whole situation has turned around him, and Mrs Mariner. Nahom Selassie trusts him – and perhaps Aman Kifle does as well, for he and Mrs Mariner saved *his* life into

the bargain. And I trust him, Major. If I could not have you to
back me up, then there is no one else I would trust as much.'

'Now, wait just one minute . . .' Robin began.

'The sergeant is right,' said Ibrahim. 'This is a suggestion that
might work. It finds favour with me.'

'Well, it doesn't find much favour with *me*,' Robin snarled.

'It's all right, darling,' said Richard. 'Sergeant Sabet will keep me
safe. Major Ibrahim might even allow me to carry a weapon . . .'

'Now that is out of the question,' said the major. 'You are a
tourist, Captain, not a member of the Egyptian Security Force.'

'Just thought I'd ask,' said Richard amenably, thinking *if push
comes to shove, I can probably pick one up somewhere along
the way . . .*

And that was that.

Ibrahim and Robin went back to the airstrip in Captain Fawzi's
staff car, a quarter of an hour later, accompanied by the man
himself – who was probably very glad to see the back of them,
Richard suspected. The pair of six-wheeled, two-ton military-style
trucks eased themselves forcefully out of the bustle of the market
and back up on to the Taba road. The two squads of policemen
told to accompany Sabet and Richard came forward and climbed
aboard. Ibrahim's men saluted respectfully as they passed their
sergeant. Fawzi's men did not. Already there was a simmering
tension building between the two commands, one which Richard
found more than a little worrying. There were only two men Sabet
could count on if the going got tough – three counting Richard
himself, though he of course had been forbidden to carry a weapon,
so he would be of limited value in a whole range of violent situations. And there were ten of Fawzi's men, all fully armed, any
number of whom might conceivably be working with the smugglers. For a disorientating moment, Richard found himself
wondering how much Sergeant Sabet would fetch at a Saudi slave
auction if things went really badly wrong.

Richard and Sabet went to join the two trucks as the last of
the police privates climbed aboard, Richard registering for the
first time that the six-lane highway which joined Suez to Taba,
and came through Nekhel as it did so, actually stood on a kind
of steep-sided causeway a good few metres above the level of

the desert with which it was surrounded. There was nothing much to look at, he thought, and a good deal to think about. But in the cab of a big truck on top of a well elevated roadway he would be in a prime position to look at what little there was to see as he tried to think this new situation through.

Just before they climbed aboard, however, Richard tackled the first of the imponderables that had been occupying his mind. 'Sergeant,' he said to Sabet, who had vanished to remove the burqa disguise during the fifteen minutes it had taken to get everything organized and was now back in her white uniform and headscarf, 'that was surprising – what you said to Major Ibrahim. I really was not expecting you to volunteer yourself for this. And never in a million years would I have thought you'd volunteer *me* to go along with you.'

The dark eyes regarded him, suddenly as cold and hard as Arctic brown granite. 'You heard what the major said earlier,' she snapped. 'So far these people and the imbeciles in the helicopter have made him look powerless and foolish. That is not a situation that I will allow to continue. He cannot chase and apprehend these men himself. Therefore you and I will do so on his behalf. And so his honour and reputation will be restored. We will do this. Or we will perish in the attempt.'

Richard paused for an instant, his mind racing. Somewhere along the line he had failed to register just how deep the sergeant's regard for her commanding officer was, just as he hadn't really registered how high above the desert sand the roadway actually stood. He felt the lack of Robin, her acute observation and her uncanny insight immediately. She had said nothing but he would have laid handsome odds that she knew exactly how Sabet felt about Ibrahim.

'Well, what are we waiting for?' he answered after a moment. 'Let's go for it: *Do*, as they say, *or die!* After you, Sergeant . . .'

Nahom and Tsibekti Selassie were sitting side by side in a vehicle that was almost identical to the ones Richard, Sabet and their men were pursuing them in. It was a venerable but virtually indestructible REO M35 two-and-a-half ton, six-wheeled truck that had rolled off the conveyor in Lansing, Michigan, pretty soon after the Second World War. It had passed through service with the American Army and then the Israeli Army, which was why it was in such good condition nearly seventy years after its first deployment. It was the first of the middle pair of a six-truck convoy, third back from the front. The Eritrean twins were seated immediately above the offside rear pair of wheels, on a naked metal bench running along the length of the truck's aft cargo section with their backs against the flapping canvas side. They were not secured, but they were squashed between Aman and Bisrat Kifle, who were in turn sandwiched between two of the largest smugglers. The smugglers in turn were nursing two of the largest semi-automatic rifles Al-Ayn's men possessed.

The trucks were running east, so the twins and the men beside them were looking north – not that there was much to see beyond the three metre gap between them and the canvas on the far side straining in towards them and the grim-faced, heavily armed smugglers sitting in front of it. They all had their keffiyehs over their faces and sunglasses over their eyes. The keffiyehs were up because the wind pushing the hot canvas against their backs was becoming increasingly laden with sand, and the ancient canvas was nothing like proof against it. Indeed, if Nahom squinted a little it was just possible for him to make out the vague outlines of the Gebel el-Tih mountains in spite of the sandstorm that seemed to be gathering in the north through a slowly widening rent in the straining material between the sturdy shoulders of the men sitting opposite him.

Even if conversation had been possible over the thrashing of the canvas, the hissing howl of the shamaal wind, the grinding thunder of the motor and the relentless rumble of the pair of tyres immediately beneath them, the twins would have had little to say to each other. They had somehow found themselves at daggers-drawn from the moment Aman and Nahom turned up at the convoy, which was parked at the roadside just outside Nekhel's eastern outskirts, waiting for them. Or rather, suspected Nahom bitterly, waiting for his money belt and the two-faced Aman, who had apparently been as deep as Bisrat in this business right from the start.

Nahom had managed to give his sister the details of his adventures but instead of the grateful praise he had expected, he had received a telling-off that reminded him of his mother and his two grandmothers all combined.

Tsibekti sat and seethed silently while her stupid brother sat sullenly at her side. That Nahom's attempt to buy her freedom had simply led to his own bruised body being added to the human merchandise on its way to market and another fortune raised by their terrified family in the treacherous hands of Al-Ayn and his men! That he should have got himself so dreadfully beaten up and battered on his way to rescue her! Bitten by a snake into the bargain, involved in a car crash and left for dead! Relying on the good graces of some Westerner like a beggar in the *kasbah*! That he hadn't even thought to arrange some sort of back-up or Plan B in case what had just happened, happened! Indeed, the stupid boy was only still alive because Aman convinced Al-Ayn that Nahom would fetch a good price in the Saudi souk where they were all bound. So, all in all, he was just one more burden to be borne by their poor, terrified, bankrupt parents at home.

However, there was probably more to it even than Aman's cunning treachery, she thought darkly – the arrival of a battered Nasr car and a couple of shifty-looking men who had been simply stunned to see Nahom alive – and who had immediately gone into close conclave with Al-Ayn also had something to do with it. If Tsibekti looked past Nahom and Aman sitting beside him, she could see the half-wrecked motor rolling along a few metres behind the truck, in the middle of the convoy. Its lights smashed, its front bumper a distant memory, its side door dented and blood-smeared. Its bald front tyres nakedly on show as it weaved from side to side under the varying strength of the sand-laden shamaal.

Now it so happened that, although Tsibekti and Nahom were twins, she had been the first born. She was all of thirty minutes older than her brother, and that fact had coloured their relationship all their lives. She was the big sister; he was the little brother. As her mind ranged over their current situation, their likely future and their ultimate fate, Tsibekti began to mellow. Nahom had come after her bravely and suffered three terrible near-death experiences in his attempt to secure her freedom. Suddenly, and unexpectedly, her breast flooded with an aching warmth of affection. How battered he looked, with his head bruised and his face still swollen from the car crash.

How brave he had been to come after her in such a way, she thought, performing a mental U-turn. To risk death on the boat

that had been wrecked on the Blind Reef. To leave the safety of
the hospital and come on foot into the desert and the mountains
of the south. To come on again, time after time. To risk a charge of
theft having stolen this infidel crusader Mariner's credit cards
and to have offered to use them only when the police confiscated
the money belt their parents had managed to fill. To have come
again as venom and anti-venom were still at war in his veins.
To have gone with the men in the battered Nasr, and to have
survived the collision with the goat, and yet still to have come
on, seeking only to rescue her . . . Suddenly her eyes were full
of tears. But the burning affection for her little brother was
replaced by an equally hot determination to get the pair of them
out of this predicament. And to make everyone from Al-Ayn to
Aman and Bisrat Kifle pay for what they had done to their family.

Nahom, on the other hand, did not feel any burning beyond
that in his eyes, though, like hers, they were overflowing. His
mind was still full of brooding resentment against his ungrateful
sister and the first stirrings of genuine outrage that he had been
betrayed by Aman and Bisrat, who he counted as among his
closest childhood friends. He was also angered by the fact that
the relentless blast of the south-blowing shamaal was filling his
eyes with grit, so that his cheeks were streaming with tears. He
was certain that the men opposite, hidden behind their keffiyehs,
their rip-off Oakleys and counterfeit Ray-Bans, were all laughing
at him and his apparently childish weeping. He had been teased
and bullied during his early days of National Service, but he had
learned to stand up for himself then and he was not going to
allow the experience to be repeated now. He dashed his hand
angrily across his face and cleared his vision for a moment. He
looked up, paused as his mind shifted gear, and frowned.

Because the nearest of the red-sand spurs of the Gebel el Tih,
visible through the widening rent in the ancient canvas, seemed
to have detached itself from the mountain range sometime in the
distant past and was rearing up over the elevated roadway they
were travelling along like a great wave on the Red Sea that was
standing, frozen, just on the point of breaking. As they entered
the wind shadow of its near-vertical face, so the air became
clearer and Nahom was able to see all too vividly what was just
about to happen. He opened his mouth and gasped in a breath

to shout out. But because he was wearing the tails of his keffiyeh down, the sand got into his mouth and choked him. By the time he had finished coughing, it was too late in any case.

Richard and Sergeant Sabet sat side by side on the right-hand side of the lead truck's bench seat. Her men were in the back but it was one of Captain Fawzi's men at the wheel. His ID badge said صقر, which Sabet translated as 'Saqr'. Richard's shoulder was hard against the passenger door and Sabet was keeping carefully clear of Captain Fawzi's driver. Every gesture of the silent private's rigid body made it clear that he did not approve of the woman he was driving, what she was doing and where she was taking them. Particularly as they were driving through a blinding sand storm which made the road immediately ahead very difficult to see – and therefore to follow, even though it was six lanes wide. The sand filled even the near distance with a whirling red fog which danced in a dazzling display of movement so distracting as to make their eyes water. That was driven by a wind which seemed to have come straight from the hottest part of *Jahannam* – Hell, itself.

The icy silence was the only cool thing in the overheated cab, Richard thought. Though silence was a misnomer in any case. The wind was roaring southwards forcefully enough to be trying to tear the truck off the road. The coarse sand grains it carried were almost large enough to count as pebbles and were hissing across the metal and glass surfaces all around like an army of tap-dancing serpents. On top of that, the big motor was roaring fit to burst, with the driver Saqr's foot crushing the accelerator hard against the floor and the *hamsa* Hand of Fatima good-luck charm that hung from his rear-view mirror obviously working overtime but rattling like castanets as it did so. Conversation was pretty much out of the question, therefore, even had their driver been cheery and garrulous, and Sabet up for a chat. As things stood, it looked like this police private would be one of the more difficult ones for Sabet's men to whip into line, thought Richard wryly, looking past her rigid profile at Saqr's equally stern profile.

But then Richard's gaze was tempted beyond the sand-blasted window and out into the windy desert. Because the wind died suddenly, as though the gate of Hell had slammed shut. The sand slid down the driver's window, letting the glass come clear. But all it showed was yet another red rock wall. For a moment he thought that one of the nearby foothills which reared the better part of a hundred feet vertically from the roadside was in some kind of motion. He blinked as his mind tried to come to terms with what he was seeing. 'Sergeant . . .' he said.

She looked at him. 'Yes?'

But by the time she reacted, he was looking straight down the road ahead. In the wind shadow of the red mound sitting to the north of them and reaching for the best part of a mile along the dead-straight Taba highway, the sand was settling out of the air as well as down the driver's window. The sudden clarity distracted him, particularly as it allowed him to see the tail-end of a convoy of trucks surprisingly close ahead.

'What is it?' demanded Sabet.

'I think that might be them,' said Richard.

'Yes!' she agreed, her voice suddenly full of excitement. 'You!' She turned to Saqr, the driver, switching into Egyptian Arabic. 'Can you make this thing go any faster?'

'No,' he answered in the same language.

None of which Richard understood, but followed easily through their body language.

But then, once again, his gaze was tempted out through the window on the driver's side by a movement that made him swing round to look through the windscreen more closely at the red wall towering over the northern edge of the road. And as he looked, scarcely able to believe his eyes, the crest of the wall came streaming downwards into the still air of its wind shadow. And he understood what was happening. The wall on their left was made of sand, not rock. It was a massive barchan sand dune migrating south under the power of the shamaal. Its characteristic horns – a pair of which normally preceded the inner, hundred-foot slope, had been blocked by the elevation of the road. The whole thing seemed to have been stopped by the height and width of the elevated six-lane highway. But it was on the move again now, breaking like a hundred-foot surf to come cascading down on to the road. 'Right!' he bellowed. 'Go right!'

Sabet saw at once what was happening and added her orders in a shout almost as loud as his. 'Yemeen!'

Saqr looked arrogantly down at the woman who had the gall to be giving him orders. His patrician nostrils flared. His thin lips parted and twisted, no doubt about to utter something dangerously inappropriate.

But Sabet prevented him. '*Shoof!*' she screamed, gesturing ahead. '*Look!*'

He looked, obeying automatically.

'*Bismillah!*' he shouted and swung the wheel right, sending the big truck lurching across the road and down the slope on to the mercifully solid southern sand as the Hand of Fatima cheerily applauded the action.

The whole wall of the dune to the north was collapsing on to the roadway dead ahead. Driven by the relentless power of the shamaal, tripped up by the elevation of the Suez to Taba highway, the entire dune was toppling over to collapse across the blacktop like a million-ton ocean breaker.

Nahom looked in simple, horrified disbelief as the avalanche of sand which a moment before had been a seemingly solid cliff came cascading into the roadway behind the truck. Ali and Tariq never stood a chance as ton after ton of coarse red grit smashed down on to the half-wrecked Nasr. One moment it was there, bouncing along with its tyres on show and its smashed headlights jiggling merrily, the next it was gone beneath an expanding explosion of red dirt. Nahom had an instantaneous vision of its roof smashed flat and its bald tyres bursting silently as it was swept sideways and under, amongst the thunder of the catastrophe. Then it – and they – were gone. And the trucks behind it must be buried as well, thought Nahom, stunned. For the whole hundred-foot wall of sand was coming down all at once, apparently right along its entire length, starting in the middle, from the highest point and spreading eastwards and westwards like a breaking wave.

Only then did it occur to Nahom that this truck was also in danger of being buried. He heaved himself to his feet only to topple back on to his seat as the truck lurched sideways as the men opposite raised their guns threateningly. The hole in the canvas between the two gunmen burst wide, torn by the weight of sand piling directly against it. A modest avalanche cascaded over the men as they dropped their guns and leaped to their feet. The red river of grit piled itself unsteadily on the floor at Nahom and Tsibekti's feet. He looked down at it, up at the two shocked smugglers and back through the rear opening. The monstrous red earth back on the spot where Ali's Nasr had been was already higher than the truck's canvas roof, though it was mercifully falling further and further behind. The truck lurched again. The two smugglers were slammed back into their sand-covered seats by the movement. Their sand-covered guns slid back beneath their feet. Nahom threw a protective arm round Tsibekti at exactly the same moment as her arm went round him. They looked at each other, wide-eyed.

Then Nahom looked up. The roof was bulging down, taut as a drumskin, hanging like hammocks between the struts supporting it. Struts that were beginning to bend and buckle under the weight of the sand pouring down on them. The truck lurched sideways again and suddenly tilted as it left the main highway and began to slide sideways down the outer slope of the causeway. At once the sand began to slide off the top and the truck surged forward, down and out into the flat sand south of the highway. Nahom got a strangely angled view of the collapsing red wall rolling right across the highway, its foundations massively solid – for all they were spreading like a tidal wave. The air above filled with a red mist of finer grains, whipped away southwards as the shamaal pushed the last of the great sand obstruction out of its way. And, oddly, before the red mist closed around the truck, Nahom was granted one last clear vision. For there, less than a mile away, behind them on the desert floor, there were two trucks almost identical to the one he was in at the moment. His heart leaped automatically. Perhaps the tail end of the smugglers' convoy had escaped after all, he thought.

But then he realized, no; these trucks had police markings. And his heart leaped once again, for exactly the opposite reason. Perhaps Captain Mariner and Major Ibrahim were still on his trail after all!

Richard shaded his eyes, wishing poignantly that he still had Saiid's incredibly powerful Zeiss Victory 8 X42 T*FL binoculars. That way at least he would be able to make out a little more about the three trucks less than a mile ahead on the flat sand and get some idea of who was in them. On his left, up in the cab, Sabet was speaking calmly and forcefully into a portable radio. Beyond her was the highest part of the collapsed dune, the midpoint at which they proposed to start looking for survivors once Fawzi was up to speed. On his right, the twelve soldiers of the police command stood, awestruck, just waiting for someone to take command and tell them what to do. Sabet was speaking in Egyptian Arabic but Private Kareem, one of Ibrahim's men, was standing closest to Richard and translating for him.

'The road is completely blocked, Captain Fawzi,' Sabet said in Arabic, and Kareem echoed a moment later in strongly accented American English. 'But it is worse than that. We have driven along the sand to the site of the main collapse where we saw the trucks go under. I estimate that at least three trucks, as full of people as our trucks are, all buried beneath the sand. That's at least thirty-six, not counting drivers and anyone else in the cabs. It is unlikely there will be many survivors but I urge you to send as many men as possible as quickly as you can with the necessary equipment to start digging them out. If Captain Mariner and I are correct then there will be innocent captives as well as smugglers guarding them in all of the vehicles. Of course, I and the men with me will do what we can starting at once, but I urge you to be as quick as you can with back-up.'

Richard gave a curt nod. The sergeant was right. Time was of the essence here. It would mean losing sight of the other trucks further up ahead. In fact, they had started moving off as soon as Sabet's truck began to roll forward, and they had kept going even when the police trucks stopped and they got down to start searching for survivors. Somehow it never occurred to him that the smugglers would come back for their buried colleagues or their captives. But there was at least a chance that Nahom and Tsibekti were buried here somewhere under the drifting sand in any case. They'd better get busy if they were going to save anyone at all. 'Are there spades or shovels in those trucks, Private?' he asked.

'Sure,' Kareem answered. 'Shovels, flashlights, all kind of emergency equipment.'

'Right. Then let's get on it. Time is of the essence.'

Sabet joined them and the three of them went to the back of the trucks and called the men over to join them. They unloaded the emergency equipment as fast as they could – everything from spades to first aid, then, spades in hand, they ran over to the long slope of shifting red sand and set to work as best they could.

Richard was not in the least surprised to note that Sabet led from the front. She could have hung back, giving orders; she could have busied herself with sorting out the first aid stuff. Instead, she rolled her sleeves up, tucked her headscarf across her nose and mouth, then fell-to with such energy that you might have thought it was her own family buried beneath the shifting red slope. Richard mimicked her in every regard and buried his spade in the sand just beside hers.

As they dug feverishly in spite of the bludgeoning heat of the sun, Richard felt rather than saw the others joining them. It was no great surprise to find Kareem and Ibrahim's other man beside them, but after a few moments the men from Captain Fawzi's command joined in as well, led by Saqr, the driver of their truck. Richard had a fleeting thought that the sergeant wasn't going to have too much trouble keeping this mixed bunch of half-soldiers and half-policemen behind her after all. Not after this.

Just as it was Sabet who started digging first, it was Sabet who found the first truck. She was at the bottom of a wide depression, with Richard and several others fighting to keep the sloping sides from slithering down on top of her, when her spade hit metal. She stopped digging at once and, as she had done every few minutes since they started, she called out. There was no reply. Gently, gingerly, she began to ease the sand away from whatever she had found. And so she revealed the rib of a cage that had supported the canvas covering to the rear passenger compartment. A moment more of careful exploration revealed several things – none of them very positive. The rib led to a downward curve at one end and a low metal side at the other. The truck had been knocked over by the pressure of the sand, therefore. And the rib had almost certainly only survived because the canvas shrouding it had been torn away by the sand that was filling the vehicle before the weight of the grains on the cloth could damage the hollow strut. In all probability, whoever had been in the rear section of the vehicle would now be piled one on top of another hard against the road surface. The odds were that they would have been dragged some distance – either as the truck skidded forward or was pushed back by the weight of the sand. And even if this had not happened, they were still somewhere beneath several more metres of red soil. Several more tons of it, in fact. And none of them was likely to be alive.

Sabet stopped digging, apparently exhausted. The others also paused, and as they did so heard a muffled tapping sound from the sloping pile of sand on the east side of their depression. 'That's about where I'd guess the driver's cab to be,' said Richard. 'Now that we know where the truck itself is, thanks to Sergeant Sabet, perhaps we should extend our excavation in this direction.'

It took them another fifteen minutes to uncover the miraculously unbroken driver's nearside window. Beneath the glass, like a swimmer trapped under an ice sheet, a bearded face peered up at them, eyes wide with terror and wet with relief. 'Do we risk opening the window?' wondered Richard. 'Or do we try and uncover the whole door?'

'Go with the window,' ordered Sabet. 'To uncover the whole door we'd have to make the hole much, much wider – and risk standing on the glass into the bargain.'

'Right,' said Richard, standing back, unsteadily, on the slope of sand. 'See if you can get him to wind the window open, otherwise we'll have to break it.'

Sabet moved forward until she was looking down into the submerged cab. Richard noted that her usually immaculate white uniform was so completely covered in red sand that her badges of identity and rank were completely obliterated. She pulled the headdress off her face and smiled down at the man in the cab. When she gestured for him to wind down the window he must have thought he had been transported to paradise and was about to meet an immortal *houri*. With his wide eyes fixed unwaveringly upon her, he obeyed and the window squealed down as the sand grains on the rubberized edge scored the glass. Once the window was open, he reached upwards and Sabet stood back while two of her men pulled him up to safety.

'Is there anyone else in there?' Sabet asked gently as the rescued man stood unsteadily, uncertainly on the shifting sand beside her, safe at last. Richard understood the question from her gestures.

Kareem supplied a quiet translation of the answer: 'Only the fool, Basir, and he broke his neck when the truck tipped over. Then he smashed the window with his head and left most of his face on the highway. He wouldn't have been worth your time even if he had still been alive.'

Oh, this guy's a charmer, thought Richard ironically. We did the right thing pulling him out. But his description of what happened to the unfortunate Basir gave him a sickeningly clear idea of what probably happened to the people in the back before the collapsing dune brought the truck to a final halt and buried what was left of them.

Sabet wasn't finished with the rescued driver. 'I heard there were several Eritreans with you,' she said, and Kareem stumbled over the word Eritreans. 'Were they in your truck?'

'No. They were up ahead, in the lead trucks with Amir.'

'Amir?'

'The leader.'

'I see. And you are?'

'Hakim. What is your name, beautiful saviour?'

'I am Sergeant Sabet of the police service. And you are under arrest for people smuggling. But I suspect that will only be the first of many charges . . .'

Captain Fawzi and his rescue team arrived mere moments after the arrest of Hakim, whose name, Kareem explained, meant *wise*.

'He turned out to be less than wise after all,' chuckled the policeman as Sabet, Richard and he led the sand-covered but elated team back to their trucks, content to let Fawzi and his men take control of the disaster area, keen to get moving in pursuit of the ill-named Hakim's heartless, cowardly smuggler colleagues, especially now that they were certain their primary objectives, Nahom and Tsibekti, were still alive and in dire need of help.

While Fawzi's men piled out of their transports and earth-movers, ready to begin their painstaking work, Sabet and her men gathered round their two trucks and began to dust each other down. Because of her rank and gender, Sabet had to do the best she could without anyone else's help. Richard looked over

Kareem's shoulder as they patted clouds of red grit off each other and frowned with sympathy, all too well aware that he himself could not offer any aid or advice without destroying his colleague's standing and reputation. Unless they went back to Nekhel for a shower and a change of clothes, they were all going to find their various skin-folds and creases packed with highly irritating lines of grit, and the intrepid sergeant was likely to suffer more than most because there was no question of going back. They were headed for Taba and the last of the smugglers, no matter how dangerous and uncomfortable the ride was likely to be.

After ten minutes or so, they had done the best they could, so they stowed the emergency equipment and piled back aboard. Ironically, the only man there who was anything like clean was the prisoner, Hakim the Wise, who was now – willingly or not – going to join the rescue attempt. Had the cab been squashed before, now it was like a sardine tin with the ex-smuggler's lean, clean body wedged between Richard and Sabet, whose positions on the bench seat had been reversed so that Richard was now beside the driver and the sergeant was wedged hard against the door. This time the driver looked respectfully across at the sergeant before he switched on the engine, clearly waiting for her orders.

'It's like Major Ibrahim observed,' she said in English for Richard's benefit, though her icy gaze was fixed on the prisoner. 'There is one trail. It leads from here to Taba. One road. One trail.'

'I don't think he foresaw that the one trail would get buried beneath a passing dune, though . . .' countered Richard.

'It was the will of Allah,' opined Saqr suddenly, and revealing that he spoke some English at least.

'It was certainly unexpected,' allowed Sabet. 'But now, in case there are any more surprises, we have a guide.' Then she turned to Saqr and began to give her orders in liquid Arabic. This was clearly as much for Hakim's benefit as for Saqr's, because as the quiet directions proceeded, the wiry little prisoner stiffened and glanced across at Richard with a look reminiscent of a rabbit caught in a speeding steamroller's headlights.

It was the best part of ninety miles to Taba, with the sprawling little Bedouin township of El Thamad roughly halfway along the mostly deserted desert highway. For the hour it took them to get

there, Sabet quietly but efficiently grilled Hakim, who had already
been petrified by her conversation with Saqr. And clearly, whatever she had said must have made a profound impression on the
prisoner, thought Richard, to whom the flow of Arabic meant
nothing at all. For the rat-like little people trafficker was already
terrified at the thought of what Amir, the leader with the evil
eye, might do to him when he found out that his erstwhile
colleague was alive and in police detention.

But to be fair, Sabet's questions seemed innocent enough at
first – even though the information that meant so little to Hakim
was in many ways of vital importance to her. As he drove, with
swiftly increasing confidence and speed – applauded once again
by the Hand of Fatima hanging from the rear-view, Saqr suddenly
took over Private Kareem's duties as translator – though his
English was at once a little less American and a lot less fluent.

'She ask how many trucks carry Amir men and prisoners. He
say six. Three gone under earth pile. He was last he saw other
two go down.'

That means they have only half of their men left, calculated
Richard with brutal practicality. How many would they need to
guard Nahom, his sister and their other victims? Four per truck?
Six? Suddenly twenty-four well-armed policemen looked as
though they would easily outgun their quarry.

'Hakim ask did we see Amir trucks? Sergeant say we did
but they drove fast away. Hakim ask did we see brown car?
Brown car was with the trucks. Sergeant say we see no car.
Hakim say car likely buried also. Two men in car. Men from
hospital in Sharm, work with Amir long time. Bring African
boy and crusader's AmEx cards with PIN number. Lose boy.
Keep cards. Thought boy was dead. Big mistake. Look for ATM
in El Thamad. Try cards there.'

So, thought Richard, my cards are now buried under a couple
of thousand tons of Egyptian desert, unless the men in the car
gave them to Amir, the leader, before the dune stamped on them
like a couple of ants at a picnic. Thank God I cancelled them.

'Captain Mariner, can you call Captain Fawzi on the radio and
warn him there's a car under there as well, please? The two-way
is in the glove compartment in front of you. The frequency is
pre-set.'

It took Richard an instant to realize that this was Sabet and she was talking to him. 'Yes,' he said. 'Of course.'

He pulled the walkie-talkie out of the glove compartment and put it to his ear. He pressed the button on the side and waited for connection. As he did so, a thought occurred to him, prompted by the probable fate of the car – something he hadn't thought of while considering what had happened to the trucks. Fuel. A squashed car would likely result in a ruptured petrol tank. Trucks on their sides, under tons of dry sand would also likely be leaking – and the sand might well be soaking the gas up rather than letting it run away. The connection came through. 'Captain Fawzi, this is Richard Mariner. Sergeant Sabet has asked me to alert you to the probability that there is a motor car buried alongside the trucks. You might also want to be alive to the possibility that there is a danger from spilt petrol soaking into the sand where you are working.'

'Thank the sergeant for her information. We will take care,' answered Fawzi stiffly. 'Is there anything else?'

Richard looked across at Sabet. She shook her head decisively. She was clearly keeping Fawzi on a 'need to know' footing. In case he tries to muscle in on whatever happened in El Thamad or Taba, taking credit away from Ibrahim.

'Not at the moment, Captain. Out.' Richard broke contact.

As Richard put the walkie-talkie back in the glove compartment, Sabet's interrogation of the unfortunate Hakim went up a notch. Once again, Saqr came to his aid. 'Sergeant say what is plan? Hakim say what plan? Sergeant say what will Amir do with Africans? Hakim say he knows nothing. She better ask Amir if she ever catch up with him. She say we catch up in El Thamad if he's waiting there to find ATM for crusader's AmEx card. We arrest the whole lot. Unless they want to fight it out. But we have soldiers well trained and fully armed. Amir and his people better give in or else they die.'

El Thamad, thought Richard. The Tombstone of the Sinai. It looked as though they were heading for an Egyptian OK Corral. But at least he was on the same side as Wyatt Earp.

NINE
Taba

As they pulled into El Thamad, Richard began to suspect that the chances of a shoot-out here were slim after all. And that was probably just as well, now that he thought of it. Because he remembered suddenly the clear view Saiid's Zeiss binoculars had given him of what looked like the business end of a Man-Portable Air Defence system sticking out of the load on one of the smugglers' camels. It was just conceivable that what he'd seen was something else – something actually harmless – and he'd mistaken it for a lethal MANPAD. Certainly, Amir's men hadn't shown any inclination to use it against the chopper – and they could have done so quite easily if they had wanted to. But they had made their escape without escalating matters – and retained a very valuable sale item if what he had seen was what he thought it was: a Russian 9K38 Igla. And the fact that they had not wasted their weaponry on the helicopter which posed an immediate, nearly overwhelming threat, made it seem to him highly unlikely that they would set up an ambush to use the same precious weapons on a couple of trucks in pursuit at least an hour or more behind.

Then again, if the smugglers were carrying anti-aircraft and anti-tank systems like that, perhaps they had all been in the three trucks lost beneath the sand. There was a logical argument suggesting that they might well be in the rearmost trucks – ready to see off any pursuers who came too close. But somehow he doubted it. Anyone firing an Igla over the tailgate of a truck would likely immolate everyone and everything behind him. Air defence systems were by no means indoor fireworks. Had he been Amir, the leader of a group of smugglers, he'd have kept artillery like that close at hand. In the lead truck, where he would ride himself. And he just knew in his bones that Amir would be doing the same.

Sabet might well have more men with her now that Amir's caravan had been reduced by half. But a couple of Igla missiles would more than even the score if they ever did catch up and get close enough to force Amir's hand.

It was with these dark thoughts in his mind that Richard began to look around the outskirts of El Thamad, for it seemed to him like an excellent place from which to mount an ambush. Half the houses of the little Bedouin township were empty and on the verge of ruin. There seemed to be no people about – no one, at any rate, who might need the services of a bank or an ATM. The first life he saw was a little herd of scrawny, flop-eared black and white piebald goats that ambled across the highway as blithely as the one that the late, unlamented Tariq had crashed into, nearly killing Nahom. There was no one herding them. Nor was there anyone seemingly in charge of the next living thing – a camel sitting by the roadside with its legs folded under its swollen belly, its head turning to watch them pass with all the disdain of an outraged duchess. The shamaal was still blowing powerfully enough to be carrying sand out of the Sinai's extension of the Great Sand Sea in the north and depositing it on the slopes astride the Wadi El Thamad to the south. The air over the little dustbowl of a town was thick and red. The light blood-coloured and shadowy. Even as they neared the town centre, all Richard could make out were dark, distorted figures hurrying between ill-defined buildings, their robes billowing in the wind, their keffiyehs over their faces and their dark glasses over their eyes, like alien life-forms in some strange and sinister Sci-Fi movie.

The desolation of the place abruptly gained a further edge of danger as Sabet observed quietly, 'We're in the Red Zone now. The border with South Sinai is down there beyond the hills to the south. We'll be in the Red Zone almost all the way to Taba, so keep an extra eye out.'

'Is safe,' opined Saqr. 'Jihadists, Ansar Bayt al-Maqdis men and ISIS men are all up in the north near Gaza. But we watch out for army . . .'

'And keep our ID to hand,' added Sabet.

'Has Hakim got any ID?' wondered Richard. 'I didn't see him bring anything out of the truck.'

'I'm his ID,' said Sabet. 'Me and the handcuffs.'

'Even so,' said Richard, 'let's hope we're not stopped by any trigger-happy security patrols.'

'Let's hope Amir and his crew are stopped instead,' said Sabet thoughtfully. 'I doubt they'll even have slowed down here by the look of things. But if a security patrol or checkpoint stops them, then we'll have a better chance of catching up.'

'And even more guns on our side,' added Saqr with quiet satisfaction.

Richard nodded and kept to himself the thought that if this road was one of Amir's regular routes then he either knew the men in the patrols and check points he was likely to encounter or he knew ways to get past them unmolested.

The only sign of modern life in the town came as they pulled into the petrol station. The place looked battered and only half built. But there were petrol pumps, a little glass-fronted shop with a promising array of ill-stacked shelves and half full fridges and freezers. And there were facilities – what the Americans called 'comfort facilities', without much comfort, thought Richard as he went through the door to the men's room to find that it consisted of a long wall of red mud stained with the leavings of the men who had visited the place before him. He fervently hoped that Sabet's facilities were less basic. Whether she used them or not he never knew, because as he came out of the men's room while the others all piled in, Saqr and Kareem with the prisoner between them, he found her in earnest conversation with the proprietor of the petrol station in the front of the mercifully cool little shop.

The trucks had an operational range of five hundred miles on full tanks and they had both been filled that morning in Nekhel, so Sabet didn't need any fuel. But she needed water for her command; though by the look of the nearest packages, jars and tins, the use-by dates were so long past that they would be better waiting until they hit Taba before they looked for anything to eat. Apart from the water and the facilities, she was also keen to glean any information that the petrol station owner might be persuaded to part with. Richard wandered around the dusty shelves as the sergeant interrogated him. To begin with he understood nothing of their conversation, but after a few moments Saqr joined him.

'Sergeant ask if man see three trucks like ours. Man say yes. Trucks stop here an hour ago. Fill up with petrol. Not take much – tanks half full already. Lucky. New supplies not due from Belayim Petrolium till next week. Men used the facilities. All men from the trucks use facilities, take water. But not much petrol. Sergeant need petrol? Sergeant say no. She ask, What were men in trucks like? Man say he see only one of them up close – Bedouin chief with one bad eye. This man pay for what they take. Three men put fuel in trucks then come to shop for to carry drinks. Everyone else stay in trucks. Bedouin man pay. Not like army and police requisition now, pay later, much, much long time later – if they ever pay at all. Bedouin man offer AmEx cards but AmEx machine out of order here. Ask for ATM. None in town. Pay cash. Egyptian pounds. Pay for petrol. Pay for drinks. Coke, Fanta, Sprite, Hayat water. Man ask, Sergeant need water for men? Sergeant say yes. Sergeant pay cash like Bedouin man, not Security Force requisition. Only water left. But Sergeant say water is all she wants.'

Sabet called the driver over then. He loaded up with gallon plastic bottles of water from the fridges and staggered out. A moment or two later Private Kareem and several others came in and also loaded up. By the time they were finished, the shop was out of water and Sabet, by the look of things, was a good deal poorer. Richard briefly considered buying himself a two-litre bottle of Fanta but almost immediately decided against it. He was one of Sabet's men at the moment. He would drink what the troops drank, though it went against the grain to take what he could easily afford from a woman who was probably cash strapped herself.

But then, on the other hand, thought Richard, she was another several notches more popular with her parched and sand-covered command. And the water waiting for him in the lead truck's cab was cold, clear, and as welcome as the finest champagne.

As soon as they were back on the road, Sabet returned to her interrogation and, as the eastern outskirts of El Thamad faded into the red mist in the rear-view, Saqr took up his translation duties once again. Or at least Richard thought he had until he realized that Saqr was voicing his own thoughts. He had changed

into the cheerily garrulous character Richard had briefly wished
for earlier. Saiid's amused voice echoed in his memory: *Be careful
what you wish for. The djinn of this place have a wicked sense
of humour.*

'The road itself dangerous between here and Taba,' Saqr
observed. His grasp of English got no better, but Richard became
more adept at filling in the blanks. 'The floods of May 2014 did
much damage to this road, and to the side road from Dahab and
Newebia that runs up Wadi Watir, as well as to the town itself
and the Taba Heights resort. Under the circumstances, repairs
have been slow to start and even slower to complete.' His foot
eased off the accelerator and the Hand of Fatima stopped jumping
and rattling.

'Floods?' enquired Richard. 'I don't think I heard about them.'

'They were not widely reported,' explained Saqr. 'I don't think
anyone was killed but a good deal of damage was done both to
the town and the resort as well as to the roadways. I think they
were even planning to close the airport. Not that any of your
tour companies or airlines fly in there any more. Like Dahab,
and like Sharm to a certain extent, Taba is squeezed between the
mountains and the sea. The floods rushed down the wadis on the
mountainsides and straight through the buildings. I have seen
pictures on YouTube. It looks like the Japanese Tsunami. But the
water is red, not black.'

'If that was back in 2014,' said Richard, 'there's been time to
make repairs, surely.'

'Some have been started. Some have not yet been completed,
including repairs to this roadway. Most of the hotels on Taba
Heights have been seen to. They are supported by international
chains. Sol Y Mar, Movenpick, Hyatt, Hilton. Money comes in
from Spain, Germany, America . . . Especially as Taba Heights
is in the Amber Zone, and still a popular tourist destination,
though not for tourists from Spain, Germany or America who,
like the British, have been warned off by their governments.
People still come from Russia, Eastern Europe, Israel.'

'But Taba City itself is in the Red Zone, isn't it?' asked Richard.

'That is so,' confirmed Saqr. 'Local money – money from
Cairo – has been a little slower to flow towards Taba City.'

Suddenly Sabet was joining in the conversation. 'That is why,

according to Hakim, Amir and his smugglers are heading for
Taba Old Town, down by the docks. There are areas there which
are effectively still derelict. They can get themselves sorted out
before they move on.'

'Move on from the docks?' probed Richard.

'On to boats and away across the Gulf,' she confirmed grimly.
'Out of our jurisdiction. Unless we stop them first.'

They were coming up out of the erg-type sand desert now into
the more mountainous reg. Richard was reminded of the
Wilderness of Sin as the red, green and black-banded hill slopes
gathered themselves into wadis, all of which seemed to flow
north or south, at right angles to the all too weather-beaten road.
The truck ground up a steepening incline as, on either side, but
especially to the north, even deeper in the Red Zone, the sharp
red peaks scored the sky like the claws of the leopards that once
roamed here.

Suddenly Richard's attention was distracted. For low in the
sky immediately above them a passenger jet came roaring through
its short finals, flaps down and wheels unfolding from the
fuselage. Richard ducked without thinking. That massive under-
carriage looked low enough to take the top off the truck. The air
behind the huge turbofans wavered, hotter even than the shamaal.
As though approaching Kai Tak through the high rise apartments
of old Hong Kong, the jetliner seemed to be swooping between
the rock walls of the north-facing wadi, its wingtips seemingly
mere feet from the jagged peaks. 'He's getting ready to land at
Taba International,' observed Sabet.

'Must be Russian,' said Saqr. 'Or Swiss.'

'The markings look like EgyptAir,' offered Richard, 'and they
both only fly Airbuses and Boeings. But you're right. I think it
was a Tupolev.' He craned forwards to see the great jet slide
away along the valley, settling towards the nearby airport. 'Maybe
its Czech Airlines,' he said. 'Or Orenair. I hear they still fly in.'

So they were all looking upwards as they came over the crest
of the hill. The road ahead fell steeply into a complexity of land
forms gathered round an unexpected road junction. Most obvious
was the wadi coming up from the south, containing a wide,
black-top road which joined theirs at the bottom of the slope
down which they were suddenly rolling. Rocking and rolling,

actually, thought Richard as he dragged his gaze away from the plane and looked down at the state of the disintegrating road beneath their wheels. The wadi the jet was apparently following had caused some serious degradation here when last it flooded. Beyond the junction with the road from the south, the Nekhel–Taba road ran on across a short, flat plain before starting to climb another hillside more than half a mile distant. But the road surface on the far slope was in even worse shape than the one they were bumping over now. Once again a red-walled valley led off to the north over there, and it was clear that sometime in the recent past this too had flooded, not only tearing the road surface into tarmacadam boulders, but washing most of them away down the slope into the bargain.

Which, all things considered, explained why the three trucks they had been pursuing all day were apparently stuck halfway up it.

The moment Sabet's trucks came over the crest, however, the smugglers, who must have been keeping careful watch, fearful of this very eventuality, came piling out of the stranded vehicles, brandishing their rifles.

His mind suddenly full of forebodings and Igla anti-tank rockets, Richard shouted, 'Look out!'

Sabet demanded, 'Can you get off the road?'

'Up that wadi,' suggested Richard, gesturing to the valley that the low-flying plane had just followed. But the quick-thinking Saqr was already in action, slewing the six-wheeler round in a tight curve and doing yet more damage to the crumbling road surface as he roared down the slope of the road's raised causeway and into the shelter of the mercifully dry wadi. Richard glanced in the rear-view above the waving Hand of Fatima and was relieved to see the second truck was hot on their tail. As soon as the valley wall had them safely hidden, both trucks skidded to a halt, kicking up swirling clouds of yet more red dust, which was whipped away instantly by the shamaal as it came funnelling fiercely down the valley as though one of the jet's engines was wedged up there, running at full blast.

That's certainly how it felt, thought Richard as he jumped down on to the slippery, pebble-strewn slope. But he had no real time for reflection, for he was in action at once following Sabet, Kareem and Ibrahim's other man up the slope to the edge of the valley from where they could look down at their enemies. All around him, Captain Fawzi's Nekhel contingent came running wordlessly up from the trucks on the valley floor, the only sounds coming from them the clatter of their boots on the stony surface and the metallic clicking of their weapons being cocked. Last of all came Saqr, dragging Hamid along by the chain between his handcuffs. The reluctant prisoner was not coming quietly. A nonstop whine of pleading, alternating with a little threatening and some self-righteous indignation, tumbled from his thin, down-turned lips. Richard went with these two up to the ridge beside Sabet. '*Ekhres!*' she spat at Hamid and he was instantly silent. 'Get down,' she added in English, but Richard was already flat on his belly on the furnace-hot ground.

Richard slithered forwards, bitterly regretting yet again that he had not thought to borrow Saiid's Zeiss binoculars, especially as the sun was beginning to sink westwards behind them, so there was little chance of anything reflecting in the lenses to give his position away. In fact, taking everything into account, Sabet's little command were not in too bad a position here. They had the high ground. They could move if they wanted for their trucks were OK and the road still holding together. The sun was behind them and shining into the eyes of Amir's smugglers, who might have taken shelter on the lip of the lower wadi now, but who would have to expose themselves if they wanted to get back to their trucks. Had Sergeant Sabet been a little more like Julius Caesar, things would have gone from bad to worse for Amir and his men.

And the smuggler seemed to know this. He did the only thing he could do under the circumstances. Relying on the old maxim that attack is the best form of defence, he opened up with everything he had. Everything, thankfully, except the MANPAD missiles, thought Richard as he ducked beneath the rock wall as ricochets and splinters began to fly. He looked around the police privates who were also exercising a sensible amount of self-preservation and made a mental list of the firepower at their disposal. Sabet had a Helwan nine-millimetre handgun. The others of her command were all clutching Al Maadi-made AKM assault rifles. It was hard to assess what the opposition had, but Richard was rapidly beginning to suspect that although there were fewer of them, they were better armed – not even counting the MANPAD missiles. He racked his brains and taxed his photographic memory to the limit, but he couldn't remember seeing any identifiable small arms when he was looking through Saiid's binoculars. The Egyptian security forces had Minimi light machine guns and he could have used one right at this moment. For he suspected most forcefully that they were being shot at with something equivalent – or even heavier. Something along the lines of an FN MAG 7.62mm GPMG, for instance.

Even so, Sabet was not about to sit still. She rapped out several orders which clearly added up to 'Stay down till I tell you different!' and was in motion, even before Richard had finished his train of thought, snaking her way over to the lower slope at the mouth of the wadi which had not yet received any enemy fire. Kareem and his buddy followed her. Saqr and Hamid the Foolish followed them so Richard joined the little sortie, falling in behind the reluctant smuggler. The move was a wise one and the position Sabet chose gave a good view across the crossroads without exposing them to any more enemy fire. It was immediately clear why Amir had ordered his heaviest guns to lay down such a weight of fire. The trucks were surrounded by people – smugglers and prisoners alike by the look of things – who were busily heaving the massive vehicles forward, lending their shoulders to help the snarling motors as they eased the vehicles forward in the lowest gear up on to the more solid section of the road ahead.

'This is a good position,' Kareem said in English. 'We could do some damage from here.' He caressed his AKM meaningfully.

'No,' said Sabet at once, also in English – not so much to benefit Richard as to keep Hakim in the dark for the moment. 'We only have a field of fire on the trucks and the people around them. We can't tell from here whether they're smugglers or victims. I don't want any more of those prisoners dead. We don't open fire until we can see whatever machine guns are firing at us. Then we fire back at them.'

'We need to get even higher to do that,' said Richard. 'Mind if I try?'

'I'm not sure Major Ibrahim would allow it,' said Sabet.

'But the major's not here. Let me borrow a really good shot and his rifle and we'll see what we can do without putting ourselves at too much risk. A little sniping, at least.'

'That would be me,' said Kareem. 'I'm the best shot in the major's command except for yourself, Sergeant . . .'

'Very well,' she said. 'But if you get yourselves killed I'll have you up on a charge when we get back!'

'That was a joke,' explained Kareem as they ran, crouching back up the wadi.

'Was it? I'd never have worked that out!' gasped Richard.

'Yes. A joke.' Kareem was very serious. And heart-warmingly protective of his superior. 'She is a most unusual sergeant!'

'She's certainly the strangest one I've ever come across,' agreed Richard cheerfully.

The conversation, such as it was, took them past the others, from whom Kareem collected some more ammunition for his AKM, and deeper into the wadi. The walls here were steeper but not impossible to climb. The pair of them scrambled upwards, glad of the afternoon shadows which were allowing the lower slopes to cool a little. The rocks were searingly hot as they reached the top of the slope however. The crest of the wadi was lined with rocks and boulders varying conveniently from the size of a head to the size of a Halloween pumpkin. It would take a very acute pair of eyes indeed to discriminate between stones and skulls. They eased forward and found themselves looking down over the lip of the opposite wadi half a mile distant, beside the stranded trucks. With the light behind them, it was easy enough to see down on to the little machine gun nest that the smugglers had set up. And they were using a Minimi light machine gun by the look of things, though there were more men with semi-automatics around the lip of the little depression also blazing away. Even had Richard and Kareem not been so well positioned, the muzzle flashes and the smoke of discharge would have given the enemy position away. But as things were, Richard reckoned Kareem had a clear shot. And if he was as good as he boasted, the men behind the hyperactive Minimi were in for a very nasty surprise.

And they didn't have much time for playing around, thought

Richard, because two of the trucks were already up on the solid
roadway, and every pair of shoulders at the smugglers' disposal
was jammed against the tailgate of the third. Richard knew
better than to hurry a sniper, and in any case, Kareem could
see the larger picture as clearly as he could himself, so he held
his peace and watched as the young policeman set himself up
for his first shot. In order to do this, he slid down into a deeper
incline that looked straight down at the machine gun emplace-
ment, but closed off the wider view like a pair of blinkers on
a thoroughbred racehorse.

'It's the wind,' said Kareem conversationally in English, and
revealing the soul of a gun-lover as he spoke. Charlton Heston
reborn, thought Richard as he listened. 'I have to make allowance
for the shamaal. Over half a mile or so it will make a difference.
But at least it's blowing steady, not gusting too badly. And this,'
he added, 'is not a sniper rifle. Although it is the most accurate
AKM I have ever handled. I'd like a scope to be sure, though.
And of course I'd rather have a Dragunov, a British L115A3. Or
one of those new American M24's that are accurate at nearly
two miles . . .'

By the time he finished speaking, Kareem was set up. He fell
silent, concentrating. Richard waited, equally silently. He would
have given much to climb back up to where he could see more
clearly how the third truck was progressing up the slope, but the
position they were now in looked down on the machine gun nest
and not much more. While he considered this fact, Kareem
squeezed off his first shot. One of the men firing the Minimi
slumped sideways. His mate sprang up and ran down the hillside
shouting and waving his arms, followed by the others from the
little nest. Kareem squeezed off another series of shots to hurry
them on their way, but they were all still upright as they vanished
from sight. The surprise was so effective that they even left the
Minimi and a couple of their own guns behind. The withering
rate of fire ceased immediately. As soon as the last of them was
out of sight, Richard rolled back down the slope. 'I think there's
another machine gun somewhere out there,' he said. 'See if you
can spot it. I need to see what's happening with the last truck.'

But as he joined Sabet once again, it was not the last truck
that claimed his attention. It was the sight of the smuggler standing

beside it, out of everyone's field of fire unless someone wanted to risk standing on the spot where Richard's head was concealed, hopefully indistinguishable from the surrounding rocks. A smuggler standing, looking very much as though he knew exactly what he was doing with a shoulder-launched missile in position ready to fire, its tell-tale green tube, so dark it had looked black when Richard had first glimpsed it, sitting snugly beside his right ear. It was the nightmare scenario Richard had feared. 'Down!' he shouted. 'That thing's designed to take out tanks and aircraft. It could kill most of us with one shot!'

Obediently, they all slid down into the relative safety of the wadi floor. Richard actually found that he was holding his breath.

But instead of the roar of ignition he was expecting there came the whip-crack of a rifle shot, followed by a good deal of shouting and the revving of truck motors, all of which faded into near silence with unexpected rapidity. After a moment, Richard climbed back into position, with his head amongst the boulders. All the smugglers' trucks were gone. Providentially, so had the man with the MANPAD. In their place, sitting at the crossroad, clearly having just come out of the road leading south to Newbia and Dahab, was the familiar shape of a battered white Land Rover Defender. And Richard didn't need his Zeiss binoculars to make out the unmistakable figure of Saiid standing beside it with a nasty-looking Enfield SA80 assault rifle still smoking at his shoulder.

'One shot took out the man with the Igla,' said Saiid a few moments later. 'Though I don't think I killed him. And the rest seemed keen to move on when they realized they were between a rock and a hard place.'

'I'm not surprised at that,' answered Richard. 'But I am surprised to see you. What on earth are you doing here?'

'Ibrahim sent us,' Saiid explained. 'Though I'd have come in any case. And I suspect the others would have accompanied me no matter what.'

Richard looked past Saiid into the Land Rover's interior. Ahmed the dive master and Mahmood, Captain Husan's lieutenant, both from *Katerina*, waved at him, grinning cheerily. The last time he had seen them was on the way back from the

Wilderness of Sin. 'Ibrahim?' said Richard, raising a hand and a smile for each. 'But why?'

The Bedouin's strange eyes flicked past Richard to watch Sabet as she stood at the mouth of the wadi back up the slope, guiding her two trucks reversing back out on to the road. 'I have no idea,' he said blandly, tongue in cheek. 'None whatsoever. But he did ask me to bring some extra paperwork which he suggests may make things easier for Sergeant Sabet if she has to negotiate with the military authorities in Taba.'

'Still,' said Richard thoughtfully, 'it's an amazing coincidence that you caught up with us when you did – just in the nick of time.'

Saiid smiled and shouldered his rifle. 'Less of a coincidence than you suppose, perhaps. We are part of the twenty-first century, even out here. Captain Fawzi's trucks have GPS beacons on them. All our major police vehicles do. Ibrahim has been tracking your progress all day and keeping me up to date on my cell phone as I drove up through Dahab and Neweiba.'

'Could he track the smugglers as well?'

'No. They aren't carrying GPS beacons. Or cell phones, come to that. Well, they probably are, but they have them disabled for the moment to prevent Ibrahim from doing that very thing. They are also more modern than they look.'

'They've certainly got some modern weaponry.'

'As, you may remember, we do too. But nothing to match an Igla MANPAD guided missile.'

'Yeah. We'd better be extra careful if we come too close to cornering them again.'

'Not *if*,' said Saiid. '*When* . . .'

Alerted by the trouble the smugglers had got themselves into, Sabet ordered her trucks to unload everything and everyone they reasonably could and to drive up the hill along the still solid causeway slope instead of the ruined tarmac of the highway itself. While Saqr and his opposite number ground slowly and carefully up the hill, Sabet led her men in a swift sortie, checking over the positions that the smugglers had taken up in the fire fight. They found one dead man that no one had dared go back for, one Minimi light machine gun, with a good deal of ammunition beside it, and a couple of assault rifles including a new-looking AK 12 which on closer inspection turned out to be chambered to take the same 7.62mm ammunition as the police AKMs. Richard, at last, had the weapon Ibrahim had forbidden him.

And he had a more comfortable ride. As the little convoy pulled away over the crest and down the winding road towards Taba, he was sitting in the Land Rover's front passenger seat beside Saiid. He regretted leaving Sabet, but practicalities as well as comfort dictated the move. Now that the chase was so much closer and his varyingly reliable input no longer so vital, Hakim had been dispatched into the back of the truck. Sabet needed the extra space between herself and Saqr to go through the paperwork that Saiid handed over on Ibrahim's behalf. The last Richard saw of the sergeant before turning back to the Land Rover was her pink-stained figure bent over a large map of Taba and environs spread out across her lap and the empty sections of the truck's bench seat on either side. Piled on the map was a stack of paperwork covered in official-looking Arabic script, in the top corners of which were several photographs, his own included.

They rolled forward soon after he settled himself in the Land Rover and soon the road became better maintained so they picked up speed once again. Several more planes swooped low above them, heading into the International Airport, but the next incident of any note came when they arrived at the crossroads north of the airport itself. Four roads, including the one they had just travelled, stretched away across the hilly desert and Saba stopped them all in the middle. She climbed down and by the time Richard joined her, she had Hakim standing unhappily by her side. 'Talk about *The Road to Hell*,' said Richard as he came up beside her. The look of total incomprehension she shot him established that she was not a Chris Rea fan. But the point was well made. The road they had been following east from Nekhel stretched straight ahead, shimmering into the dusty distance. Its ill-maintained surface spoke of little usage, and the thick covering of sand on the tarmac showed no trace of tyre tracks. 'That's the road down to the border with Israel,' said Sabet. 'I guess they could have gone down there, then swung north and run up towards Gaza.' She swung round to glare questioningly at Hakim, who looked down the road less travelled and shook his head. They had not gone that way. His gesture and the undisturbed sand made that quite clear.

Sabet, Richard and Hakim walked over to the left. 'This road leads north immediately in any case,' she said, shading her eyes to look along a highway that seemed no better maintained or more recently used than the road heading east. 'It eventually leads to Rafa. And a world of sorrow.' Once again, she glared questioningly at Hakim, who twisted his body placatingly like a misunderstood dog.

'This, on the other hand,' she said, turning through one hundred and eighty degrees to lead them over to the road running south, 'this is the road past the airport. The main road down to Taba.' The road surface was well-maintained and, in spite of the shamaal, it was dust-free. 'You did say Amir and his men were definitely going to Taba,' she said, still lost in thought. Then, in the face of Hakim the Ignorant's blank incomprehension, she repeated the question in Arabic.

'*Naam*,' he said, nodding feverishly. '*Naam*.'

'Then that's the way we go,' she decided, and the three of them went back to their vehicles.

The road down to Taba was steep and spectacular. There were near-vertical cliffs on each side that seemed to grip the high, steel-blue sky like the jaws of massive pliers crushing a metal strip. 'I drove down here in May 2014,' said Saiid conversationally. 'I had business in Taba Heights. There were waterfalls pouring over the edges of those cliffs and cascading on to the road here every hundred metres or so. Big waterfalls. Some of them huge, in fact. And the downhill slope of the road channelled it all like an artificial wadi.'

'I saw the videos on YouTube,' added Ahmed's deep boom from the back seat. 'Some of the hotels in Taba were built on the outwash plain of the real wadi. There was water pouring through them, through the reception areas, the ground floor rooms, on out into the gardens and pool areas and on out into the bay. It was incredible. So much damage . . .'

'And we thought the floods in England were bad,' said Richard thoughtfully.

They were silent for a while after that, Richard for one

sidetracked into imagining what the waterfalls flinging themselves off the high skyline must have been like – and how the increasingly steep roadway would have channelled all the millions of gallons down towards Taba and the coast increasingly swiftly and catastrophically. But long before they actually reached the town, the mountain slopes fell back and Richard understood with some relief that the water Saiid described flowing down the road must have washed away across the flat desert areas before it could do too much damage. The junction of the road down from the airport and the main Sharm to Taba coast road was completely undamaged, therefore, and the little convoy was able to swing left with a minimum of fuss, and follow the main road northwards.

The road ran along the edge of the coast for the most part, on that slim little ribbon of level land between the mountains and the sea. The views on either side were spectacular and reminded Richard of diving holidays in Dahab. Almost at once, they found themselves rolling past a small but exclusive-looking hotel complex, dotted with trees and well-packed with buildings. Richard craned to see what was there, and the fact that the road was elevated allowed him to look down on a couple of piers, an unexpected jut of hillside and a good number of beach umbrellas. The hotel buildings were designed in the Moorish style and that feature seemed to run from the roadside down to the beach itself. And then, beyond it, a little way out across the bay, to an island whose steep, rocky sides rose to become the walls of a forbidding-looking fort with unusual crenulations almost in the shape of arrow-heads, similar to those he remembered from the Alhambra palace in Grenada. The castle was tall and strong looking, grey-walled and uncompromising. It dominated the little island on which it sat, seeming to encompass the whole rocky outcrop from the little docking facility on the landward side to the crest of the red rock cliffs on which it stood.

'What on earth is that?' asked Richard, awed. 'It looks almost like Mont St Michel in France.'

'It is the Pharaoh's Island,' said Saiid. 'And the castle is the Fortress of Salah ed-Din. Whom you crusaders call Saladin, I think.'

'It's certainly spectacular,' said Richard, awestruck. And he thought nothing more about it as the road swung inwards and mountains gathered on either side before it swung outwards again and continued to follow the coast.

Less than a mile later, the trucks slowed and the Land Rover followed suit. Slowly, carefully, clearly with eyes skinned, they rolled through what looked like the main port facility near Taba. On the left there were warehouses, blocks of offices, secure areas. To the right, a proper, good-sized commercial pier reaching out into the still, blue water straddled by two smaller jetties suitable for pleasure craft or swimmers. But everything looked deserted. There were no trucks parked among the warehouses. No vessels secured alongside the pier. No lights on amid the gathering shadows on the dark side of the mountains. No activity of any sort – not even goats, dogs or cats. As they eased suspiciously along the road, nothing whatsoever moved. Then they were past the facility and back out on to the coast road, heading north towards Taba Heights – Taba proper – and the border with Israel.

The only time the coast road moved significantly inland again was when it fell back to become the promenade through Taba Heights, which was the next point of interest. Suddenly there were trees on either side of the highway, through which hotels, their pools and their verdant, flower-bright grounds could be glimpsed as the trucks and the Land Rover rolled on. Hotels on the left and beach umbrellas on the right; the hotels becoming blazes of light amid the gathering shadows of evening. Tourists bustled excitedly from shop to shop, hotel to hotel, slowing the little convoy further as they wandered across the road between a maze of sleeping policemen, filling the beach with sunbathing bodies and the sea with swimmers and snorkellers, even though the full weight of the sun was well down behind the mountains now, and the only real brightness came from the red-tipped mountain tops of Saudi Arabia across the bay. Then, just as Richard was getting used to the new, upmarket ambiance and wondering whether the difference in atmosphere came from the fact that he was briefly back in the Amber Zone, the road swung out round white cliffs once more and there was only a stony breakwater between him and the Gulf of Aqaba. Back in the Red Zone almost at once, he thought, looking out at the empty sea as the light on the mountaintops opposite faded and they paled with unsettling rapidity from red to rose to grey.

But then, 'There it is,' said Saiid, and the road swung round another steep cliff outcrop to reveal the outward thrust of Taba itself.

Richard's eyes narrowed automatically, as though if he squinted he would be able to see the smugglers' trucks more clearly. But all there was to see at first was the municipal area of the town – what looked like offices and public buildings on the left – overlooking a square tarmac heliport on the right, then the dark blue of the sea with the red mountains of Saudi and Jordan increasingly close beyond. Here also, there was movement, but nowhere near as much as there had been in Taba Heights. There were tourists hurrying to and from the Movenpick and Hilton resorts. There were gardens, trees, shops and restaurants, all blazingly lit. There were no dark and half-ruined dock facilities. But there were jetties. 'Are any of these big enough to take the kind of vessel the smugglers would need?' wondered Richard. His tone made it clear he didn't think so.

'These are jetties for pleasure craft, swimming and scuba diving,' said Saiid. 'We've only seen one actual pier.'

'Right back along the coast, almost as far as Saladin's Fort,' agreed Richard. 'Where all those apparently deserted dock facilities were.'

The conversation, short as it was, took them past the snowy mound of the Hilton and almost as far as the Israeli border crossing. 'So . . .' said Saiid.

'Turn us round,' said Richard. 'We go back as fast as we can.'

'And hope Sabet sees what we're doing and decides to follow us?'

'Yes. Given only that we don't want her backtracking so suddenly and so quickly that she upsets the Israelis. God alone knows what they'd start throwing at us if they thought we were up to some Jihaddist trick.'

'Ansar Bayt al-Maqdas are called Supporters of Jerusalem because they will kill to bring it under their rule, not because they want to protect it the way it is now,' Saiid observed. 'They're apparently linked with ISIS. And they've supposedly killed people at this very checkpoint early in 2014. If the Israelis think we're anything to do with them, they'll be sending drones.'

'Oh, great,' said Richard. 'Whatever happened to *my enemy's enemy is my friend*?'

Even so, Saiid swung the Land Rover round and headed back through town as fast as the pedestrians and the sleeping policemen would allow. Richard kept an eye on the rear-view mirrors until he was sure that Sabet had come to the same conclusion he had and was turning the trucks to follow the Land Rover. It took a good ten minutes to get back to the municipal area and the heliport, but then the road was clearer and Saiid was able to put his foot down hard. The trucks initially fell much further behind – slowed by the tourists and the traffic calming bumps even more than the Land Rover was, but by the time Saiid was powering down the straighter road towards Taba Heights, they were at least beginning to get free of the busy main drag. They swung right, following the road in from the coast past a facility Richard had hardly registered. Another road led up into the hills closed off by a wall and a gate. Then they were down on the shore again and barrelling into Taba Heights. Once again, pedestrians, crossings and traffic calming measures took their toll. Another ten minutes passed before Saiid got them free of the bustle, and this time there was no sign of Sabet's trucks in the rear-view as they pulled out on to the next clear stretch. 'Nearly there!' said Saiid as he swung the Land Rover round the tall white outcrop and the docking facility was laid bare before them. 'Damn!' swore Richard. The view this time could hardly have been more different. There were three trucks drawn up at the outer end of the jetty and, moored beside them, there was a battered but powerful-looking boat. '*Go!*' shouted Richard, and Saiid floored the accelerator. The Land Rover swung on to the jetty and roared down towards the trucks. Shadows were gathering and there were no lights either on the jetty, in the trucks or aboard the boat – but it was still possible to see the prisoners being roughly herded out of the trucks and over towards the boat. There was only one long, thin gangplank down, however. And at the moment that looked to be blocked by Amir and his immediate cohorts who were apparently going aboard to arrange a reception for their prisoners, and taking aboard the weapons, drugs or whatever else they were smuggling in an assortment of bundles, packages and crates. The deck was bustling with contraband, crewmen and smugglers. The gangplank was jammed and the men and women Richard was here to rescue stood under the guns of the guards on the concrete pier head.

Saiid hit the headlights and the brakes all at the same time. The Land Rover skidded to a halt and the three passengers leaped out, guns at the ready. Richard opened fire first, aiming high above the heads of the dazzled men and women. The other two joined in, doing the same. Then all three dived for cover as their shots were returned, but the smugglers and the boat crew did not aim high. Miraculously none of them was hurt, though one of the Land Rover's headlights and its passenger window were shattered.

Richard hardly had time to catch his breath before Sabet's trucks came roaring round the corner from Taba. Even before they swung on to the pier, their arrival caused confusion among the smugglers. The prisoners were being herded towards the gangplank even though it was still blocked. The men in charge of the smugglers' vessel were shouting at the guards to hurry up and the boat itself was pulling away to the limit of its mooring ropes, putting the gangplank at serious risk of falling into the water, taking everybody with it.

From the top of the wheelhouse a single white searchlight struck back at the Land Rover's one headlight. Saiid put it out immediately with a shot that Kareem the sniper might have envied. Sabet's trucks arrived and the police contingent began to pile out of the back. The smugglers began to panic then. From his position behind the Land Rover, Richard watched them herding their screaming victims off the pier head and on to the gangplank faster than the unstable walkway could be cleared at the inboard end. The result was inevitable. People started falling into the sea. And, Richard saw all too clearly, the first two to go – either by accident or because they were taking a desperate gamble – were Aman and the slight figure next to him.

No sooner did the Eritrean couple tumble into the water than the crew got the gangplank clear. The rest ran aboard with the guards fighting a rearguard, still firing at the Land Rover and the trucks.

Richard wormed forward, consumed with concern that the smugglers would shoot the pair in the water as well, but their focus seemed to be exclusively on the police trucks and the Land

Rover from which a steady stream of fire was issuing. Because of his position, a little further forward than the rest and at an angle to the smugglers' trucks and the boat, he saw the movement on the top of the wheelhouse, just beside the shattered light, before anyone else. He saw it and understood it.

'Watch out!' he bellowed. '*Incoming!*' He rolled away and pulled himself to his feet, sprinting across the concrete pier. Behind him, the others did the same, scattering like a flock of starlings that had just seen a hawk.

The boat pulled away, leaving its mooring ropes and its gangplank to fall into the sea. The smugglers along the main deck rail kept up their automatic fire, emboldened by the fact that their pursuers all seemed to be running away. But then they too were ducking down and looking up, wonderstruck, as the missile from the Igla MANPAD came roaring off the top deck like a space rocket gone astray. It streaked across the pier in an instant and impacted with Saiid's Land Rover like the stroke of doom. The whole vehicle vanished into the heart of a ball of fire that lit up the whole area and released a blast wall that starred the windscreens of the five trucks on the dockside and reduced their canvas coverings to smoking rags. But, mercifully, that was all the damage the explosion caused. While the Land Rover burned like a Viking at his funeral, the men who had been riding in it and hiding behind it began to pick themselves up, safe in the knowledge that even the most warlike of the smugglers was standing, awestruck, watching the destruction as their boat pulled away into the gulf. As they stood up, so did Sabet's men, slowly and shakily. Richard was first to come fully erect. Giving the immolated Land Rover a wide berth, he ran down to the pier head, where he crouched on one knee, looking down into the water. And there, clinging to the discarded mooring ropes, were a lovely woman who could only be Tsibekti and, beside her, looking a good deal less lovely, Aman.

'Are you all right?' he called.

Tsibekti disregarded his question. 'They still have Nahom,' she called in thickly accented English, her tone desperate. 'We have to go after them!'

'You'd better pray,' snarled Aman, 'that they don't decide to come back after *you!*'

'Nobody's going after anybody at the moment, as far as I can see,' said Richard. He looked across the water, feeling, for the first time since he had become involved in this adventure, helpless.

Saiid joined him, towering silently behind his left shoulder. And no sooner had he done so than the cell phone he carried in his right trouser pocket started ringing. He pulled it out and put it to his ear. After a second, he looked down. 'It's for you,' he said, and handed it down to Richard.

Disorientated, almost in a dream state, Richard put the little instrument to his ear. 'Mariner?' he said.

'Hello, you bloody man,' came Robin's brusque voice. 'I'm here on *Katerina*'s bridge with Captain Husan and we're just coming past something that I believe is called Saladin's Fortress. Do tell me if I'm wrong, but I assume you are somewhere near that massive column of fire we can see burning almost dead ahead. Assuming you're not actually *responsible* for it . . .'

TEN
Shamaal

Pushing *Katerina*'s impending arrival to the backs of their minds, Richard and Saiid concentrated on the far more important business of pulling first Tsibekti and then Aman out of the water.

As they eased Tsibekti up into the dancing light of the Land Rover's funeral pyre, Richard was struck with three main impressions about the young woman. The first was her similarity to her twin. The next was her radiant loveliness, which was even more apparent in the flesh than it had been on the pictures on Nahom's phone. Her face was all sculpted lines, huge eyes, sharp cheekbones and a square jaw which should have looked mannish but which somehow seemed the epitome of femininity. A wide, full-lipped mouth parted as she gasped to reveal perfect white teeth. And she had a riot of hair that contrived to look lovely even when reduced to rats' tails by the dirty dockside water.

The third thing that struck him was her modesty, though her culture, religion and her recent experiences should have warned him. Even as Saiid and he were pulling the rope to which she was clinging up the side of the pier, she was dangling one-handed, little more than a black shadow against the shimmering darkness of the water, fishing in the heaving waves for her burqa, which she slung over her shoulder before taking a firm, two-handed grip on the rope, and began to walk up the pier wall into the flickering golden light. She put it on as soon as she was able to stand, and became at once a pair of huge dark eyes staring around guardedly, as though the two-dozen policemen observing her silently were just another set of people smugglers with evil on their minds. And she could be right, thought Richard, as his gaze flashed from her to them and back again. Her clothes were soaking and, under the gathering power of the shamaal, adhered to her in a disturbingly revealing manner – even though she kept pulling the clinging material away from her long thighs and deep chest. Sabet came over at once and moved her to the gathering shadows where the eyes of the men could not follow her so easily. This gave Tsibekti the chance to speak more forcefully, repeating that they had to chase the smugglers' vessel and rescue her brother.

Even before Tsibekti was under Sabet's wing, Richard and Saiid had turned their attentions to Aman. The double-dealing smuggler had used their focus on Tsibekti to try and escape, letting go of the rope, turning and blundering clumsily out into the bay, hampered by his clothing, even though it consisted of little more than jeans and a T-shirt. When Richard and Saiid looked down over the edge of the pier he was some way out in the dark water, fruitlessly following his smuggler friends – a black beach ball of a head with eyes and teeth that glittered when the light caught them. 'It's hopeless,' Saiid called down to him. 'You can't catch the dhow and you can't swim all the way to Saudi. Especially if this wind kicks up much more of a chop. And there are sharks . . .'

'If you keep splashing around like that, you'll be talking to a tiger long before your friends get back,' emphasized Richard. 'Even if you're right and they are about to turn round when they find Tsibekti's gone.'

Aman twisted clumsily and floundered back to the rope. 'They already know she's gone!' he shouted as he took firm hold and pulled his torso clear of the heaving surface. 'Bisrat and I stopped them going over together. Then I slipped and fell in with the silly bitch. But they know. Amir saw what was happening. Just because he has a cast in one eye doesn't mean he's blind. He sees *everything*. They're probably just getting their weapons ready, then they'll be back!' His sneering tone showed how much he wished for his smuggler friends to revenge his pain and humiliation, and how little he understood or cared about the vital information he was giving away.

But the first vessel to come nosing alongside was *Katerina*.

Robin jumped nimbly from the upper deck straight on to the pier even before Captain Husan could order the mooring ropes attached and the gangplank secured, even though the powerful vessel was frisking about like a skittish Derby winner in the gathering wind and the choppy water. She strode across to Richard

194 Peter Tonkin

as Ahmed and Mahmood hurried the other way, heading back to the vessel they usually crewed, worried that whoever was handling the mooring ropes and securing the gangplank might have replaced them as permanent crew members.

In spite of her harsh words on the cell phone, Robin stood on tiptoe to kiss Richard's lean cheek as he handed the bedraggled Aman over to Saiid. 'Everything shipshape, Sailor?' she asked quietly, her wise eyes taking in the blazing wreckage, the serried trucks, the well-armed soldiers, and the fact that Saiid immediately put the protesting Aman in a hammerlock and frogmarched him towards Sergeant Sabet, clearly minded to have the two-faced smuggler under close arrest like his erstwhile colleague Hakim the Silent.

Richard slid one arm around Robin's trim waist and gave her a swift hug. 'Shipshape and Bristol fashion,' he answered. 'Especially now that you're here.'

'Hmmm . . .' she answered, unconvinced. 'I don't think I'm going to be the only new arrival. Any minute now, whatever Taba has in the way of police, security and fire-fighting services are going to come in like Gangbusters. You'd better have a pretty good story to tell them.'

'You're right. But Major Ibrahim sent a load of paperwork up with Saiid. Sergeant Sabet's got it. Hopefully that will cover us and keep the local authorities happy. But there's more than the Taba people to worry about. Aman says that the smugglers will be back.'

'Really? I would have thought their best bet was to cut and run.'

'I'd have thought so too. But apparently not. Maybe there's something we're missing in this nasty little equation. However, my next plan was to chase them and see whether we could rescue Nahom somehow. It's the first thing Tsibekti asked us to do after we pulled her out of the water.'

'Tsibekti? You've rescued Tsibekti?'

'Well,' he allowed. 'She rescued herself. She threw herself off the gangplank while there was some confusion on the pier. She would have brought Nahom with her, but she got Aman by sheer bad luck.'

'So the shoe's on the other foot now: we have her but we still have to rescue Nahom.'

'Looks like it. Tsibekti's certainly up for it in no uncertain terms. And I thought we were in with a chance. I reckon *Katerina* is faster than the battered old dhow they're using. But appearances can be deceptive. They could have a couple of big Perkins turbocharged diesels in her for all I know. It's not unusual for smugglers' vessels to appear deceptively decrepit on the outside but be geared up like powerboats on the inside. Then, if Aman's right and they're coming back after Tsibekti anyway . . .'

Apparently apropos of nothing, Robin suddenly asked, 'What actually happened to Saiid's Land Rover? I assume this *is* his Land Rover doubling as something out of Bonfire Night?'

'Ah,' said Richard. 'That was hit by an Igla . . .'

There was a brief pause. The shamaal gusted again, bringing the stench of burning rubber and a breath of wind from the hottest hole in hell to join the overwhelming roar of the trusty old vehicle's immolation. 'I see,' said Robin. 'So, when Aman's friends return in search of Tsibekti, at the very least they'll be armed with Russian shoulder-launched *missiles* will they?'

'Possibly. They've been reluctant to use them so far though,' answered Richard at his most positive *cup half full*. 'They're probably planning to sell them on at an enormous profit, you see. Using them too often would be like throwing packets of heroin, crack or crystal meth at us. Costly.'

'And that's what you call being *in with a chance*, is it?'

'Yes. They've had lots of chances to use the MANPADs so far but they haven't made much use of them.'

'Tell that to Saiid's poor old Land Rover.'

'I think someone will have to tell it to more than the Land Rover,' observed Richard, tightening his grip on her as several official-looking vehicles led by a fire engine roared off the Taba road and on to the landward end of the pier. 'Sergeant Sabet,' called Richard. 'We have company. I think it's time to get Major Ibrahim's paperwork out.'

But Sabet had seen the new arrivals coming as soon as they swung round the outcrop of cliff, lighting up the tall white rock face with their multicoloured flashing lights; only seeming to move in silence because the roaring of the Rover's funeral pyre drowned out the screaming of sirens and the rumble of racing engines. As she moved towards the newcomers, so the men of both the Sharm and Nekhel commands fell in behind her, leaving Tsibekti standing beside Saiid, who was armed with her handgun and was in charge of Aman and Hamid.

As the fire fighters set up and prepared to hose down the burning wreckage of the Land Rover, Sabet and her men strode past them and closed with the first of the police cars. Except that, thought Richard acutely, because they were in the Red Zone here, the term 'police' would probably actually mean Egyptian Army security. He found himself hoping quite fervently that whatever paperwork Ibrahim had sent up with Saiid would serve to further inter-agency cooperation and keep them all out of the Egyptian military prison.

As it turned out, Ibrahim's documents had an almost magical effect. By the time the Egyptian army fire fighters extinguished the Land Rover, which they managed to do in less than ten minutes, Sabet was back, with the bundle of paperwork tucked under her arm, giving the spreading puddle of fire-fighting foam the widest possible berth as the steadying wind blew it towards the south side of the pier. 'The Taba command will take over here,' she announced as she came up to Richard and Robin. 'I have talked to their commanding officer who knows Major Ibrahim well and is happy to help in any way he can. Private Saqr and the men from Nekhel may stay the night – facilities will be provided – and then take their trucks back to Captain Fawzi in the morning. All five trucks will be impounded in safe storage tonight so that the arms and equipment aboard ours will be secure . . . And any evidence left aboard the smugglers' will be untouched.' Sabet added this almost as an afterthought as, out of the corner of her eye, she saw Saiid, Ahmed and Mahmood disappearing into the rear of one of her own soon-to-be impounded trucks. Saiid had passed her gun to Tsibekti, who was now very competently in charge of the prisoners. 'I and my men from Sharm may please ourselves. We can stay here overnight and then go with the Nekhel men. We can stay and make arrangements to be picked up by someone from Sharm tomorrow. Ourselves and also the smugglers' trucks, unless Major Ibrahim wants to send a forensics team up to go over them for evidence before they're moved. In which case, the trucks can stay where they are, under armed guard, until we're finished with them.'

She took a deep breath, looked around and concluded, 'Or we can go back to base at once and sort out the smugglers' trucks later. If you will take us aboard *Katerina*.'

There was another brief silence, this time underlain by the dying hiss of the cooling wreckage. Sabet added, 'I assume you will be heading straight back to Sharm . . .'

'That's our plan at the moment,' said Richard. He stepped back, apparently thoughtlessly, taking Robin with him, for he still had his arm around her waist. Sabet automatically swung round to maintain eye contact. Her back, therefore, was to the truck from which Saiid and his men were unloading some bulky equipment that was impossible to identify in the shadows. But Richard knew well enough what it would be.

'Then if we may go aboard when you leave . . .' continued Sabet, apparently unaware of the byplay behind her.

'Of course,' said Richard. 'And our three guests?'

'Slightly more problematic,' Sabet shook her head. 'But as the men, Aman and Hakim, are under arrest and in my custody as arresting officer, I may take them with me. And, as Major Ibrahim and I are the ones building the case against the smugglers, we may take our witness Tsibekti too. We have two private soldiers from the Sharm command with us as well, of course.'

'Kareem and his mate.' Richard nodded.

'Will there be room for all of us aboard *Katerina*?'

'I should think so,' said Richard. 'She's designed to sleep twelve guests.'

And so it was agreed. Sabet, her witness Tsibekti, her men and her prisoners would go aboard *Katerina* with Richard, Robin, Saiid, Ahmed and Mahmood. They would all head for Sharm tonight, due to arrive there in a few hours' time. The various contingents split up. The Nekhel men prepared to drive the trucks for which they were responsible into secure accommodation, then go to the Taba command area and mess down. Saiid and the prisoners under Sabet's jurisdiction went aboard *Katerina* – easily enough now that Ahmed and Mahmood had reappeared from wherever they had vanished with the bundle they had liberated from the back of Sabet's truck and were available to hand people off the gangplank and on to the deck. Even people unhappily in handcuffs.

Richard, Robin, Sabet and Tsibekti followed them. Kareem the marksman and his mate brought up the rear. Ahmed and Mahmood then released the gangplank and pulled it aboard as soon as the other crewmen had loosened the mooring ropes. *Katerina* turned, and under Captain Husan's direction began to ease back into the south-running sea lanes, heading back down past Pharaoh's Island and Saladin's Fortress towards Sharm el-Sheikh. Sabet took her prisoners below and locked them – still in handcuffs – in the most secure of the cabins. Then she and Tsibekti explored the yacht's facilities until they found showers, towels and the kind of towelling robes that a Muslim woman could wear in the presence of believers and crusaders alike. As this was the plaything of a Russian oligarch to whom outrageous excess was a way of life, each of the six double suites below had en-suite facilities, so once the women were satisfied it was easy enough for the others to start washing off the red sand the shamaal had showered them with so far today.

As they did this, Robin and the still-grimy Richard joined Husan on the bridge. At once, Richard glanced automatically at the location system, noting that Sharm was one hundred and eighty kilometres to the south. At *Katerina*'s top speed, that was several hours' hard sailing, he thought, even with the strengthening shamaal behind her. And that fact started the short hairs on the back of his neck prickling uncomfortably. It was well past sunset now, and the next few hours were likely to be just about the darkest of the night. If everything went well, they would be back in Sharm soon after one a.m. tomorrow.

But if Aman's threat held any water, then they were likely to be chased – at the very least – almost every metre and minute of the way.

These thoughts were sufficient to occupy Richard as he watched Captain Husan carry the Russian billionaire's bath toy into the southward lanes. Until, in the rapidly deepening darkness, Richard saw the citadel of Saladin's Fortress illuminated by its security lighting. Full of restless tension, he crossed to the starboard side of the bridge, looking vaguely westwards towards the spectacle. But no sooner had he done so than Saiid appeared at the starboard bridge door. 'Come, Captain,' he said quietly. 'We have something to show you.'

Without a further thought, Richard followed Saiid out on to the exterior companionway that led down to the main deck. Robin remained beside Captain Husan, her eyes busy on the boat's displays as well as on the movements of her errant husband. With one last glance back, Richard followed Saiid down on to the weather deck. 'You look,' whispered Saiid. 'You see.'

The pair of them crept up the length of the foredeck to the forecastle, such as it was. There, Richard found Ahmed crouching over the traffickers' Minimi machine gun that Sabet's men had recovered after the fire fight in the mountains north of the airport and which Saiid had smuggled aboard while Sabet was talking to Richard. It was perfectly set and positioned to give the widest possible arc of fire over the bows. Richard smiled, wondering silently what other armaments they had smuggled aboard from Sabet's trucks. What undeclared weaponry, indeed, they might have stowed below from earlier, even less legal, voyages. 'This is excellent,' he said supportively. 'Let's hope we're the ones chasing the smugglers down to Sharm.'

Saiid shrugged. 'It makes no matter,' he said. 'There was nowhere on the poop deck to mount it. We cannot fire backwards – only forwards. If we are chased, we will just have to hope for the best.'

Richard nodded and smiled, even though Aman's bitter words still rang in his head.

And, indeed, as *Katerina* powered past Saladin's Fort, sailing south into the darkness, so the prow of the smugglers' dhow swung southwards into her wake. The one-eyed smuggler chief Amir stood on the cramped little rear-mounted bridge, peering through the bridge windows past the two tall masts with their lateen-rigged sails tightly furled. Like the rest of the big smuggling vessel, the rigging was as deceptively old-fashioned as the wooden hull and the huge wheel of the helm. The dhow had not relied on the ancient sails for many years. It did rely on lookouts, watch-keepers and the captain's most intimate knowledge of its home waters, however, for its usual, limited smuggling routes around the great mountain desert wedge of the Sinai, made complicated and expensive electronics redundant. Like the man who effectively commanded it, the dhow was partially sighted but enormously powerful. Amir pressed a pair of powerful binoculars to his eyes – though a telescope would have done as well. These were the same binoculars through which he had watched the men pull the priceless Tsibekti and the stupid Eritrean from the water and then usher them aboard the big white billionaire's plaything that they were now following as he perfected his simple plans to recapture the girl.

With these grim thoughts in his head, Amir called for more speed from the huge diesel motors down below, so that the seemingly half-derelict smuggler could keep up with the fleeing gin palace, and at the very least keep its distinctive running lights well within view of Amir's binoculars. For the time-being, at least. Because he planned, at the earliest feasible moment, to take control of the vessel and everyone aboard her and bring Tsibekti back into his possession – no matter who got slaughtered in the process. Assuming, in fact, that everyone aboard *Katerina* who could not be sold would die. It galled him to face the prospect of losing another potential fortune, but he saw no immediate alternative to sinking her after he had boarded her, reclaimed his property and got rid of all the witnesses.

Passing the binoculars to the captain's mate, he ordered, 'Keep that boat in clear sight and call me the moment we can catch up to her without being observed.' Then he went below, walking carefully down the interior companionway that led to the main accommodation area. This big wood-walled space was currently packed with the full range of his merchandise – human, military and narcotic. He glanced coldly over the cowed men and women sitting under the guns of his gang, noted that the troublesome boy who had tried to rescue the girl was still unconscious from the beating he had received in consequence. The boy was only still alive because Amir proposed to kill him personally in front of the girl to show her what disobedience inevitably led to. He caught the eye of Bisrat, sitting beside the unconscious body, and nodded. Bisrat nodded back with a silently conspiratorial smirk, as though he and his chief shared some secret bond. The stupid Eritrean had no idea that he and his brother had outlived their usefulness as well and they would be sharing the unconscious boy's fate. They too would die screaming, to keep all the others in line. After that infinitesimal pause and silent nod, Amir went on through into the only private area aboard, the little master's cabin immediately above the lower engine areas. It was a strange little place, whose hardwood walls and decks were constantly vibrating to the pulse of the big motors; the air was constantly filled with their powerful rumble, and with the faint fragrance of wood dust shaken free of the joints and seams all around. Here he had set up his laptop, which, this close to the Sinai coast, had excellent Wi-Fi contact.

While he was being driven down the Taba road, Amir had used his cell phone to conduct an auction, as though he was the people-traffickers' equivalent of eBay. And now that he had access to his laptop and a good signal, he was in the process of completing it. On one side of his screen was the picture of Tsibekti – without her burqa, most becomingly partially dressed, all flashing eyes, bared teeth and wild hair held between two of his strongest men – with which he had tempted his bidders. On the other side of the screen were the bids. The winning bid was highlighted in red and the sum was fabulous; certainly the greatest he had ever earned in an internet auction without allowing his bidders more intimate access to the bodies on sale. The only problem was that the man who had purchased Tsibekti was famous for his ruthless-ness and cruelty. Should Amir fail to deliver the woman, the disappointed bidder would certainly take his head in her place.

Although he would never show it – *could* never show it – Amir, the chief of all Sinai smugglers, was in a situation that was rapidly making him very nervous indeed. If he recovered Tsibekti, safe, sound and unscathed, he would become rich enough to retire. If he did not, then he was as dead as the three Eritreans.

Richard's suspicions that they were being followed were confirmed within half an hour. And it only took him that long to become certain because the sea lanes at the northern end of the Gulf of Aquaba were unusually busy that night. *Katerina*'s main radar display showed a circular pattern on a video screen with *Katerina* herself at the centre. Dotted all around the circle were the ships and boats of all shapes and sizes moving within or across the rings designed to measure one, five, ten and fifteen sea miles distance from the centre. Most of the bustling crowd of contacts showed as lines of letters and numbers as their electronic identities registered with *Katerina*'s system. But some were registered simply as anonymous electronic targets because they had no identification systems aboard.

Ships ahead were given highest priority by the computer-controlled collision alarm radar, especially those following a reciprocal course, coming north where *Katerina* was heading south. But vessels heading southwards ahead of her or astern of her registered as well – particularly if their speed or course made it likely that they would come too close for comfort.

Or rather, the display would have been circular had *Katerina* been out in the wide waters of the Red Sea proper. Here in the narrow Gulf of Aquaba, the eastern and western sides of the electronic array were truncated by the cliff-edged coastlines of Saudi and the Sinai. *Katerina*'s electronic layout made everything look dangerously constricted by these cliff-edged, reef-fanged jaws of land which, at this point, were scarcely ten miles apart. To east and west, therefore, only the five-mile circle was alive. As *Katerina* headed south, so the rear-facing northern display began to lengthen past the five-mile line. Only the southward-facing section of the display stretched to its full extent, showing the state of water traffic almost as far ahead as Dahab. And so all vessels moving north and south were forced into close proximity with her by geography as well as by desire. In the constricted little square to the north of them, the best part of a dozen contacts showed, including big freighters heading to or from Taba, Eilat in Israel or Aqaba in Jordan, their identities bright and clear – their radio officers available for contact if Richard desired it. Smaller boats heading for haven as the night gathered and the wind continued to rise, some with electronic identities, some without. Most, again, happy to make radio contact. But there were others, too. Vessels of varying size, according to the display. Without identities. Stubbornly silent. Of which three seemed to be sailing south in *Katerina*'s wake.

'Those are the ones I don't like the look of,' said Richard.

'There might be safety in numbers, though,' mused Robin. 'If one of those contacts is the smuggler, the other two are potential witnesses and could be causing him to hold off.'

'That's true but, even so, I'd like to know which one of them is our prime suspect. Husan, what speed are we making?'

'Seven knots.'

'Can you take her up to twelve?'

'In a few moments, yes. I just want to get clear of the facilities north of Tala Bay in Jordan. There's quite a lot of traffic around there, a good deal of it heading in and out, cutting right across our path. And we'll have to keep an eye out for traffic round Haqi in Saudi just south of it,' he added in a lower voice, clearly talking to himself. But even as he was speaking, Husan was easing the throttles forward and the big diesel motors below were pushing *Katerina*'s sleek hull through the busy sea lanes with gathering speed. Richard and Robin pored over the display as the head of the gulf, with Taba, Eilat and Aquaba clustered around it, fell more rapidly astern. So did two of the vessels that had aroused their suspicions. But the third, the largest of the contacts, also began to gather way, keeping pace with them as though the vessels were attached to each other with a tow rope. 'Right,' said Richard. 'Looks like that's our man. Can I borrow those binoculars?'

Five minutes later, Richard was standing on the poop, the front of his thighs pressed against the aft safety rail as he brought Husan's identical twin to Saiid's Zeiss binoculars into focus. Their field of vision swept up over *Katerina*'s RIB, which was bouncing along on a short line astern. Then there was only a wilderness of white horses catching the light of a low moon, their tops whipping forward down the wind towards him. As he searched the horizon, Richard found time for one or two wry thoughts. First and foremost among them was relief that he hadn't had the chance to shower and change yet. Because the thick, hot, wet wind that was boiling out of the north seemed to be increasingly laden with sand. He should have brought his keffiyeh, though. There was a tell-tale saltiness on his lips while gritty grains were crunching between his teeth and tickling his nose already.

'Can you see anything yet?' asked Robin, who should have known better than to venture on to the sand-blasted deck beside him, and was beginning to regret her decision to do so.

'Not yet,' he answered, trying not to open his mouth too wide.

But no sooner had he said the words than he realized they weren't quite true, because there was something out there. An absence of light. A slightly amorphous shape that blocked the gleam of the white horses that blotted out the lower stars. That was, if he looked carefully, given some sort of definition against the receding glow of the three cities at the head of the gulf behind them. He realized he had only managed to see their pursuer because the radar contact had given him a good idea where to look. Once again, the short hairs on the back of his neck began to prickle. And not because they were getting full of sand.

Robin sneezed explosively. 'Well?' she demanded.

'Got him,' he said. 'About a mile behind us. Almost invisible. Running without any sort of lights. That's so illegal and plain bloody dangerous in these waters under these conditions that only a pirate would chance it.' He turned round with his back to the wind, lowered the binoculars and looked at *Katerina*. She was a blaze of light. Shafts of brightness streamed from her command and accommodation areas, given extra definition by the sand and spray-filled wind. She was as well-lit as a Christmas tree even before he took her bright running lights into account. Not only that, but what moonshine made it through the scudding overcast and the thick atmosphere beneath it gleamed off her glass superstructure and her white-painted hull. She was in every regard the opposite of the black ship following her. He turned back, dazzled, and it took him a good long time to focus on their dark pursuer once again. 'God, he looks sinister,' he said.

'Right,' said Robin. 'Unless you want to hand Tsibekti back to him without a fight, then it's time for a council of war.'

They all met in *Katerina*'s palatial lounge. Husan sent Ahmed and Mahmood down. Saiid accompanied them, boasting that he and his cousin could read each other's minds so he would speak for the captain. Sabet and Tsibekti, clad in flowing and extremely modest – though probably priceless – robes from Anastasia Asov's wardrobe in the Owner's Suite, brought Kareem and his silent partner.

Sabet began the discussion. 'The situation is simple,' she said. 'If we really believe that the dhow following us is full of pirates and people being trafficked, then we should call the authorities. Major Ibrahim . . .'

'How long would it take the authorities to get to us?' asked Richard. 'Would Major Ibrahim drive up to Dahab and get a police launch from there? Or are there suitable vessels nearer at hand?'

'No!' cried Tsibekti. 'The instant Al-Ayn sees an official-looking vessel, he would simply throw the cargo over the side. Better the sharks for them than prison for him.'

'I'm sorry, Sergeant, but I have to agree with Tsibekti,' said Richard. 'She knows the men we are dealing with better than any of us. And they're the sort of men who allow hundreds and hundreds of refugees to drown each year – either here in the Red Sea or up in the Mediterranean.'

Sabet nodded once, in reluctant agreement. 'Then what will we do?' she asked quietly.

'As Kareem, I think, observed during our stand-off on the Taba road, *the best method of defence is attack*,' Richard said, to get discussion under way.

'We cannot attack the dhow until Nahom and the other prisoners are safe,' snapped Tsibekti at once.

'Of course we can,' answered Richard. 'We just have to be careful about how much damage we do.'

'Is there any way,' wondered Robin, 'that we could launch an attack that doesn't look like an attack?'

'Yes,' said Richard. 'Of course there is!'

Ahmed had warned Richard it was going to be tough, even for a fairly experienced diver such as himself. Even so, when the pair of them hit the water, side by side, they were still moving at the better part of ten knots. And, because they didn't dare go over at the stern where the smugglers might see them, they went over the side and hit the water from a considerable height. Richard lost his grip on the bundle they were carrying and would have been swept away into the rushing black oblivion beneath *Katerina*'s keel had he not been securely tied to it. As the water pummelled him like the fists of a bare-knuckle boxer and the great bright vision of *Katerina*'s hull sped away through the water above him, her engines pulsing like hammer blows in his ears, he experienced a moment of utter disorientation. His face mask nearly came off and he risked adjusting it, squashing it

brutally against his nose before he grabbed hold of the rope and
started to pull himself back towards his dive buddy and the bundle
they were carrying, both of which were utterly invisible in the
dark water now that *Katerina* had sped away, where the only
glimmer of light came from the face of Richard's dive computer.
He took a glance at it as he pulled himself forward into the inky
blackness. He wasn't interested in the facts it was supplying
about dive depth, water temperature, how much air he had left
in his tanks or any other information it was displaying. The only
thing he was interested in was the countdown in the top right
corner. It told him he had five more seconds to get a grip.

Literally.

His gloved knuckles bashed into the bundle. A tiny glimmer
beyond it was Ahmed's dive computer. He felt along the side of
the invisible bulk, and found the padded handholds just as the
first countdown reached zero. The bundle jerked forward. Richard
and Ahmed became submarine shadows of the RIB above them
as *Katerina* towed them forward. But no sooner did she do so,
the next carefully calculated countdown began, the line attached
to the bundle began to be paid out so the two divers started falling
swiftly, silently and invisibly along *Katerina*'s wake towards the
black dhow sailing ever more closely behind her.

Katerina was just coming south of Nuweiba now, heading for
Dahab. Her course had taken them past Haqui on the Saudi coast
and almost right back across the Gulf to the Egyptian bank once
more, the canny Captain Husan making sure they stayed in
crowded waters for as long as possible as they plotted, planned
and prepared, while their speed had slowed infinitesimally, and
the black dhow pursuing them sailed closer and closer to her
stern. The long run between Nuweiba and Dahab was likely to
be the first section of the Gulf where the shipping would get
dangerously sparse, not least because the coast below the water-
line was composed almost entirely of reef after reef of ship-killing
coral heads. So this was where they had to take action before
the murderous smugglers aboard the dhow took action first.

In the lightless abyss of the benighted water, the only senses
the sightless divers could rely on were those of feeling and
hearing. They could feel the way the water was racing past them
with dangerously numbing speed, its effects almost like those of

frostbite. But as they felt the rope lengthening, so they began to angle their bodies carefully to take them and the bundle they were hanging on to deeper into the water. Richard's photographic memory threw up a random picture of *Katerina*'s radar display as he had last seen it, and his whole right side seemed to flinch as he remembered how close they were to the reefs he had dived in previous years a few miles north of Dahab's notorious Blue Hole which had claimed so many lives. But at least there was deep water beneath them, for the coral reefs plunged like cliffs from just below the surface to a sea bed the better part of two thousand metres down.

Katerina's engines faded as she powered on a couple of hundred yards ahead. They were hardly audible above the sound of rushing water in Richard's ears. But he could hear the increasing throb of the dhow's massive diesels increasingly clearly as she swept invisibly above them. Like Chinese martial arts masters, they were using their enemy's strength to overcome him. Had the dhow actually been powered by its ancient sails, they would never have been able to find it. But once they were in the water, those powerful motors became a beacon just as clear as the great pool of brightness spilling out of *Katerina*. As soon as the buffeting roar passed its crescendo, Richard and Ahmed jerked on the line and started finning upwards. The tow-rope stopped being paid out as their signal registered at the far end like a fish taking a hook. Now, praying that all eyes aboard the dhow would be focused forwards towards *Katerina* or westwards towards the reefs, Richard did switch on the heavily masked head-torch, which emitted a narrow blade of light, just sufficient to reveal a variable pitch propeller spinning on a shaft protected by an efficient-looking Spurs anti-fouling system and the bottom of a solid-looking rudder. Like the rest of the ship's original design, the steering system was almost medieval. The rudder was hung from a stern post and would, Richard knew, basically be controlled by a more modern adaptation of the classic two-rope system described by al-Muqaddassi, the Arab ship engineer more than a thousand years earlier. Up, somewhere just above the water, would be two chains or cables running from each side of the rudder in through openings in the transom to servo motors that would tighten or loosen them, swinging the rudder from side to side, depending on whether the captain wished to go to star-board or port. With the equipment they had brought in their bundle – makeshift though it was – Richard reckoned they could affect and maybe even control the dhow's speed and heading.

With calculated care, they had prepared for the worst-case scenario. So the bundle they had brought with them contained various nets and coils of all-but indestructible polypropylene and Kevlar-strengthened mooring rope and even a length of ancient woven steel cable. With any luck, these would overcome the Spurs system. But the rudder was a different matter. To control that they would have to come to the surface and get at whatever ran in from the rudder through the transom. What they were doing now was dangerous enough, for they could all too easily be seen. If they took the light up to the surface they would be discovered at once.

Unless the dhow's crew had something much more immediate and important to look at. Richard looked at his dive computer as the second countdown hit zero.

Robin was kneeling on *Katerina*'s main deck, with only the top of her head showing as she peeked over the stern rail. The whole aft section was designed to fold down flat and form a shelf just above water level to allow the owner and her guests easy access for swimming, boating on the RIB or playing on the vessel's pair of Dan Rowan custom built Yamaha Rickter two-seater jet skis. But at the moment, it was raised to form a low wall. Over which two long lines reached away into the dangerous darkness aft. Each line was secured around one of the aft docking winches so that it could be paid out and winched in with absolute control and millimetre precision. The man controlling the winch for the line pulling Richard and Ahmed was Mahmood. The man controlling the other one was Saiid, who knelt beside it on one knee, eyes narrow, beard wild, clutching in his right hand the biggest pair of bolt-cutters they could find among the engineers' equipment.

'It's time,' said Robin tersely, speaking to both of the winchmen and the third man, who was kneeling by her side. Though to be fair, both Sabet and Tsibekti, who were also here, crouched on the solid cover that was closed over the swimming pool, heard her and nodded their agreement.

Kareem the police marksman's English was more limited than Sabet's, but he understood better than Tsibekti what the woman with hair the colour of dahab was saying. And what it meant for him, as the next link in the chain, the next element in the plan. The RIB was almost as far back as the divers now, right at the furthest edge of his vision and almost at the end of its tether, as close as humanly possible to the bow wave of the dhow that was pursuing them. The RIB and everything it contained was a big black bundle, hopefully utterly invisible to the watchmen on the dhow – and to those on *Katerina* as well, except for the circle of white paint immediately above where the rope was tied, on the end facing Kareem. The circle that he had to hit. Ideally with his first shot.

But he was by no means in the best position. He was kneeling where he would have preferred to be lying. His rifle was resting on *Katerina*'s raised aft wall, not on a steady rock or on his own still hand. The wind was blowing gustily from the north, carrying veils of sand and spray that made the target come and go like a blinking eye. The RIB and the target were by no means stable as they wallowed through the rollers at the far end of their rope. At least, from Kareem's point of view, it was framed by the white scar of the dhow's bow wave. But *Katerina* was nothing like a perfect platform from which to be shooting. She was heaving and pitching, rocking and rolling. Only the weight of the two long lines and what they were dragging through the water gave her any kind of stability at all.

But he had to take the shot. Everyone was relying on him. Especially, it seemed, the three women by whom he was distractingly surrounded, and the men who in turn were relying on them. He breathed out until his lungs felt empty, then slowly began to breathe in. When his chest was at full stretch, he began to breathe out again, steadily and with absolute control, like an opera singer holding a perfect note. As he did so, he began to squeeze his rifle's trigger, telling himself that only this afternoon he had pulled off an almost miraculous shot to neutralize the Minimi machine gun nest.

The rifle spat, jumping back against Kareem's shoulder. The casing flew out towards the dahab-haired woman whose husband's life depended on his hitting that distant, dancing target, like the

life of the Eritrean woman's brother and the reputation of the
sergeant's commanding officer. He blinked. Nothing happened.
He gritted his teeth – literally, with the sand grains crunching. He
breathed in, calming himself, all too well aware that time was
of the essence now – not only was he running late but someone
on the dhow would probably have heard the shot. When his lungs
were full and his aim steady once more, he began to breathe out
again, blanking everything except the next shot and what he had
to do to make it.

The rifle spat, jumping back against his shoulder. The casing
flew towards the gold haired woman. And the RIB exploded,
transformed in an instant from an anonymous, scarcely visible
bundle into a raging ball of fire. A column of white flame leaped
up and back, seeming to lick right round the dhow's forecastle
head. Then the flames spread across the water. Rearing into an
unsteady wall, fanned by the wind. In the instant between these
two actions, everyone on the aft deck ducked as Saiid cut the
tow-rope with the bolt-cutters. The tow-line whipped away into
the night with a crack like a whip. The blazing RIB fell back,
surged up over the dhow's bow wave and wrapped itself around
the wooden cutwater, still fiercely ablaze, as the wings of floating
fire closed in on her from each side.

Amir the smuggler could hardly believe his one good eye. Never
in his long and brutal career had any of his victims made a
serious attempt to stand up to him – let alone to fight back. And
now the forecastle of his precious dhow was alight. He stood on
the bridge, beside the huge helm, gazing down the deck in disbelief, hesitating for an instant, torn between his immediate desire
to start slaughtering his prisoners in retribution and the need to
get the blaze under some sort of control before it spread to the
rigging or the sails and barbecued them all. The skipper of
the burning vessel made up his mind for him. 'Amir,' he called.
'You must get the fire under control at once. The spare diesel
for the motors is in the forecastle storage holds. If it gets too hot
it will explode!'

'Are your men not trained?' snarled Amir.

'Of course! Fire is the one thing we all dread more than running
aground on some uncharted coral head. But they need a leader.

Find the mate. Stop them from panicking and get them to use the pumps. I must stay here, there is something wrong with the steering and we are beginning to swing to starboard!'

'So what?' raged Amir.

'That is where the reefs lie. Amir, in the name of Allah, you must take charge of manning the pumps and fighting the fire while I try to keep us off the reefs. Have you any idea how many wrecks there are in these waters?'

Amir capitulated and ran towards the inner companionway. The last thing he heard before he exited the bridge was the skipper yelling at the helmsman, 'Hard over to port, you imbecile, and give me more power! Why is there no more power?'

At the bottom of the first companionway, Amir had a choice. He could run out on to the main deck or he could go down one more level and check the cargo that was sitting in the hold under the guns of his men. Once again, he hesitated. He was an able leader, but he was no seaman. He looked to his own people first, therefore. He ran down the steps and thrust his head into the hold. It seemed as though hundreds of terrified eyes met his one. And many of the most fearful belonged to his men. 'There is a fire,' he told them calmly. 'I am just about to put it out. Stay here, all of you. He fixed the man he trusted most with his most piercing stare. 'If the cargo make any trouble, shoot them!' he ordered. Then he raced up on to the deck once more.

The deck was a scene of worrying confusion. Flames were licking up over the forecastle, reaching dangerously close to the lateen rigged foresail which hung almost as far forward as the forecastle head. Had there been a bowsprit, it would have already been ablaze. The smell of burning was as disorientating as the roaring of the flames. The wind, at least, seemed to be on their side, for it was blowing the worst of the fire southwards towards the vessel whose occupants had started it. Amir caught his breath and looked around. The dhow's crew were beginning to take action, flinging buckets on the ends of long ropes over the side and pulling up water to pour on the flames. But as often as not, the full buckets coming in were topped with burning fuel, likely to do more harm than good. 'The pumps,' he bellowed. 'Where are the pumps?'

A crewman he recognized as the mate ran over to him. 'The

pump team is just assembling. We have to break out the hoses.
Why are we turning to starboard? Why are we slowing? What
is going on?'

'I have no idea. The captain sent me to find you. Can you take
control here?'

'Yes.'

'Good. You fight the fire. I will fight our enemies.'

Amir turned on his heel and sprinted back along the deck. He
jumped down the steps and swung back into the main hold. His
men were all standing now, their guns trained on the restless
cargo. Even down here, the air smelt of smoke. They turned
towards their leader as he entered. He looked at the forward wall.
Behind that flimsy wooden partition was gallon after gallon of
fuel, all of it heating up rapidly. 'You two,' he said, gesturing to
the men he trusted most. 'Come with me. We're going to get the
missiles and blow these cursed crusaders out of the water.'

Richard released the last of the netting from his bundle and
watched as it wrapped itself round the propeller and its shaft.
The steel cable was giving the Spurs system a hard time. The
propeller was serious trouble for the moment at least, and
the dhow was making hardly any headway at all. *Katerina* too,
would be all but hove to a couple of hundred yards ahead if
everything was still going to plan. Certainly, there was no pull
on the long rope that still tied the black bundle to *Katerina*'s aft
port docking winch. Then, uncoupling the line at last and pulling
the bundle after himself, he finned to the surface. Ahmed was
up here, working in the flickering moonlight. He had taken from
his section of the waterproof bundle the tools he needed to attack
the dhow's rudder. The cables that attached the ancient blade
to the rather more modern servos were just within his reach and
he had been able, therefore, to wedge the rudder over to the right
so that the dhow was swinging slowly but inexorably to the
starboard. To the west shore of the Gulf, to the reefs along
the coast north of Dahab.

Richard switched off his head torch as he joined Ahmed and
the pair of them looked up, catching their breath with their regulators hanging on their chests and their face masks up. They were
joined in mild frustration. Richard had half-remembered seeing

a series of wooden hand- and foot-holds running up the sheer wall of the dhow's transom. But for once, his prodigious memory had let him down. What looked like footholds were just patterns in the timbers of the vessel's high stern. There was a pair of windows immediately above the two divers, but they were far out of reach. Richard had hoped to sneak aboard and create more mayhem, but the only place where the ship's side dipped near enough to the water was mid-ships – and it would be suicidal madness to try and board her from there.

But then good fortune took a hand. A hand that Richard might almost have planned for had he thought things through in sufficient detail. A rope ladder was dropped from the poop rail immediately above their heads. Its bottom rungs splashed into the water just beside them, and one of the dhow's crew came swarming down it to try and discover what was wrong with the steering gear. One of the tools he had brought with which to work on the gear in question was a screwdriver the better part of eighteen inches long with a heavy wooden handle. It made an excellent cosh. The dhow's crewman never knew what hit him. They left him hanging just above water level, tangled safely in the bottom rungs as they slipped off their flippers and climbed halfway up the sheer stern, then forced open the wide windows to the deserted cabin below the command bridge and silently climbed aboard. Their compressed air tanks hampered them, so they slipped them off and laid them gently on the carpeted deck, slipping their regulators over their heads and removing their face masks. Richard also took off his head torch. Then they opened the last section of the waterproof bundle, took out their guns and padded forwards. Richard opened the door a crack and looked forward on to the main deck. Everyone seemed to be up at the prow, fighting the fire there. But a quick glance established that the desperate fire fighters seemed to be winning, so time was limited. They turned sideways, therefore, and stepped on to the internal companionway that seemed to be full of flickering shadows, silent on their rubber-soled dive boots, almost as invisible in their black and blue-panelled wetsuits.

Richard was armed with Sabet's nine-millimetre Halewan. Ahmed was carrying an old army issue Webley & Scott break-top .455 revolver that Husan and Saiid had produced from heaven knew where. There was a bag of ammunition to go with it, just as Richard had a couple of extra clips for Sabet's automatic. Not that they were here to start a fire fight like a couple of desperadoes from the Wild Bunch. Their aim was to help get the prisoners free when the final elements of the plan came to fruition. Or to save as many as they could if everything went to hell in a handcart.

Five steps down led to the wide opening into the main hold. Richard, in the lead, squashed himself into the angle between the wall and the doorframe. He didn't need to look in – not that he would have risked putting his head round the doorway in any case. He could feel the heat of the close-packed, terrified bodies, hear the murmuring of their desperation; smell the fear. One of the impatient smugglers guarding them snarled something Richard could not understand and cocked his semi-automatic – a metallic double click that he understood all too clearly. He gestured with his chin – *let's go back up*. He wanted to be out on the main deck, hidden in a choke point where the action was likely to be most intense when the final sections of his plan all came together. Now that he knew where the prisoners were, he needed to know where the leader of the traffickers was. The pirate captain, he assumed, would still be on the bridge, trying to steer and power his vessel out of danger. Power was likely to be returned to him at any moment – the one imponderable in the equation being how quickly the Spurs cutters would clear the tangle of netting round the propeller. The helm was in Richard's control after Ahmed's sterling work on the rudder cables.

Richard eased the door on to the main deck open and sank to his knees. The shadows were darkest down here. He fell forward on his belly and oozed on to the main deck, invisible in the shade like an oil slick spreading over tar. Ahmed followed immediately behind him. To right and left, immediately in front of the bridge house, stood the two lifeboats designed to take the dhow's crew in a crisis such as this. They sat on the deck, supported by wooden rests – there were no davits designed to lift them overboard. They were open, uncovered. Each of them was twelve feet long and the better part of six feet wide. Beneath their elegantly curving sides were pools of even deeper shadow from which it was possible to watch what was happening along the entire length of the deck. Richard took the boat on the starboard, Ahmed took the one on the port. They squeezed beneath their inner sides and began to look around. The only things limiting their worm's eye view were the series of raised hatchways down the centre of the deck that were obviously designed to open into the main hold on those occasions when legitimate, non-human cargo needed to be lowered aboard because it could not walk. They could see well enough what was going on. The fire on the forecastle was all but out now. But the crew were taking nothing for granted. They were pumping water on to the forecastle as fast as they could.

Suddenly the door through which Richard and Ahmed had just crawled slammed wide. The leader of the smugglers strode forward, with a couple of his men in tow. The tall, commanding Bedouin was carrying an SA 24 Igla MANPAD. The two men running behind him were carrying another. Of course they would be wasted shooting at a boat thought Richard – but these men had used the anti-aircraft system to total a Land Rover, so they weren't going to be too picky. The leader shouted something Richard did not immediately understand, but the reaction of the crew made it clear he was demanding whether the forecastle was going to be safe to shoot from. Richard tensed himself for action as the tall, white-clad figure walked purposefully on to the still-steaming forecastle. Nothing the matter with his nerve, he thought with grudging admiration.

But just as the three men reached the point of the prow, even as the characteristically generous thought entered Richard's head, the next section of his plan kicked in. The Spurs system cleared the propeller of the cordage he had wrapped so carefully around it. The dhow's captain was holding the throttles on full ahead, trying to compensate for the loss of power. But now, suddenly and unexpectedly, it was fully restored. The freed propeller bit into the water and threw the dhow forward. Or it would have done so had Ahmed not sabotaged the steering gear. As it was, the dhow lurched forcefully to starboard, and with all the strength of her newly liberated propulsion system behind it, the massive diesel motor ran her up on to the reef.

The dhow rose up as she grounded, then crashed down as the

keel beneath the forecastle was torn open by the claws of coral. Miraculously, the masts did not go by the board but the sails came roaring down. They smashed open the tops of the hatches, spilling sailcloth, splinters and cordage into the hold, from whence erupted a deafening cacophony of howls and screams, which Richard fervently hoped came from sudden shock rather than serious injury. Fortunately, the lifeboats stayed firmly in their place, so that neither Richard nor Ahmed was crushed. However, a good number of the crew, still fighting the fire, were incapacitated beneath the heavy spars, the nets of rigging and the sheer weight of the sails. The leader's acolytes went overboard, tumbling helplessly and probably fatally from forecastle to coral, taking the second shoulder-fired missile with them. But the leader remained standing. His howl of outrage was so loud that Richard actually heard it over the Armageddon on the deck.

Richard reckoned he would probably be safe enough to get moving. In mayhem like this he could have dressed up as a gorilla and still gone unobserved. He rolled out from under the lifeboat and sprang erect, then he began to run down the length of the deck towards the back of the leader who had put the Igla to his shoulder and clearly had every intention of firing it as soon as he had acquired a target. And the target was *Katerina*. As Richard ran, he glanced down into the hold through the openings of the smashed hatches. It was difficult to be certain, but it looked as though the smugglers had lost control – or maybe just given up and tried to run. There seemed to be no one in charge down there, and there were no guns in evidence. But all he had was a fleeting glance, for his main objective was dead ahead, standing on the steaming forecastle, snuggling the long green tube of the Igla into the crook between his shoulder and his neck.

And Richard realized he wasn't going to get to the smuggler in time. He had been able to run this far pretty quickly and nimbly – even given that the dhow was still settling on to the reef. But in front of him was a maze of sails, spars and rigging. He came to a halt, raised Sabet's pistol and shouted. Shouted the only name he knew for his foe – Tsibekti's nickname for her brutal captor, Al-Ayn.

Amir the smuggler swung round as he heard the nickname he had so hated as a child. He was stunned that anyone should know what his contemporaries had called him in his youth. Contemporaries he had loathed, using a name he hated. Such was his outrage that he momentarily forgot that he still had the Igla on his shoulder.

There in front of him stood a tall man in a black, blue-panelled diving suit. He hardly registered the gun that was pointed at him. 'Put the rocket down or I will shoot,' Richard commanded. But he spoke in English and the Bedouin did not understand. The words of gibberish made him pause, however. And that pause made him remember that he still had the Igla on his shoulder and a target at his mercy. He swung back, traversing the lethal missile system towards the bright-lit yacht which sat so helplessly at point-blank range.

And, seeing the movement, Kareem, still kneeling on *Katerina*'s transom, at last had a clear shot at the man armed with the deadly missile as he stood on the dhow's forecastle high above. He was already breathing out in that carefully controlled manner. He squeezed the trigger at once. The rifle spat as it kicked back into his shoulder. He saw his target stagger and thought *job well done*.

The bullet took Amir in the left shoulder. It was the same heavy load that had dropped a machine-gunner in a nest at the better part of half a mile. At this range it was enough to spin Amir round. Richard's shot also hit him high in the torso, but on the other side of his chest, completing the job that Kareem's rifle bullet had started. So that, when Amir's fist closed convulsively on the trigger, he was facing in exactly the opposite direction he had been facing a moment before. The missile, therefore, streaked back along the dhow's deck. It sped just above the wreckage of the sails. It went just west of the masts because Amir had staggered sideways when the dhow struck the reef. But it hit the solid front of the bridge house with all the force it possessed and it blew the entire structure into atoms. Richard, who had automatically flinched away as the missile streaked past him, was thrown headlong on to the deck by the blast. And he was by no means all that was felled by the force of the explosion.

The dhow's main mast, weakened by the grounding, began to topple forward, and it collided with the foremast so that both of them came crashing down. Amir the trafficker, frozen with the shock of the damage to his shoulders and the mayhem wrought by the Igla, hardly even registered that the masts were falling inexorably towards him until the foremast smashed down, hurling him overboard to go crashing on to the reef beside his two most trusted men. Who were also, by this stage, dead.

Richard pulled himself erect and ran across the deck to the gaping hatch-tops. No sooner had he reached the nearest, than the first of the prisoners pulled himself up out on to the deck and stood, looking around, stunned by his freedom. It was Nahom. Richard went over to him and thrust out his hand. 'Hi, Nahom,' he said cheerfully, just as though they were friends meeting by chance on a familiar city street. 'I have someone over on *Katerina* who wants to talk to you. But I think she's going to give you an even bigger telling-off than Robin's going to give me!'

The main terminal at Sharm el-Sheikh airport, aptly enough, is designed to look like a series of Bedouin tents. It sits, almost ethereally, seeming to waver in the desert heat, hard up against geometric red mountains that, from a distance, look exactly like pyramids. Richard and Robin were sitting comfortably in the first-class lounge three weeks later with all their paperwork done and all their luggage handed in, waiting for the London flight. The lounge was cool, quiet, and almost empty. Those few who were there, tourists for the most part, were, like the Mariners, dressed in holiday gear. Shorts and T-shirts, light skirts and blouses. All of them colourful, fragrant, diaphanous.

So that when Major Ibrahim and Sergeant Sabet entered, they stood out immediately. Richard watched the pair of them in their smart white uniforms marching across the marble floor towards him. He nudged Robin who looked up from her book. Then they stood, side by side, and waited for the police officers to join them.

'We have come to say goodbye,' said Ibrahim, holding out his hand.

'And good riddance, I should think,' answered Richard cheerfully, returning the major's cool, dry clasp.

'Not at all,' the moustache twitched and the wrinkles at the outer edges of his eyes deepened. It was as close as Ibrahim came to smiling. 'Because of your involvement—'